A Time for Peace

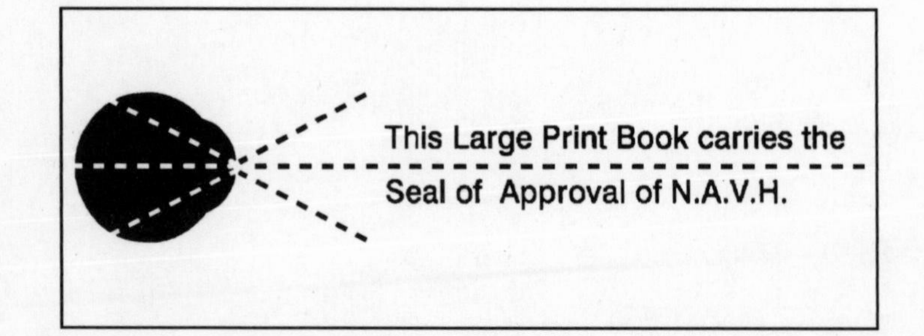
This Large Print Book carries the
Seal of Approval of N.A.V.H.

A Time for Peace

Barbara Cameron

THORNDIKE PRESS
A part of Gale, Cengage Learning

GALE
CENGAGE Learning®

Detroit • New York • San Francisco • New Haven, Conn • Waterville, Maine • London

Thorndike Press, a part of Gale, Cengage Learning.

Thorndike Press® Large Print Clean Reads.
The text of this Large Print edition is unabridged.
Other aspects of the book may vary from the original edition.
Set in 16 pt. Plantin.

LIBRARY OF CONGRESS CATALOGING-IN-PUBLICATION DATA

Cameron, Barbara, 1949–
A time for peace / by Barbara Cameron.
p. cm. — (Thorndike Press large print clean reads) (Quilts of Lancaster county series)
ISBN-13: 978-1-4104-4475-2 (hardcover)
ISBN-10: 1-4104-4475-9 (hardcover)
1. Amish—Fiction. 2. Quilting—Fiction. 3. Lancaster County (Pa.)—Fiction. 4. Large type books. I. Title.
PS3603.A4473T48 2012
813'.6—dc23 2011046231

Published in 2012 by arrangement with Abingdon Press.

Printed in the United States of America
1 2 3 4 5 6 7 16 15 14 13 12

For my friends who keep me going

ACKNOWLEDGMENTS

This book would not have been possible without the enthusiasm and support of Barbara Scott, my wonderful editor at Abingdon Press.

Barbara encouraged me in writing the Quilts of Lancaster County series and provided a warm, supportive atmosphere for me to write stories that are different about the contrasts and conflicts between the Amish, a people I love, and the *Englisch* as they call us. I didn't meet Barbara in person until a year later, when my first book of the series was out and we were attending the American Christian Fiction Writers (ACFW) conference, but when I did, it was as though I'd met a dear friend I hadn't seen in years.

I also met my new editor, Ramona Richards, there and immediately felt I'd met another dear friend. I particularly appreciated Ramona's warm, concerned reaction when I let her know I ran into difficulties delivering the manuscript on time when I experienced a stress-related illness working on it. I enjoyed working on this book with you, Ramona, and look forward to working on many more with you.

Ramona and Barbara are such wonderful, intuitive editors. I feel so blessed to have been led to work with both of them and hope Ramona and I will do so for many years to come. And Barbara, please enjoy your retirement. You have worked so hard to bring quality to Christian fiction.

Thank you to Becky Lee, who checked the manuscript for accuracy. I so appreciate your help.

My grown children — Justin and Stephany — are supportive of my writing. They have always been, and I appreciate them so much. Writers are a strange breed and not everyone understands us. But even when my house becomes a mess, and I talk about characters like they're real people, they don't look at me oddly. My son has worked on my website and my daughter has made posters and offered marketing advice. Family is everything — particularly the special grandchildren they've given me!

Sometimes as you're living life it seems like things don't always make sense. My heroine, Jenny, calls it "unanswered prayer" when you feel God isn't listening. But then later, when you look back, you can see a real pattern, a reason why some things worked out and others didn't. When I look back at my life, so much joy sprang from my writing and my family. I can't ever thank God enough for that!

1

It was official.

She wasn't a saint.

But Jenny had never claimed to be a saint. None of her Amish brethren did, either.

She knew she should be grateful for her family and she was. Her husband's *kinner* were as much hers as they were his — especially Annie who had been so young when her mother died that she didn't remember her and thought of Jenny as her *mamm.* And Joshua and Mary treated her as a beloved mother even though they remembered their mother.

But ever since Hannah had announced that she and Chris were going to have a baby, Jenny had felt the unaccustomed and very unwelcome emotion of envy. They'd only been married a year. She and Matthew had been married for three.

It wasn't fair.

Almost immediately, she was ashamed of

herself. But she couldn't seem to help it. She wanted a baby of her own. A *boppli.* She loved that word. It sounded so sweet. So happy and bouncy. So cherished.

Instead, so many months had passed and she'd found out she wasn't pregnant. She wouldn't be carrying a baby close to her heart. She wouldn't share the miracle of creating life with Matthew and watching it come into the world.

Sometimes she wondered if she was showing God she didn't appreciate all He had brought into her life. After all, he'd brought her back here to have a second chance with the man she'd never forgotten. She'd gone through such a valley of despair when she'd been seriously injured, scarred, in her work as a news reporter overseas.

Yet Matthew had seen past that, cherished her, and shared the most precious children in the world with her. He'd said that if they had *kinner,* that would be wonderful, but if they didn't, then that was God's will and he seemed fine with that. Content, even.

God had even found a way for her to continue to write about the children affected by war she'd grown to care so much for, right here on a farm in the heart of peace and love and simplicity.

She and Matthew had talked about how

she felt when she didn't become pregnant. He'd been kind, understanding, and had tried to comfort her. He had been everything she had hoped for about it.

But he wasn't unhappy that they hadn't had children together yet. He reminded her that before they'd gotten married he'd told her he didn't care if her injuries prevented her from having their child. He had three to share with her, he'd said, and if they were meant to have a child together, that God would send one. It was a matter of God's will, he told her. And he was content.

But she wasn't. If she tried not to think about it, every month she got a reminder that she wasn't pregnant.

And this was the way she rewarded Him. With a lack of gratitude, with mental whining. With tears when she found that another month had come and gone and a tiny glimmer of life wasn't beginning inside her.

Sighing, Jenny threw down her pen and got up from the big table that dominated the kitchen. She was tired of working, couldn't seem to stay focused on what she was writing. Best to just get busy doing something else. Idleness wasn't encouraged here.

Not that she'd ever been an idle person. But everyone pulled their weight here, contributed, from small children with chores appropriate to their age and ability to older family members doing what they could after they moved into a *dawdi haus,* the sort of mother-in-law apartment at the back of the family home.

She glanced at the clock. Half an hour before the *kinner* got home. Time to do something constructive. If she couldn't write, then she should at least get supper started or *redd-up* the place a little.

Funny how she'd gotten to where she thought in Pennsylvania *Dietsch.* If anyone had ever told her that one day she would return to her grandmother's house here in Paradise and marry her girlhood crush, and become Amish, she would never have believed them.

But she had, and here her dreams were coming true, dreams of having a husband, children who loved her, and her writing career as well.

Her life was nearly perfect.

Nearly.

Sighing, she got up. Nearly was *a lot* better than much of the world had. She knew that better than anyone did after her job as a TV news reporter covering issues involving children in war-torn countries.

Every time her own family gathered

around this big wooden kitchen table and she saw how healthy and how happy they were, how they had so much abundance of food and love and security, she made sure she thanked God.

Spring was coming. The cold of the winter had passed and she'd seen little green buds on the trees around the house that morning when she'd said goodbye to her family as they rushed off to work and school. That was probably why her thoughts had turned to new life.

She was only in her early thirties and had years to have a baby, her doctor had told her. Women could have them safely into their late forties, he'd told her.

But though she tried not to worry about internal injuries she'd suffered when she'd been the target of a car bomb overseas during her TV reporting days, there was still that little niggle at the back of her mind each month she didn't get pregnant.

Determined to push those thoughts aside, to remember to be grateful for what she had, she got up, put away her writing things, and changed to *mamm* mode, as she called it.

Supper went into the oven, Matthew's favorite: ham and scalloped potatoes. She'd endured a lot of teasing the first couple of times she'd made it. Microwaved food had been her specialty before she became an Amish *fraa.* Now she cooked from scratch with recipes her grandmother handed down to her.

She caught a glimpse of her reflection in the glass of the cupboard door when she opened it. Even though she considered herself plain with her brown hair and gray eyes, her hair center-parted and drawn back under a white *kapp,* Matthew always made her feel beautiful when he looked at her. He never seemed to see the scar from the bombing that, while faded, was something she could never forgot was there and still found herself raising her hand to cover when someone looked at her.

She was washing her hands when she heard a commotion at the door. The Bontrager children were sweet as can be, but when they came in the door after *schul* they sounded like a herd of buffalo.

They swarmed into the kitchen and engulfed her in hugs and charmed her into giving them big glasses of milk along with cookies she'd baked earlier that day.

"Three? They're small," asked Annie, giving Jenny her most charming smile.

"Two," Jenny said, smiling at her. "They're big." All of the children looked so like Matthew with their almost white-blond hair and deep blue eyes.

Seven-year-old Annie normally talked so much no one else had a chance to talk for a few minutes at the end of the *schul* day, but with her mouth stuffed with cookies, Joshua and Mary were able to talk.

"I helped Leah with John and Jacob today. They're still having trouble with arithmetic. It was fun."

"Maybe you'll be a teacher one day."

Mary smiled. "Maybe."

Jenny looked at Joshua. He was most like his father with his quiet intensity and willingness to work hard. After his snack, he'd go out and help with the horses for hours. "And what did you do today?"

"I got 100 on my vocabulary test."

"Very good. All your studying paid off." She was careful with praise. *Hochmut* — pride — wasn't encouraged here.

Joshua wasn't as good at schoolwork as the girls. Annie had decided that she wanted to be a writer like Jenny, and Mary enjoyed teaching the younger children so they both worked hard at lessons. Joshua liked working with animals and with his *daedi* in the fields and didn't think schoolwork was all that important. He was dutiful about studying but so obviously didn't enjoy it.

The snack finished, the children got up, put their plates and glasses in the sink, and set about their chores. Mary began mixing up a bowl of corn bread and Joshua went to help his *daedi* in the barn.

Jenny glanced out the window as she washed up the dishes from dinner and set the plates and glasses in the drying rack. She hadn't seen Phoebe all day. Usually she came over in the afternoon to have a cup of tea and a visit.

Wiping her hands on a kitchen towel, she turned to Annie, who was setting the table.

"Would you go over and see if Phoebe would like to have supper with us?"

"Ya!"

"And don't charm her into giving you more cookies."

Annie's face fell. "Not even one?"

Jenny's lips twitched as she tried to keep a straight face. "Not even one. We'll be eating soon."

"Okay."

She dragged her feet out of the room and left the house. But then when Jenny turned and looked out the kitchen window, she was racing across the field that separated the two houses. Jenny wished she had half the energy Annie did.

A few minutes later, she was slamming

the front door and racing into the kitchen.

"Whoa, a little quiet—" Jenny started to say and then she saw Annie's face.

"*Mamm,* I can't wake Phoebe up."

A chill ran down Jenny's spine. "She's taking a nap?"

"On the kitchen floor! I think she's sick! I think she's sick!"

Jenny reached over and turned the oven off, then called Mary.

"Come help me see what's wrong with Phoebe. Annie, you go get your *daedi.* He's out in the barn."

Jenny raced across the field with Mary in tow, praying that nothing was seriously wrong with her grandmother. She had looked a little tired when she visited the day before but hadn't said anything was wrong.

But then again, she wouldn't. Phoebe always acted like she wouldn't let the passing years slow her down.

"Grandma! Grandma!" she called as she ran into the house.

Just as Annie had said, Phoebe lay on the floor in the kitchen.

2

Jenny knelt beside her grandmother. Phoebe lay lifeless on the floor, her face white, her small, thin body motionless.

Her fingers shaking, Jenny touched the vein in Phoebe's neck and felt for a pulse. It was thready but it was there.

"*Grossmudder?* It's Jenny. Wake up. Please, wake up."

But Phoebe lay still, her eyes closed, her chest barely moving beneath the apron covering her thin chest.

Swiveling around, Jenny saw that Mary was standing there, eyes wide with fear.

"Mary, go get —"

The door slammed. "Jenny?"

She turned. "Matthew, thank goodness you're here! Phoebe won't wake up. Call 9-1-1. Tell them we need an ambulance. Hurry!"

He backed up, turned, and ran for the

door to go to the phone shanty next to the house.

Jenny looked at Mary. "Soak that dish towel in some cold water from the tap. Maybe she just collapsed from the heat from baking."

Mary went to the sink and did as Jenny asked her, squeezing the moisture from the cloth and rushing over with it. "Is she going to be *allrecht?*"

Jenny stroked the cool, damp cloth over her grandmother's face, so frightened of the way her lashes stayed still on her cheeks. Age was so evident in the woman's face, in the way there were crinkles around her eyes from laughing and from staring into the sun as she worked in the yard hanging clothes, planting, harvesting her kitchen garden, and helping her late husband with their farm. Lines bracketed her mouth that in repose seemed so stern but which framed a smile that always warmed Jenny's heart.

She looked so old and frail, so vulnerable at that moment, tears rushed into her eyes. Furiously she blinked them back. She didn't want to upset Mary. And she prayed that it was just a faint, not something more serious. She couldn't remember a day that Phoebe hadn't bustled around working, working, working. And caring for everyone in her family. Someone that strong could have a weak moment without it being one of their last, couldn't they? Just look, she thought. The counters were covered with bread and cookies and a pie she'd baked just that afternoon from the looks of it.

Reaching behind her, she took Mary's hand. "Where's Annie?"

"She went for *Daedi.* I'll find her and make sure she's safe."

They both turned at the sound of sirens in the distance. The sirens grew louder and then were shut off.

"They're here!" Matthew called and he hurried in with paramedics carrying their equipment.

Jenny stood. "Annie found her on the floor. She's breathing but she won't wake up."

Matthew took her hand and drew her into his arms, offering wordless comfort.

Together they watched as all through the steps of their exam Phoebe didn't move a muscle, not even after her oxygen level was checked with a pincher thing on the tip of her finger and an oxygen tube was hooked up.

One of the paramedics set a laptop on the kitchen table and began asking Jenny questions. Another opened cupboard after cupboard and rooted around inside.

"What are you looking for?" Jenny asked, confused.

"We're supposed to look around for any medications the person is on. Do you know if she's taking anything?"

"I've never seen her take anything, not even an aspirin."

"Sometimes the family doesn't know, even if they live in the same house. Where's her medicine cabinet?"

"I'll show you," Matthew said.

Jenny wanted him to stay, to continue to hold her. Instead, she watched him leave the room with the paramedic, and when the men returned, the other man was holding several prescription bottles.

Two men came in with a gurney and Phoebe was gently lifted onto it.

"Ma'am? Do you want to go to the hospital with us?"

"Yes, please." She looked at Matthew and he nodded.

"Go. I'll take care of the *kinner* until Hannah gets home and then I'll see you at the hospital." He hugged her and then set her from him. "She'll be *allrecht,* Jenny."

Phoebe's gurney was being loaded into the ambulance as Jenny ran outside and climbed into it. Gathering her skirts, she climbed inside and sank onto the bench seat opposite Phoebe.

Then the doors were shut, making her feel claustrophobic. The driver accelerated out of the driveway and turned onto the road in the direction of the hospital. He activated the siren and the noise reverberated in her head.

Being inside such a vehicle brought back memories, such painful memories of riding in one in pain and terror after the car bombing overseas, and later, stateside, going from hospital to hospital. Jenny forced them away, took one of her grandmother's still, cold hands in hers.

Silently she watched as the paramedic stood next to Phoebe and took her blood pressure, inserted an IV with fluids, and checked her pupils, swaying but never losing his balance like a sailor on a shipboard deck as the vehicle sped up and turned.

He called ahead to the hospital, relaying Phoebe's condition.

It was the longest ride of her life.

But when they arrived at the hospital, Phoebe was taken away and instead of being able to stay with her, Jenny was urged to go to admissions and fill out paperwork and then sit in the waiting room. It was then that she knew the time in the ambulance wasn't going to be the worst of her life because the wait was going to be longer.

A nurse came out, looked around the room, then signaled to Jenny. "Your grandmother's awake."

Jenny closed her eyes, said a silent prayer of thanks, then opened them. "Can I see her?"

"Sure. Come with me."

Phoebe still looked entirely too pale when Jenny walked into the cubicle but she was awake and talking to the doctor. She looked up and smiled at Jenny. "I'm sorry I gave you a scare. I'm fine now. I'm just trying to persuade the doctor to let me go home."

Jenny looked at the doctor and saw that he was frowning.

"I don't advise it," he said bluntly. "With your history —"

Puzzled, Jenny glanced from her grandmother to the doctor and back again at her grandmother. "Her history?"

The doctor looked at Phoebe then and it seemed to Jenny that something passed between then.

"Her age, the approximate amount of time she was out, her blood pressure reading," the man said. "I'd like to run some tests. We've ruled out a concussion from her falling. But I'd like to know what *caused* her to be unconscious."

Phoebe opened her mouth and as she did, the doctor straightened and looked stern.

"Fine," she said at last. "I'll stay for your 'observation time,' young man. For twelve hours and no more."

"You drive a hard bargain," he said.

He offered his hand and they shook on it.

Jenny moved to Phoebe's side as the man left the cubicle. "You frightened me."

Phoebe held out her arms and Jenny went into them. "I'm sorry, *liebchen.* I just got warm and fainted. It's never happened before. And it's not going to happen again."

"You don't know that."

"I do. Now, don't fuss. You get back home and make sure the *kinner* aren't upset."

But Jenny wouldn't let her shoo her out of the cubicle. She fluffed the pillow behind Phoebe's back, unpinned her *kapp* and laid it on the folded bundle of her grandmother's clothes lying on the nearby chair, and generally fussed over her until the nurse came to ready her to be transferred to a room.

"Go, now!" Phoebe ordered sternly but Jenny saw the kindness in her eyes. "I'll be fine. Just remember to send someone to fetch me home in the morning."

"Matthew and I will be here for you," Jenny promised.

Leaning down, she kissed her grandmother's pale, lined cheek and then, unable to prevent herself, she gathered the woman up in a hug again, careful of the tubes and IV bound to her, and held on. "I love you. I'll see you in the morning."

Turning her head, she rushed from the cubicle so that Phoebe wouldn't see the tears in her eyes.

She was so grateful to see Matthew rise from a chair in the waiting room when she walked out.

"Where's Phoebe?" he asked, looking around her.

"The doctor wants to keep her for observation."

Matthew nodded. "Since she was unconscious? Did she hurt her head when she fell and get a concussion?"

Jenny shook her head. "She doesn't have a concussion. I don't understand why she's here. She won't let the doctor tell me anything."

"Your grandmother is a strong, independent woman," he said. "I'm sure she's going to be *allrecht.*"

Jenny wasn't so sure. "I hope you're right," she said, taking his hand and walking with him through the waiting room and out of the hospital.

They'd been here several times since they'd married, always for some emergency for the children. Joshua had had stitches for a gash in his arm once because he'd fallen and landed on a rock. Matthew liked to tease that Joshua was growing so big and so fast he tripped over his own feet as he walked across a room. Mary had a high fever last winter when she got the flu. Even Annie had had her turn here when she slammed a door on her fingers and broke two of them. She tended to be a little klutzy because she was always thinking about something she was writing and didn't look where she was going.

But Jenny had never had to leave a loved one here at the hospital to be cared for by strangers. She'd never had to worry about why one of them had come to the hospital. Or what might happen while she stayed. Things happened sometimes when people stayed in the hospital.

Something didn't feel right.

Matthew had never seen Jenny in such a state.

He knew why she was so upset, of course. She'd lost her mother in her early teens, her father in her twenties. Phoebe was the only family she had left of her birth family.

They'd grown so close since Jenny had come to heal here after being so grievously wounded in a car bombing overseas where she'd served as a television reporter.

They'd talked often of God's will, he and his *fraa,* as she struggled to understand why such a horrible thing had happened to her when she thought she was doing good, when she thought she was doing what God wanted her to do. She'd healed here, not just physically but emotionally and spiritually.

And both of them had come to realize that they were being given a second chance to renew the love they'd had for each other when they were younger. Jenny had spent two summers here visiting her grandmother and he was what she often teasingly called "the boy next door."

They were from such different worlds — she, from the *Englisch* world, he an Amish man. But she'd slipped seamlessly into the way of life here, into the Amish way of looking at life and God when she visited those summers. He'd been on the verge of asking if he could court her. Something had happened to prevent that — some*one* — but in the end, things had turned out as God willed. She'd been brought back here to him, they had realized how deeply they loved each other, and they had married.

Now they lived as a family with the children he'd had with his late first wife.

He knew how she struggled with God's will again after they were married; these past couple of years when she didn't conceive had been a spiritual challenge for her. He knew how much she wanted a baby; she battled unhappiness so often because each month she was presented with proof that she hadn't conceived.

Now, as they traveled back home after leaving Phoebe in the hospital, he tried to comfort his beloved, wrapping one arm around her, letting her rest her head against his shoulder, and listening to her worry aloud about a woman he'd come to think of as his own *grossmudder.*

"I don't understand why she couldn't come home," Jenny was saying. "They let me go home even when I had a concussion, remember? She looked after me all night. I'd have taken care of her."

"I know you would," he told her. "You'd take good care of her. I've seen how you care for the *kinner* when they've been hurt or sick."

He pressed his lips to her forehead and looked ahead to their farmhouse coming into view. "The doctors know what they're doing. There must be some reason why they want her to stay."

Jenny looked up at him and she frowned. "It was so strange. The doctor started to say something and I felt he stopped because she looked at him."

"What was he saying?"

"Something about her history." Jenny fell silent. "But what could that be? I don't remember even seeing her take an aspirin even though I've seen it's more difficult for her to move around these days. But —"

"But what?"

"That paramedic found prescriptions in her medicine cabinet. Did you see what they were for?"

He shook his head. "Sorry."

Matthew guided Daisy into the drive and the *kinner* spilled out the door, their young faces expectant.

Suddenly Jenny thought about how the children considered Phoebe their own great-grandmother. "Oh, Matthew, I didn't think about — what do we tell the children?"

He kissed her cheek. "The truth. We tell them the truth. They're old enough to understand and not be frightened."

3

"*Daedi,* where is Phoebe?" Annie, the youngest, asked, her forehead puckering in a frown as she peered inside the buggy.

"The doctors wanted her to stay tonight," Matthew told them.

"Did she need an operation?" Mary asked. She was gnawing at a fingernail, something he hadn't seen her do for years.

The newest member of the family, Hannah's husband Chris, strode onto the porch. "Where's Phoebe?"

"They wanted to keep her overnight."

"Why? What's wrong with her?" he asked and held open the door for Jenny to walk inside.

"They didn't seem to know why she passed out. She was conscious not long after she got to the emergency room but they're concerned that she was out for a while."

"*Kumm,* children, let's go put Pilot and the buggy up and start getting you ready for bed," Matthew said.

"But we want to find out about Phoebe," Mary began.

He put an arm around her. "I can tell you. Let's give your *mamm* a chance to sit down and rest."

Jenny sank down in a chair at the kitchen table, bone-weary.

"Are they back?" Hannah called down the stairs.

"Yeah, they're home!"

Hannah rushed into the room and looked around. "But where's Phoebe? Has she gone to her room? I'll go see if she needs —"

Chris grasped her arm as she started past him. "They're keeping her overnight."

Hannah stared at him, then Jenny. "What's wrong with her? She's going to be okay, right? She was fine when I left this morning to teach my quilting class in town and then when I come home this afternoon I hear she's been taken off in an ambulance. Did she have a heart attack or something?"

Chris pulled out a chair and made her sit down. "Hannah, calm down. It can't be good for you or the baby to get so upset."

Nodding, she drew in a deep breath and exhaled as she rubbed a hand over her protruding stomach. "I know. I'm sorry."

"Jenny? Was it her heart?"

"What?" Jenny blinked, aware that she'd been staring at her sister-in-law's stomach.

"Was it her heart?" Chris asked again, his gaze intent.

"He said she didn't have a heart attack."

Chris sat back, looking relieved. "That's good to know."

Jenny found herself staring at the place on the floor where she'd found her grandmother earlier that day.

"I just don't understand," she said. "If she fainted because of the heat then why didn't she wake up sooner? She didn't until we got to the hospital. She's one of the healthiest people I know — I've never seen her take any medicine and yet the paramedic found pills he took to the emergency room."

She sighed and looked at them. "I don't know. I feel like something's going on but I don't know what it is. Has she said anything to either of you?"

"No," Chris said and he stood. "Let me fix you some tea." He looked at Hannah and she shook her head.

"Hannah? Did Phoebe say anything to you?"

She shook her head. "No."

"The paramedic went through her medicine cabinet. He said they always take any medications to the emergency room so the doctors can see what the person was taking. But I didn't see what he took."

Hannah patted her hand. "You look exhausted. I fed the *kinner* and saved supper for you and Matthew. Let me get some for you."

"Thanks, but I'm not hungry. I'll just have the tea." She smiled gratefully at Chris when he set a steaming cup before her.

"You have to eat." Hannah rose, pulled a casserole from the oven, and set it atop the stove.

And then, to Jenny's surprise, she handed the oven mitts to Chris who carried the casserole to the table.

Hannah shrugged when she saw Jenny's expression. "I gave up on fighting him over whether I can carry a casserole."

Chris turned from setting it on the table. "Wise woman, eh, Jenny?"

Rolling her eyes, Hannah brought over a plate and began spooning a serving of the chicken and rice onto it. "I'm lugging around a considerable amount of baby. A little casserole is nothing."

Chris placed a hand on her stomach. "Since, as you say, you are lugging around a considerable amount of baby, you shouldn't be adding more to the burden." He kissed her cheek and sat down at the table.

Even as distracted as she was by worry over her grandmother, Jenny couldn't help noticing how the interaction between the two of them had changed so much since they'd fallen in love and gotten married. Hannah was outspoken, unlike her brother, and there'd been some tension when Chris had arrived here.

It had taken Hannah a long time to believe that Chris hadn't come to pursue Jenny after he met her at a veteran's hospital. Jenny hadn't known until much later that Hannah had given Chris a hard time about that. If she had, Jenny would have let her know that wasn't going to happen. She and Chris had become friends after they met at the hospital — nothing more. Matthew was the love of her life.

Two worlds in one house, she thought, just like her own. So much for cranky Josiah, a church elder who didn't think the *Englisch* and the Amish should mix. Not only had she and Matthew just celebrated another anniversary, his sister and this man who'd served as a soldier and come here for healing had found happiness together.

The chicken and rice casserole was delicious. Once she started eating, Jenny realized that she was, indeed, hungry. Lunch had been a lot of hours ago.

There was a knock on the door and Joshua came inside. "I told *Daedi* I'd walk you home when you're ready."

"Thank you, *Sohn,*" she said, feeling her eyes tear up. He was so like Matthew with that quiet, intense manner; neither of them said much but their actions spoke loudly.

He wrapped his arms around her and patted her back. "Phoebe will be fine, *Mamm.*"

Phoebe had been a surrogate great-grandmother to him, Jenny knew. "I'm just so worried."

Releasing her, he stood back and regarded her. "Remember what Phoebe likes to say."

She smiled and felt her lips tremble. "She always says, 'I try not to worry about someone. After all, it's arrogant to do so when God knows what he's doing. He has a plan for each of us.' "

Phoebe would be upset with her if she knew that she was worrying now.

"How about some pie?" Hannah asked.

"No, thanks. I'm full." She looked at her plate, surprised to find that she'd eaten all that Hannah had put on it. "This was delicious."

She got to her feet and embraced Hannah, then Chris, before turning to Joshua and laying a hand on his shoulder. "Let's go home."

■ ■ ■ ■

"Hannah sent supper home for you."

Matthew took the plastic container from Jenny and set it on the kitchen table. "Thanks. I'll eat in a little while."

She started to object, to say that he needed to eat right then because he'd worked so hard in the fields that day before being summoned to help with Phoebe. But she realized that he was simply holding out his arms, inviting her into them.

"I know you're concerned," he said. "But God's in charge. Phoebe's a strong woman. Now, why don't you go upstairs and say good night to the *kinner* and then come down and keep me company while I eat?"

She smiled and nodded, then climbed the stairs. Annie's room was first because as the youngest she could never seem to keep her eyes open long after supper. When she peeked in, Annie's bed was empty. Her heart skipped a beat and then she took a deep breath and looked in on Mary. Sure enough, Annie was tucked up fast asleep in Mary's bed.

"She wanted to sleep in here," Mary whispered. "I told her I thought it would be okay."

"Sweet girl. Thank you." Hannah bent to kiss Mary's cheek. "See you in the morning."

"*Mamm?* You're sure Phoebe will be back tomorrow?"

No matter how many times one of the children called her mother, she got a funny little pang in her heart.

"That's what I was told," she said carefully.

She sat on the edge of the bed, careful not to jar the mattress and wake Annie. Reaching over, she took Mary's hand.

Looking down, she saw how small Mary's hand was in hers. Mary was nearly twelve now. She'd grown but was still more finely boned than Joshua. Like her brother and sister, she had big blue eyes that were regarding Jenny with too much seriousness right now.

"Did what happened today make you think about your *mamm?*"

When Mary nodded, she squeezed her hand. The children had lost their mother at such a young age to cancer.

"It made me think about my mom and my dad, too," Jenny told her. "I don't want to lose someone else, not for a very long time. We're just going to have to trust that God will send Phoebe back with us soon."

She released Mary's hand and pulled the quilt up to cover both girls. "See you in the morning."

Matthew was standing in the hall when Jenny came out. "I just checked on Joshua. He's asleep."

He took her hand and drew her down the hall, down the stairs, into the kitchen. A pot of tea sat in the middle of the table, steaming and sending out the scent of chamomile. Her favorite.

She smiled at him. "Thank you."

They sat down and Jenny enjoyed a cup of tea while her husband ate his dinner. It was quiet, so quiet.

"There's some pie."

He grinned at her, his eyes lighting up. "I never turn down pie. You know that."

"I know." She went to get it but when she reached into the refrigerator, her hand shook as she touched the pie plate.

"Did Joshua eat it all?" Matthew called when she didn't immediately return to the table.

"No," she said, bringing it to the table.

"There's enough for both of us," he said with satisfaction.

Jenny's bottom lip trembled. "Phoebe baked the pie."

"Yes," Matthew said slowly, watching her

steadily.

She looked at him with eyes brimming with tears. "What if it's the last one she makes?"

Jenny came awake with a snap.

She lay there, wondering what had awakened her. Matthew slept beside her, his arm wrapped around her. She listened, wondering if a child had cried out with a bad dream, but the house was quiet. No one needed *Mamm* to reassure them that the bad dream wasn't real. Or even that Phoebe would be back tomorrow.

Closing her eyes, she tried to will herself back to sleep. It had been a long and stressful day. Tomorrow would be here soon. Well, tomorrow was today now, she noted after a glance at the clock on the bedside table. She wanted to be up bright and early to go get Phoebe.

She pulled the quilt covering the bed up over her. Hannah and her friends had made it for her and Matthew and it was so special to her.

But as she touched the quilt, she thought of another one and wondered what would have happened, what her life might have been like, if her grandmother hadn't sent that quilt to the hospital where Jenny lay wounded. On the verge of sleep, she hoped that Phoebe was resting comfortably, that she wasn't lying there feeling scared or lonely or in pain like she'd been that day.

"You have a package," the nurse had said, placing it on the table beside Jenny's bed.

"Help — help me open it?"

"Sure, honey."

The nurse had lifted out a quilt and stroked it. "Oh, look what we have here," she murmured. "Isn't it lovely? I can't imagine how much work went into this."

Jenny watched the woman unfold it and spread it over her hospital blanket.

"There must be a card in here," the nurse said, searching through the tissue in the box. "Here, I found it."

She handed the card to Jenny. But no matter how much Jenny tried to read the writing, the lines blurred. "Can't read."

Frowning, the nurse took the card. "I forgot about your double vision. It's taking some time to go away but it will, honey, it will." She patted Jenny's hand. "Here, I'll read it for you."

The words inside had been simple and direct: "Come. Heal." It had been signed "Your grossmudder, Phoebe."

So she came back here as soon as she could, the moment she was released from the hospital. She'd come here and the first morning she was back this man beside her had come over to see Phoebe, his next-door neighbor, and through the maze that her poor hurt brain had become, the memory of being in love with him had emerged.

She'd never thought she'd walk again or talk normally and never, ever, in her wildest dreams, had she thought that Matthew could see past her battered body and failure to believe in herself or God or anything and want to marry her.

But here she was, married to this big, blond, gentle giant of a man. As if he felt her thinking about him, he stirred in his sleep and gathered her closer, cupping her head and pressing it against his chest, so that she finally fell asleep listening the slow, steady beat of his heart.

Someone was patting her arm. She opened her eyes and saw that Annie was standing beside the bed.

"Time to get up," she said brightly.

"Wha— what time is it?" Jenny asked. She glanced at the clock beside the bed and groaned. "Oh, Annie, go back to bed. It's too early to get up."

Annie gave her a winsome smile, one that showed two missing teeth. "Let's go get Phoebe before I go to *schul.*"

Jenny pulled the quilt up over her head. It

was too early to be up, even for the Amish. She nudged Matthew with her elbow. "Matthew? Tell our daughter to go back to bed."

"Annie, go back to bed," he mumbled and rolled over.

There was a tug on the quilt. Jenny lowered it. Annie still stood beside the bed but this time, Jenny saw the tears in her eyes.

She moved a little closer to Matthew then lifted the covers so that Annie could climb into bed.

"Ssh," she whispered when Annie started to speak. "Go back to sleep and we'll talk later."

To her surprise, Annie did so and after a few minutes, Jenny fell asleep again. She woke when Matthew climbed out of bed and dressed for the day.

Leaving Annie to sleep a little while longer, Jenny slipped out of bed and dressed, then headed downstairs to fix breakfast.

Matthew was standing at the stove, watching the percolator sitting atop it, his cup in his hand. She smiled. He could wait for breakfast until after chores, but he had to have that first cup of coffee before he went to work.

She walked up behind him, wrapped her arms around his waist, and laid her cheek against his back. "Love you."

"Love you, too."

"But you're looking at the coffee, not at me."

He turned and grinned at her as he slipped his arms around her waist. "Sorry. That doesn't mean I love it more."

"Sure," she said. "Sure."

Bending, he kissed her. "I didn't have my arms around coffee last night."

She returned his grin. "You're right."

"And I'm making you tea," he said as the teapot began whistling.

Reaching around him, she moved it and the whistling wound down to a sputter. "Thanks. Now, if we're quiet, we might get to have a few minutes before the children come down."

They sat at the table and enjoyed their jolt of caffeine, a morning routine for them.

Halfway through her tea, Jenny pressed her hand to her abdomen and winced. Getting up from the table, she rummaged in a kitchen cupboard for some Midol and washed it down with her tea.

When she sat down again, Matthew took her hand and squeezed it, giving comfort without words.

Another month without getting pregnant, she couldn't help thinking.

Feet hit the floor overhead and then moved around. Mary was up. Then the same thing happened in a different area of the upstairs. Joshua was up, too. No footsteps came from Jenny and Matthew's room. Annie had yet to wake.

Jenny chided herself for feeling a little depressed that she was once again not pregnant. She didn't need to be Amish to feel that children were a gift from God; wanting more than these precious three Matthew was sharing with her seemed greedy. He told her often that it was God's will if they had more and she believed that. She truly did.

It was just that she had these moments of disappointment thinking that she and God weren't on the same page. So to speak. But was He listening to her?

"As soon as I finish the chores and clean up, we'll go get Phoebe at the hospital," Matthew told her.

"I could go by myself —"

"No, we'll go together," he said firmly. "She's family."

Reaching out, she pulled him closer by his suspender and kissed him. "Thanks."

Mary came into the room a few minutes later. "Annie wasn't in my bed when I woke up and she's not in her room."

"It's okay. She's in my bed," Jenny told her. "She got up really early and wanted to go get *Grossmudder* before school."

Mary's face brightened. "Can we?"

"No, sweetheart." She hated the way Mary's face fell. "But she'll be here when you come home."

"Okay. Do you want me to go get Annie?"

Jenny smiled. "That would be wonderful. And for that, you get to choose what we'll have for breakfast."

Mary thought for a moment. "French toast?"

"French toast it is." Jenny got a skillet out, set it on the stove, and rummaged in a drawer for a spatula.

Mary passed Joshua as he walked into the room, rubbing his eyes.

"You snooze, you lose," she told him smugly.

"Huh?" He looked from her to Jenny.

"Early bird gets the worm," she said and walked out of the room.

"We're having worms for breakfast?" he asked, making a disgusted face.

"Your *mamm* would never make you worms for breakfast," Matthew chided, finishing his coffee and setting the cup in the sink.

"You never know what she might make,"

Joshua told him. "You remember she made scrapple." He grabbed his throat and made a gagging noise as he started for the door. "How can anyone eat that with what's in it?"

"Some people like scrapple," Matthew pointed out.

"You think you're so funny with the comments about my cooking!" Jenny popped him on the fanny with the spatula.

"Hey, ow!" he cried. "She hit me!" he told his father.

Matthew shook his head and tried to suppress a grin. "A wise man always compliments the cook."

"Right!" Jenny said. Then she frowned. "Wait a minute, that sounds like a backhanded kind of comment. Are you saying you compliment my cooking even when you don't think it's good?"

Matthew cocked his head. "Did you hear that?" he asked Joshua.

Joshua listened hard. "I don't hear anything."

"There it is again. Bessie's calling for us. Back soon," he said quickly and the two of them rushed out the door.

"Very funny," Jenny muttered. "Like a cow's calling you!"

■ ■ ■ ■

"I tried to call you," Phoebe said when Jenny and Matthew walked into her hospital room. "They're insisting on keeping me another day."

"Another day? But why?"

"Just more tests. You know how doctors love to run more tests."

"What kind of tests?"

"Just the usual stuff," Phoebe said vaguely. "You get older, they want to do more tests."

Jenny sank into a chair beside the bed. "Now you're getting me worried. Since when would you meekly agree to these? I expected you to be waiting at the front door when we arrived, impatient to be out of here."

She studied her grandmother, feeling that something wasn't being said, that more was going on here than —

An aide knocked on the doorframe. "Ready to go?"

Phoebe nodded. She lifted the covers and her feet emerged, covered with bright red crocheted footies. When she saw Jenny staring at them, she laughed. "The nurse on duty last night gave them to me. A friend of hers makes them for patients. They kept my feet nice and cozy."

"How about we bring you some of your own things this afternoon? Since you have to spend another night."

Jenny felt her heart warm at Matthew's suggestion. "Maybe your robe?" she suggested, smiling at the way her grandmother wore a second gown with the ties in the front, covering the one underneath that she would have felt immodest to leave the room in.

As always, Phoebe wore her *kapp* over her perfectly groomed hair.

The aide rolled the wheelchair closer to the bed and Phoebe sat in it and watched him adjust the footrests for her. Then he picked up the blanket from the foot of the bed and tucked it around her. "It can be a bit cold where we're going."

Jenny wanted to ask where that was but Matthew took her hand and squeezed it and when she glanced at him, he sent her a silent message that husbands and wives quickly learned to interpret after their wedding. This one said, "Leave it alone. Please."

Even though his look wasn't one of censure, she wanted to object, to say that she had a right as a granddaughter to ask where they were going, what tests the aide was taking Phoebe for. It wasn't nosiness, it was simply concern. If something was wrong, she wanted to know so she could do something. *Something.*

And then the sobering thought came that if there was something wrong that there was nothing she really could do about it . . . it was all up to God.

The aide pushed the chair toward them and then stopped, sensitive to Jenny's mood.

Jenny bent and hugged Phoebe and noted that her grandmother's arms felt as strong as ever. Drawing back, she forced a smile.

"I'm not going to worry," she said. "Because — because you always say that worrying is arrogant. God knows what He's doing."

Phoebe beamed. "Exactly. I'll be back home before you know it."

Matthew kissed her cheek. "See you later."

They stood and watched as the aide pushed Phoebe out of the room and then Jenny turned to Matthew.

"What was that about, that stopping me when I wanted to ask about the tests?"

Matthew touched her shoulders and his eyes were kind. "She's your grandmother but I've known Phoebe for a long time and she's a very private person. If there's something she wants to tell you, she will. And if she doesn't, you need to respect her privacy."

"But if she's seriously sick —"

"We must respect her wishes, *lieb*."

"Don't try to distract me by calling me 'love,' " she told him, trying not to pout.

His lips twitched. "I wouldn't dream of it." Then he sobered. "I'm not saying that if her health were to change seriously that I don't agree with you about talking with her about it," he told her. "But I feel she'll talk to us if things change."

Jenny nodded and sighed. "Well, let's go on home, then. Maybe the children will want to come when we bring Phoebe some of her things."

"I think if we try to leave them home we'll never hear the end of it," he said with a chuckle as they left the room.

4

"It's driving you crazy, isn't it?"

Jenny frowned at Hannah. "It's not funny."

Hannah sighed and reached for Jenny's hand. "No, it's not. I don't know why Phoebe's being so secretive, either."

"You didn't know she was taking prescription medicine?"

Leaning back in her chair, Hannah began rubbing her abdomen, a habit Jenny had noticed.

"I really didn't," Hannah told her. "I've been concerned by how hard it was on her to climb the stairs here at the house but she kept saying she was fine. Then Chris and I got married and she insisted we should have her bedroom upstairs so that solved that."

She looked around the room and her smile was soft. "You know, sometimes it seems like a dream. Everything that's happened, I mean. Did you feel that way when you first married Matthew?"

Jenny smiled. "Yeah. Sometimes I still do. Especially when I look at the children. It already felt like a miracle that Matthew and I got a second chance but to have a ready-made family. Well, I still find myself thinking I should pinch myself."

"I was remembering this conversation we had not long after I met you," Hannah said. "I thought I wouldn't ever get married. You said I should make a wish list of what I wanted in a man."

She glanced at Jenny and grinned. "A wish list for a man. Imagine, I thought. What's funny is after I did that, I realized I wanted a man much like my brother."

"You couldn't do better," Jenny said with a smile. "It's so good to see the two of you so happy. You deserve it. And Chris surely does after all he went through in the military."

She watched Hannah unconsciously rub at her arm. "Is it hurting?"

Hannah glanced down at her arm. "Talking about Chris and all he went through being injured overseas probably made me think of it. Who'd have thought someone could hate him so much and come here to hurt him."

"And hurt you in the process."

Hannah shrugged. "That's all over now.

Look at how well things turned out. Last time I saw Malcolm —"

Someone knocked at the front door. Hannah started to heave herself up out of the chair but Jenny rose and pressed her back into it.

"I'll get it. You stay and relax."

Rebecca Yoder stood on the front porch. "I'm on my way into town but I just had to stop. I heard that Phoebe was taken to the hospital. Is she okay?"

Jenny filled her in and the woman impulsively hugged her. "I'm sure she'll be fine. Is there anything I can do to help?"

"If you could make some calls and let her friends know."

"I surely will. Now don't you go worrying. Phoebe's a strong woman. I'm sure she'll be home before you know it."

Touched by the older woman's caring, Jenny walked back to the kitchen.

Her sister-in-law was doubled over as if she were in pain. Jenny rushed to her side.

"Hannah? What's wrong? Tell me you're not going into labor."

Hannah shook her head. "No," she managed to say. "It's too soon."

"Like babies ever do what they're supposed to do. You remember how Fannie Mae went into labor at the quilting two weeks ago. She thought she was just having back pain and she'd been in labor most of the day."

"I'm — I'm not in labor. Pain —" she pressed a hand just under her bust. "Feels like the baby's got his foot stuck — up under — under my ribs."

Truly alarmed by now, Jenny knelt beside Hannah's chair. "That's not possible, is it? I mean, it's in the uterus and —"

"I don't need a biology lesson right now," Hannah snapped.

Then, just as quickly, she turned and gave Jenny a look of remorse. "Oh, I'm sorry!"

Jenny patted her arm. "It's okay. Is it any better?"

Hannah grabbed Jenny's hand, pressed it to her abdomen, and held it there. "Here, feel this! Doesn't it feel like it's going to kick its way out?"

The minute Hannah held her hand to her abdomen, Jenny felt the moving lump kick. She jerked her hand away and stared, shocked, at Hannah. "Wow!"

"Hurts!" Hannah gasped.

"I think we better call the doctor."

Hannah shifted in her chair and frowned. "I'm sure it'll stop in a minute." Then she looked at Jenny. "What?"

"Has this happened before?"

"No. Really," she insisted when Jenny looked doubtful. "Trust me, I'd have told you if something like this had happened."

"I dunno," Jenny muttered. "One family member's already kept a secret from me."

"Well, I have no secrets. Well, except for telling everyone the sex of the baby. But Chris and I agreed we don't want to know so how can I tell anyone what I don't know?"

Jenny watched as Hannah broke out in a sweat. She went to the sink, dampened a dish towel with cool water, and wiped Hannah's face with it.

"That feels good."

"Where's Chris?"

"Out in the field."

"Let me go ring the bell and call him in."

"No! I don't want to worry him."

"Too bad," Jenny told her and started for the door. "You're scaring me."

Jenny rang the dinner bell, hoping Chris would hurry in, wondering why she was using the bell when it wasn't time for a meal. Sure enough, he came running up.

"What's wrong? Is it Hannah? Is she in labor?" he asked, panting.

"She says she isn't but the baby's doing something that's hurting her. I think she needs to go to the doctor."

Hannah was grimacing in pain as she bent over the table when they rushed into the kitchen. Chris grasped her by the arms and held her against his body. "Baby, are you okay?"

"This little monster's kicking me up under my ribs," she told him, sounding breathless.

"It can't kick its way out, can it?" Chris turned to ask Jenny.

She pressed her fingers to her mouth, trying not to laugh at his naiveté, and shook her head. "I never heard of such a thing."

Then, to their horror, Hannah slumped against Chris. "Ow!" she cried. "That hurt!" She looked at Jenny. "Is this how bad it's going to hurt when it comes out?"

"How would I know? I've never had a baby, remember?" But Jenny had heard horror stories of hours, *days,* of labor, of excruciating pain.

Hannah glanced at Chris and he gave her a disbelieving look. "Don't look at me! How would I know? Listen, I think we better get you to the doctor."

"I don't want to go. I don't want them to make the baby come out before it's time. Maybe if I just lie down for a few minutes it'll stop."

Chris glanced at Jenny and she lifted her hands and then let them fall to her sides.

"Let's let her lie down on the sofa and you call her doctor."

Nodding, he lifted Hannah into his arms and carried her into the living room and gently laid her on the sofa. Carefully, he tucked a sofa pillow behind her and bent over her to take her hand. "Any better?"

Jenny stood beside Chris and saw that tears were leaking from the corners of Hannah's eyes and she'd lost even more color in her face.

"I'll stay with her while you go call the doctor," she said quietly. "Here, it's the doctor's card she keeps on the refrigerator."

Chris nodded. He kissed Hannah's cheek and hurried to the phone shanty.

"He looks terrified." Hannah said, sighing. "I never thought I'd see him this way. I mean, he was a soldier in war and even after he came home he had a gun shoved in his face by the man who followed him here to hurt him."

Jenny drew a chair over to sit closer to Hannah. "I have to agree with you." She glanced at the door, then back at Hannah. "Wonder how he's going to be in the delivery room?"

The front door opened and shut and Matthew rushed into the room. "Why did you ring the dinner bell —" he stopped as he took in the sight of Hannah lying on the sofa. "What's this about? You in labor?"

Hannah rolled her eyes at her brother. "No, the baby's got its foot up under my ribs. Chris is calling the doctor."

The door opened and slammed. "The doctor said to bring you in," Chris said tersely. "I called a driver. He said he can be here in ten minutes." He sighed as he put his hands on his hips and stared at Hannah. "If I had my Mustang I could be taking you there right now."

"I'm not getting up on some horse," Hannah snapped, rubbing her hand over her abdomen.

He stared at her for a long moment and then he laughed. "It's a car, sweetheart. A Mustang's a sports car."

"Oh." She held out her hand. "Can you help me get up? Otherwise I'm going to need a crane."

"You stay right there while I get your bag."

"I don't need it!" she said but he was already out of the room and they could hear him taking the stairs two at a time.

"Anything I can do?" Matthew asked Hannah.

"Why don't you go see if you can calm Chris down," she suggested.

"I can do that."

Jenny waited until Matthew was out of the room. "How was he when Amelia had the children?"

"He was a rock when it came to having a *boppli,*" Hannah told her, grimacing as she tried to get more comfortable. "At least, that's what Amelia told me."

Good information to have for the future, Jenny thought. *If* ever she conceived.

Chris and Matthew returned minus the suitcase Hannah had packed for when she went to the hospital to deliver.

"I convinced Chris that he doesn't need to take the bag," Matthew said. "If the *boppli* decides to come, we can bring it later."

A horn honked.

"There's our ride," Chris said. "Let's hustle."

Hannah held out her hand but instead of taking it, Chris lifted her easily and started for the door.

"Oh, my purse!" she cried. "Jenny, my purse!"

"You don't need it," Chris told her but when she held out her hands, blocking them from passing through the front doorway, he stopped and sighed. "What is it with women and their purses?"

Matthew turned to Jenny. "Better go get it."

Jenny ran for the purse and passed it to Hannah. "Let us know what the doctor says. Matthew has his cell phone."

"Tell Phoebe I'll see her later."

"Phoebe!" Jenny looked at Matthew. "I have to get her a robe and some things." She pressed her hands to her cheeks. "Oh, my, what excitement we've had around here the past two days."

"Why don't you go take care of that and I'll round up someone to look after the *kinner* while we go see Phoebe?"

"It was good of Rebecca to come over and watch out for the *kinner,*" Matthew said as they pulled out onto the road in their buggy.

"Mmm," Jenny said.

Matthew glanced at Jenny. She seemed lost in thought.

He had an idea of where those thoughts were centered. She didn't know, couldn't know, that he'd heard her ask his sister how he'd been when he and his first wife had had their *kinner.*

He knew it wasn't about Amelia . . . that Jenny felt she came second to her in any way. She was just curious about how he cared for a wife when she was in need. He carried a sense of guilt that he hadn't shown Jenny how he could care for her in a time of

spiritual that I can just say, 'Okay, it's God's will.' "

He stared ahead at the road. "I went through all the stages of grief" — he stopped and looked at her. "I know about them because I didn't just talk to the bishop after Amelia died. I talked to a grief counselor and he told me about the seven stages of grief. I went through every one — some of them several times. It took a long time to come to some kind of peace about her death. Years."

Looking at her hand in his big, work-callused one, he searched for the right words — so hard for him and so easy for her since she was a writer. "The biggest thing, the most important thing I learned about watching someone I loved being ill was to take each day and live it because you never knew how many days you had left with the person you loved."

"You're saying worry destroys today, that it takes away from our being able to live and love."

"I admire how you can come up with the right words."

She elbowed him. "You're teasing me."

Picking up the reins, he glanced back and found the road clear. He called to Pilot and guided the buggy back onto the road.

"Let's go see how Phoebe's doing. She could be waiting there to go home with us instead of needing her robe."

"I pray you're right," Jenny said fervently. "I'll worry a lot less when she's back home."

"Well, Matthew said that you were coming home today and I didn't believe him," Jenny told Phoebe as they traveled home a short time later.

"Did you call the hospital, Matthew?" Phoebe asked him.

He shook his head. "I just had a feeling." He glanced at Jenny and grinned.

Jenny sighed. "He's going to be impossible and think he's right about everything from now on."

Laughing, Matthew shook his head. "I know better."

They pulled into the drive and as Matthew was helping Phoebe climb out of the back seat of the buggy, a car pulled into the drive.

"Hannah!" Jenny cried and ran to her as Chris helped her from the vehicle. "You and Phoebe, home at the same time! God is good!"

"It was all a big worry over nothing."

"Hardly nothing," Chris told Jenny as he

tucked away his wallet after paying the driver.

"We can talk about that later," Hannah told him, hugging Phoebe and then sliding her arm through the older woman's so they could walk inside together. "Phoebe's home!"

Jenny put coffee on, water for tea, and set out a plate of cookies.

"So what did the doctor say?" she asked as she sat at the table.

Hannah looked at Phoebe. "You go first."

Phoebe shook her head. "I want to know about the baby first. Jenny told me about what happened on the way home. What did the doctor say?"

"Just that this sort of thing happens sometimes."

"Hannah," Chris said in a low voice.

"Okay, he said that the pain can get bad enough that women have passed out. So he said to be careful and stay away from things like glass doors and that sort of thing so I don't get hurt."

"I see." Jenny got up when the tea kettle whistled and poured a mug of hot water. She brought it to the table with a tin of tea bags and set them before Hannah.

"Of course the baby stopped what he'd been doing just as we walked into the doctor's office." She shook her head and rolled her eyes at her husband. "Sorry."

He leaned over and kissed her cheek. "I don't care. We needed to know what was going on. And this way, if it should happen again, you'll know what to do so you don't get hurt."

"Did you find out the sex of the baby?" Phoebe wanted to know. She leaned forward, her eyes sparkling with interest.

"We don't want to know. Remember?"

"I was hoping you'd changed your mind."

Jenny secretly wished so, too. It just seemed to her that now that people could know, they'd want to. It seemed to make life easier. The prospective parents could pick out the right name and paint the room and decorate it for whatever sex the baby was. Friends and family could buy the right presents for baby showers. If there were any siblings, they could be prepared for the new little person who would appear soon.

When Hannah and Chris had first told Jenny and Matthew that they were expecting but that they'd asked the doctor not to tell them the baby's sex, Jenny had thought that it was just a whim. That they'd change their minds.

She must have forgotten how stubborn her husband's sister was, and how much

Chris was willing to do to make her happy. He had good reason to want to do it, apart from loving her. After all, how many women stood in front of a man and took a bullet meant for him?

Jenny thought about how amazing it was that two such different people — this woman raised as Amish from birth as Hannah was and Chris, a former *Englischer* raised to join the military as part of his family tradition — meshed so well as a couple. And that they had worked through Hannah's insistence to forgive their assailant and see that he was given a second chance to not go to prison.

Matthew got up to pour more coffee for them and as he passed Jenny, he paused to touch her shoulder. "You okay?"

She nodded. "I'm fine, thanks."

"So now it's your turn," Hannah said. She leaned her elbows on the table and looked at Phoebe.

"Everyone made such a fuss out of me fainting," Phoebe said casually, shrugging her shoulders. She stirred a spoon around and around in her coffee cup.

A whisper of alarm ran up Jenny's spine. She'd never known Phoebe to be evasive, to avoid looking at anyone. When she'd been attending college, earning her journalism degree, she'd attended a lecture for psychology class, one on nonverbal communication. The lecture hadn't just been interesting and helped her earn extra credit for the psychology class — it had proven invaluable when she interviewed people, among other things.

After all, like the professor had said that night, something like eighty percent of the information that people received about a person was nonverbal — it wasn't what they said, but how they behaved. Watch their eyes, their hands, their posture, the professor had said. Watch to see if they look at you directly or if they avoid meeting your eyes. See if they tap their foot from nervousness or do some other movement that seems to show they're tense.

Like stir their coffee over and over. While not meeting your eyes.

Uncomfortable, she looked around at the others at the table. Matthew and Hannah were watching Phoebe and clearly taking her at face value. But Chris was doing the same thing as Phoebe — well, not exactly. He wasn't stirring his coffee, but he wasn't looking at Phoebe or anyone else at the table. His expression was troubled. Why? Jenny wondered.

He knew something, she realized. He *knew*

something.

"One of the paramedics went in your medicine cabinet," Jenny said slowly. "He showed us prescriptions you'd been taking."

Phoebe's eyes flew up to meet Jenny's. "Why, that's an invasion of privacy."

Jenny shook her head. "No," she said quietly. "They need to know what medications people are taking so they can tell the doctors at the hospital. They need to know about those medications because they're taken for certain conditions and if the person they've been called to come help is unconscious, well, that gives them more information."

"We don't want to pry, *Grossmudder.*" Jenny reached across the table. "But we're worried. Something's wrong, isn't it?"

Phoebe sighed. "Yes. But it's not as bad as it seems."

Her words were chilling. Jenny glanced at Matthew and he'd gone still, his coffee cup halfway to his mouth. *Not as bad as it seems?*

The front door slammed open and it sounded like a herd of cattle ran through the living room. Annie burst into the kitchen and skidded to a stop when she saw the adults seated at the table.

"You're back!" she cried, flinging herself

into Phoebe's arms. "I'm so, so happy."

Phoebe beamed and hugged her. "Me, too."

Annie turned. "Mary! Joshua! See who's here!"

Phoebe flinched. "Well, I don't think I'll be able to hear for another hour, but who cares."

She held out her other arm and Mary and Joshua rushed into them so that she was holding all three in a big hug.

The sight warmed Jenny's heart. Phoebe looked at her over the tops of the children's heads. *Not now,* she seemed to telegraph. *Not now.*

5

"*Mamm,* can we have a celebration supper?" Annie asked her.

It was a family tradition to have a big supper when there was something to celebrate like a good report card or a birthday. Jenny supposed they could do it when the children's grandmother-of-the-heart had returned home.

"Sure," said Jenny. "We'll fix all her favorites."

Phoebe looked at Annie, then Mary, then Joshua. "I want macaroni and cheese. And green bean casserole. And oatmeal cookies for dessert."

"Those are all our favorites!" Annie cried.

"They are?" Phoebe pretended surprise.

"You make them for us all the time," Mary told her.

"Well, I love them, too."

"Go do your chores and I'll get the macaroni and cheese and green bean casserole started," Jenny told them. "We'll all make the cookies after supper."

She looked at Hannah. "Would you mind if I cooked for all of us here?"

Hannah chuckled. "If I had the energy I'd jump up and kiss you for that."

"Great. Whatever ingredients you don't have I can send one of the children to get from our house." She turned to preheat the oven. "I'll replace what I use tomorrow."

"Don't be silly. We're family. We share."

Jenny nodded and sighed. "Sorry. You're right."

The moment the children were gone, Jenny turned to her grandmother. "Now we can talk."

Phoebe glanced around at them and sighed. "I've been having some trouble with my heart."

Jenny's knees went weak. She sank down into her chair.

"See, I knew you'd get upset," Phoebe said, frowning. "That's why I didn't tell anyone. You've been through enough."

"That doesn't mean that you shouldn't tell me," Jenny told her. "If you'll ill, we need to know."

"I'm not ill!"

Chris patted her hand. "Of course you're not. My grandmother had it and she lived

for a long time after her diagnosis."

"What diagnosis, Chris? All she's said is she's having some trouble with her heart. She hasn't even said exactly *what* type of heart problem she's having."

His coloring was fair so even though his face was tanned from working the fields under the sun, there was a telltale reddening.

"You knew," Jenny accused. "You knew and you didn't tell me."

Hannah turned to Chris. "You knew?"

"Don't be angry at him," Phoebe said quickly. "He guessed. He saw my prescriptions and guessed I have congestive heart failure."

"Congestive heart failure," Jenny whispered, shocked.

"It's not as bad as it sounds," Phoebe rushed to say. "I've been doing what the doctor told me to. I'm managing. You can't blame Chris."

"I found out a while ago," Chris said in his defense. "She's been fine so I forgot all about it."

"When?" Hannah wanted to know. "When did you find out?"

Chris hesitated. "That day you thought I was leaving town." Chris turned to Jenny. "So you see, not telling you didn't make

any difference. Phoebe has been fine for a long time."

Phoebe nodded. "Exactly."

"Have you forgotten that she was just released from the hospital?" Jenny asked him. She turned to Phoebe. "Maybe it's time for you to move into the *dawdi haus* with us."

"Why?"

"So we can take care of you —"

"I don't need taking care of." Abruptly, Phoebe stood and walked over to put her cup in the sink.

Jenny looked to Matthew for support.

"Phoebe knows she is welcome in our home," Matthew said quietly. "She's been like a *grossmudder* to the *kinner* and me."

"*This* is my home," Phoebe said firmly.

"It is," Chris said. "That was what we agreed on when I moved in here after Hannah and I married and you sold us the farm." He smiled at Phoebe. "But it's more than a business deal. If this had been my house, I'd have wanted you to stay with us, Phoebe. You know I love you like a grandmother, too."

She gave him a fond smile and ruffled his hair. "I know. And I love you like a *grosssohn.*"

Then she looked at each of them with her

back straight and her eyes direct. "But I'm not sick and I'm not old," she insisted. "And I won't have anyone treating me that way unless and until I am."

There was silence. Phoebe had never spoken to them this way.

Then Phoebe glanced at Hannah. "What's wrong?" she asked, moving swiftly to her side.

Hannah looked even paler than she had earlier that day, Jenny saw.

"Doing it again," she gasped, using both hands to knead on her abdomen, as if it were a lump of dough she could reshape. "Kicking — kicking me under the ribs again."

"I'd say maybe it's a 'he' and he's going to be a football player but that game's not played in these parts," Chris told her. "Come on, let's get you to lie down and see if it helps."

He lifted her but she shook her head. "I'm sorry, I know you're strong. But I'm not letting you carry me up the stairs."

Chris staggered and set her back on her feet. "Well, maybe you're right — oof!" he cried and rubbed his stomach where her elbow had connected.

"I saw you grinning!" she retorted, glaring at him over her shoulder as she stomped to

the stairs.

"Tread carefully," Matthew warned, trying not to smile. "And I don't mean be careful on the stairs."

"Yeah, yeah," Chris said.

"Chris!" Hannah called, her tone sharp.

His glance slid back to Matthew. "Yes, dear?"

"I thought you were going to come up here!"

"Yes, dear," Chris said and he hurried after her.

Matthew couldn't stop laughing.

"You're watching me."

Jenny glanced at Phoebe as she piled freshly baked oatmeal cookies in the cookie jar. "I don't know what you're talking about."

"You keep looking at me like I'm going to collapse at any moment."

"You're imagining it."

Phoebe harrumphed. "I know what I see."

Jenny placed the top on the jar and turned. "Well, then, if I have — and I'm not saying that I have, then all you have to do is stay healthy and I'm sure I'll get tired of that and stop. Right?"

Her grandmother placed her hands on her hips and stared at her. "Sometimes you're

just too smart for your own good."

"I never understood that phrase," Jenny said, trying to hold back her smile. "I mean, how can it be bad for a person to be smart? It seems to me that we should want to be as smart as we can be."

Phoebe gave her a stern look. "You're trying to change the subject. What is it they call it in the *Englisch* world? You're being a smart Alex."

"Smart aleck," Jenny said. "It's 'smart aleck.' " She pressed her fingers to her mouth to still the giggles.

"You know what I mean."

Jenny sighed. "I do. But you're just going to have to put up with me. I'm still a work in progress. I'm still trying not to worry," she explained when she saw Phoebe look confused. "But I haven't mastered this not-worrying thing like you have."

She threw her arms around Phoebe. "You scared me so badly," she said. "You scared me."

She felt her grandmother pat her back. "I know. I know. Don't cry. I don't like to see you cry."

"I'm sorry." Jenny stood back and wiped away her tears with her hands.

Phoebe handed her the snowy handkerchief she always kept tucked in her pocket.

"I miss you," Jenny told her. "I miss us living together under the same roof."

"You don't have time to miss me with all that you do."

"I do," Jenny insisted.

"You see me every day. And I intend to be around for a long time."

"We don't get a say in that," Jenny told her, shaking her head and trying to smile. "Not even you get to make bargains with God."

"No," Phoebe agreed and she smiled. "You're right."

She patted Jenny's cheek as she gazed at her with her wise, faded blue eyes. "But I'm doing everything the doctor says and as much as I'd like to see my *mann,* I'd really like to enjoy this beautiful earth for quite a while longer."

She yawned. "Sorry. I'm feeling kind of tired. I think I'll go to bed early." She slanted a look at Jenny. "Tired. Just tired. Okay?"

Jenny nodded. She kissed her grandmother's cheek. "Sleep well. I'll see you tomorrow."

Two days later, Hannah surprised Jenny by visiting after the children left for school.

"I was just coming over," Jenny told her.

"I know. But I thought I'd warn you." Hannah took a seat at the kitchen table.

"I'm worried about Phoebe," she said without preamble. "She looks flushed like she has a fever and she's coughing. And all I could get her to eat this morning was a piece of toast with some hot tea."

Jenny frowned. "Sounds like she's coming down with a cold."

"She said so herself," Hannah told her. "Said all she needed to do was lie down for a little while and she'd be fine."

"I was coming over after I finished my baking." She glanced at the timer on the stove.

Hannah sniffed. "What's that I smell? It's not —"

Laughing, Jenny nodded. "It's cinnamon rolls. I made a second batch after the children left. Figured I'd bring some over to you and Phoebe."

"Did I ever tell you that you're my favorite sister-in-law?" Hannah nodded when Jenny held up the tea kettle. "*Ya,* I'd love a cup of tea."

"I'm your only sister-in-law," Jenny said, pouring them both a cup of hot water and getting out the canister of tea bags — regular for her, decaffeinated ones for Hannah, of course.

"The thing is, we have to be careful with what we say around Phoebe. I think we offended her the other day."

The timer dinged. Jenny drew the pan of rolls from the oven, placed them on top of the stove and checked them, then shut off the oven. When she turned to get a plate, Hannah was right there, holding one out and grinning.

"Can I have that one?" she said, pointing to the biggest roll in the pan.

Jenny peered at it. "Looks like it has your name on it. But I haven't put the frosting on yet."

Hannah gave her the plate and resumed her seat. "Well, hurry. There are two of us waiting, you know."

"I know. That's why you ate at your house and then here, too."

Smiling, she got out a bowl and stirred confectioner's sugar and milk together to form a thick frosting. Slathering it on the rolls, she watched it melt down into the crevices.

Hannah cleared her throat, reminding Jenny of her impatience to eat it. Quickly, she cut out the roll Hannah had pointed to, placed it on a plate, and put it before her.

"You know, one of these days I might make that recipe for cinnamon roll French

toast that Fannie Mae gave me."

"Ooh, you're killing me," Hannah said as she picked up the roll. "Imagine how incredible that must taste." She chewed and swallowed, then took a sip of tea.

Jenny wrapped up several of the rolls to take to Phoebe and made a separate package. She handed it to Hannah. "There's one in here for you and one for Chris. I trust that the one for Chris will make it to him?"

Hannah rubbed her abdomen. "Is he carrying this baby? Hmm? Is he?"

Rolling her eyes, Jenny took back the package and added another roll. Really, sometimes adults were worse than kids.

"I'm sure Chris is going to love it," Hannah said with a grin. "Ready to go?"

Jenny knocked on her grandmother's door.

"Come in," she croaked.

Opening the door, Jenny peered inside the room. The blinds were shut, so it was dim, but she could see her grandmother sitting up in her bed, her back resting against the headboard.

"You sound awful."

"It's just a cold. You shouldn't be here."

"I've been around colds with the children," Jenny told her briskly. "It doesn't mean you automatically get one."

Walking over to the bed, she lay the back of her hand on her grandmother's forehead. "Oh, my, you're burning up," Jenny whispered, alarmed. "I'm going to get a thermometer."

"There's one in the cabinet in the bathroom there."

She'd never had reason to go into her grandmother's medicine cabinet before. Now, she saw the prescription bottles she'd never known Phoebe had. Quickly, she reached for the thermometer and shut the cabinet. No way she wanted her grandmother to think she was snooping and get upset with her.

When she returned with it and persuaded Phoebe to pop it into her mouth, Jenny found that her mother's intuition about how high her grandmother's temperature was based on her hand to forehead was correct: Phoebe's temp was 104.

"I think this is more than a cold."

Phoebe shook her head. "I'm going to take some aspirin and have a nap."

"I'll get the aspirin," Jenny said quickly. "You rest."

A nap? Phoebe taking a nap was as alarming as her having a temperature.

Hannah thought so, too, when she went to tell her.

"I think we should call her doctor."

Jenny bit her lip. "This is so hard. She's an adult. We can't treat her like a child." She sighed. "I better get back with the aspirin. I wouldn't want her to think we're out here talking about her."

"Since when is it wrong to care about someone?" Hannah wanted to know. "I don't get upset when someone does that with me."

"You mean like you immediately listened to us when we wanted you to go to doctor the other day when the baby was kicking under your ribs?" Jenny asked her as she held a glass under the running faucet,

Hannah sighed. "You had to bring that up, didn't you?"

Jenny added some ice to the glass of water and returned to Phoebe's room.

Her grandmother sat up when Jenny entered the room. She took the aspirin and drained the glass of water. "I'll be fine after my nap."

Jenny wasn't so sure about that but she stayed silent. "I think I'll stick around and help Hannah with some cleaning. You let me know if you need anything."

Nodding, Phoebe lay down and Jenny could hear her deep, even breathing before she left the room, closing the door quietly behind her. She went in search of Hannah and found her sweeping the floor in the living room. Or rather, Hannah was leaning against the wall and wiping her brow.

"Hot work," she said with a sigh when Jenny entered the room. "Pregnancy and late summer don't mix well."

Jenny reached for the broom but Hannah kept her hold on it. "Sit down and put your feet up. I can finish this."

"No, it's my house. You have enough to do."

For a minute they wrestled with the broom and then they stopped and stared at each other. Jenny was the first to burst into laughter and then Hannah joined her.

"Here, you win," said Hannah, wiping her eyes. "Far be it from me to keep you from your housecleaning mania." She sank down onto the sofa and sighed as she put her feet up.

"I know it's not easy being pregnant right now. Maybe it never is, no matter what season it is when you get close to delivery. I thought I'd stick around and help you while Phoebe naps, see how she's feeling when she wakes up. I'm wondering if I should take her to see the doctor."

"You think it's more than a cold, too."

Jenny nodded. "I do."

As if on cue, they heard Phoebe coughing.

"She sounds worse than last night," Hannah said.

Jenny swept faster. "I'm going to do the kitchen, too. You stay right there."

"I'll owe you."

Jenny turned so Hannah wouldn't see her wince. Everyone just seemed to assume she would get pregnant. What were they thinking? Hannah knew as much as Phoebe about her injuries, about what the doctors had said about possible repercussions with the internal injuries; Jenny's doctor had said only time would tell if she could get pregnant.

As Jenny swept the kitchen, she kept hearing Phoebe's coughing and wondered if she was getting any rest at all. She had her answer when Phoebe opened the door and peered out. Her eyes were glassy and her face flushed. "Where is Hannah?"

"In the living room resting. Did you need her?"

"No, I don't want to take a chance of getting her sick in her condition. I was going to get a glass of water in the kitchen."

Jenny touched Phoebe's forehead. It felt hotter than before. "I'll get the water for you but let's take your temp again first."

It had gone up another degree.

"Grandmother, I think it's time we took you to see the doctor."

The older woman opened her mouth, then closed it. She walked over to the bed and sat. "Fine."

Like her grandmother saying she'd take a nap in the middle of the day, her acquiescence was totally unexpected.

Jenny rushed to the other room and found Hannah staring at the ceiling as she lay on the sofa. "I can't sleep," she complained. "I keep thinking of all the things I need to do."

"You can call Phoebe's doctor and tell him we're bringing her in."

Hannah sat up. "She's worse?"

"And she agreed to go. That scares me. I expected to have an argument."

"*Ya.* I would have, too. I'll go call now."

Jenny returned to her grandmother's room and found her still sitting in the same place.

"I'm going to get Matthew to hitch up the buggy," Jenny said quickly. "You stay right here and when I come back I'll help you get dressed."

"I can get dressed by myself," Phoebe grumbled.

But when Jenny returned, Phoebe hadn't moved.

"Back so soon?" she asked, looking a little bewildered.

"It's just that you're not feeling well," Jenny soothed, reaching for a dress. "Here, I'll help you."

She'd always thought that the name Phoebe suited her grandmother for she was a tiny, birdlike woman who flitted around with such energy and bright-eyed enthusiasm. Now Phoebe seemed even smaller and more frail. She'd never seemed old.

Until now.

Even though she was sick, Phoebe insisted on going through the laborious motions of brushing and binding up her waist-long hair and putting on her *kapp.* But the effort cost her. By the time she finished she was white and her breathing was raspy.

There was a knock on the door. "Phoebe, are you ready?" Matthew called out.

Jenny opened the door. "She's ready."

"I'm sorry for all the trouble," Phoebe said as she walked past him.

"It's no trouble at all," he told her, gallantly taking her arm and walking with her.

When she stopped and started coughing, a hacking cough that left her leaning against the doorframe, he scooped her up and carried her to the buggy.

"I can walk."

Matthew slanted a look at Jenny. "I've heard that before."

"I — haven't been — carried in years. I remember when —" she broke off and began coughing again.

"Sounds like it might be a good story," he said as he lifted her onto the backseat of the buggy. "But I think you better save your breath and tell me sometime later."

"I think we should take her straight to the emergency room," he whispered to Jenny as they rounded the buggy.

"She agreed to go to the doctor, so we're taking her there. If the doctor thinks she should go to the ER, we'll go there."

The news wasn't good.

"Phoebe has pneumonia," the doctor told them. "I'm recommending that she go to the hospital."

"No hospital," Phoebe said firmly. "Where do you think I got it?"

"Now, you don't know that."

Phoebe sniffed. "No one is sick around me but a hospital's a hotbed of germs. I bet I got it there when I went to the emergency room. I want to go home." She looked at Jenny, then Matthew. "I want to go home."

"I don't think that's a good idea," the doctor interjected.

"They'll take care of me at home," Phoebe insisted. "I don't have to go to the hospital just because I have pneumonia. Fannie Mae

had it last year and she didn't go to the hospital."

"I'd prefer it, considering the heart condition."

When Phoebe just continued to stare at him, he sighed, reached into his desk drawer, pulled out a prescription pad, and started writing. "I'll have the nurse come in and talk to you."

"I can take care of you," Jenny said slowly, an idea forming. "But you'll have to move into the *dawdi haus.*"

She raised her hand when Phoebe started to object. "Remember Hannah's condition. We can't risk her getting sick."

Phoebe looked at Matthew.

"She makes a good point, Phoebe. And you know we love you and will do anything we can for you."

Casting her eyes heavenward, Phoebe nodded. "You are one stubborn woman, Jenny Rebecca."

Jenny just smiled and held out her hand for the prescriptions. "Gee, wonder where I got that?" She stood. "Now, let's get you home."

6

The *dawdi haus* hadn't been used since Chris had stayed there when he first came to Paradise.

But nothing sat around unkempt on an Amish farm, so it only needed "a lick and a promise." Joshua swept, Mary wiped down the kitchen and the inside of the refrigerator, and Annie helped Jenny put fresh linens on the bed. Matthew went off to get the prescriptions filled and Chris helped by taking over Joshua and Matthew's chores.

Hannah contributed by sending over a big pot of chicken soup.

As quickly as she could, Jenny got her grandmother dressed in a nightgown and tucked into bed. Matthew returned with the prescriptions. Phoebe took her pills with a glass of water, tried a few spoons of soup, then confessed that she just wanted to sleep for a while.

Jenny leaned down and kissed her fore-

head and left the room. She closed the connecting door to the kitchen so that the noise of the family supper didn't disturb her grandmother and vowed to get her to eat more soup when she woke up.

Annie was the last to come to the table. "*Grossmudder's* not going to eat with us?"

"She's not feeling well enough. I'm going to take some more of Hannah's soup in to her when she wakes up."

"Maybe we can make her some Three Bear Soup tomorrow," Annie said, wrapping her arms around Jenny. "That always makes me feel better."

"We'll do that. Now let's sit down and eat supper."

The girls did the dishes after supper so Jenny went to see how her grandmother was feeling. Phoebe was still asleep and when Jenny lightly touched her forehead, it was burning hot. She thought about waking her and getting her to take some medicine for her fever but it was too early.

She pulled a rocking chair over and sat and watched her grandmother while the sunset lit up the simple curtains at the window. Phoebe stirred and pulled at the quilt on the bed.

"Cold," she muttered, half awake.

"I'll get another quilt," Jenny told her and

she got up and went upstairs for a quilt. When she returned, she spread it over her grandmother and tucked it around her shoulders.

Phoebe woke again a little while later. Jenny had turned on a battery-operated lantern beside the bed and it cast a soft glow in the room. The older woman blinked as she looked around the room.

Then she glanced down at the quilt. "It's the one I sent you when you were in the hospital."

Jenny nodded and smiled. "The note you sent with it said, 'Come. Heal.' Now you've come to my home to heal."

"Thank goodness it's just pneumonia. I don't know how you got through all those surgeries. How you kept your spirits up." Her coughing started again and by the time it stopped she was breathless.

Jenny gave her a sip of water and patted her shoulder. "I'm going to get you some soup. Is there anything else you'd like?"

"Do you have any orange juice?"

"I do. I'll be right back."

Matthew came into the kitchen as Jenny was pouring the juice.

"The *kinner* are in bed. I told them you'd come up later and kiss them goodnight."

"I'd better go now. I don't know when I'll

be able to later." She turned the flame lower under the pan of soup. "Can you watch this for a minute?"

Matthew looked at it dubiously. He had the typical Amish *mann*'s aversion to cooking.

"It'll be fine for a few minutes. I just don't like to walk away and leave something unattended on the stove."

He nodded, poured himself a cup of coffee, and sat down at the kitchen table.

"Mamm?" Mary smiled up at her sleepily. "How is *Urgrossmudder?*"

Jenny stroked Mary's cheek. "She's very sick, sweetheart. But I'm hoping she'll feel better soon."

"Give her a kiss for me."

"I will. Goodnight. See you in the morning."

Annie was reading a book when Jenny peeked into her room. "Time to go to sleep now," she told her, leaning down to kiss her cheek.

"One more page?"

It was a familiar question. "One more page."

Luke was already asleep, one foot hanging off the bed, uncovered. Jenny tucked his foot under his quilt. He woke for a moment and grinned at her.

“Love-you-’night,” he mumbled, giving her a silly grin, and then he turned over and fell asleep again.

“Love you too,” she told him with a laugh. She tousled his hair, pulled the quilt up over his shoulders, and then left the room.

When she walked into the kitchen, Jenny smiled when she saw that Matthew was engrossed in the farming magazine spread open on the table.

Then she realized that something was sputtering in the pan on the stove.

“Oh no! You were supposed to watch the soup!” she cried as she rushed to turn the heat off.

Matthew looked up. “Huh?”

“The soup!” she said, holding out the pan to show him that only an inch or two was left. Her shoulders slumped. “Now what am I supposed to do?”

“I’m sorry.”

Jenny rubbed at her forehead. “I need to get some soup into *Grossmudder.* This is all I have.”

She pawed through the freezer and came up with a container labeled “Three Bear Soup.” It was beef based, not made of chicken broth. But maybe it didn’t matter. Maybe all that mattered was that it was warm and healthy.

The trouble was, the container was frozen solid. At that moment, she wished for electricity more than she ever had. She didn't mind that they didn't have television or even air conditioning when it got miserably hot canning the harvest from her kitchen garden.

But right now she wanted a microwave so much. Then she could hit "defrost" and thaw the soup, warm it up, and it didn't matter if a husband didn't pay attention — the soup would never burn away while he sat inches away from it and read his magazine.

She plunked the container in a pan and went to the sink to run water in it. Then she placed it on the stove and turned the flame up beneath it. This time, no matter what happened, she wasn't leaving to do anything else.

"Look, is there anything I can do?"

Sighing, she turned and shook her head. "No. Well, maybe you could go tell *Grossmudder* it'll be a few more minutes."

She watched him shift his feet and cast a nervous glance at the door.

"Just knock on the door and call in to her. You don't need to go in — you shouldn't go in her room."

"Oh, *gut.*"

Jenny got out a tray, placed a plate with some crackers on it, and filled a glass with orange juice.

7

Jenny woke suddenly and wondered what had awakened her.

She was sitting up for the third night with her grandmother since she'd moved into the *dawdi haus.* Reaching out, she touched Phoebe's forehead to see if she had a fever. To her disappointment, it was back again with a vengeance.

Just as she started to rise from the rocking chair, her grandmother stirred and opened her eyes. Jenny opened her mouth to speak and then realized Phoebe was staring at the end of her bed. Glancing in that direction, Jenny didn't see anything.

"Jacob," Phoebe said and she smiled, then fell asleep again.

Jacob? Jenny went cold.

Stumbling to her feet, she rushed into the kitchen of her home, straight into Matthew standing at the stove pouring himself a cup of coffee.

"Matthew! Oh, Matthew!"

He immediately set down the cup. "What is it? Is Phoebe — ?"

She shook her head but she was shaking so hard her teeth chattered.

Matthew gathered her into his arms and held her. "Are you cold? What's the matter? You're not getting sick, too, are you?"

He held her away from him and put the back of his hand against her forehead the way she'd done with her grandmother. "You can't get sick."

She heard the fear in his voice and quickly shook her head. "No, it's not that, I'm fine. I'm not getting sick." But she was, she thought. She was sick at heart. Wrapping her arms around his waist, she clung to him.

He drew her closer and made that shushing sound he used to comfort. "I know it's upsetting to see your *grossmudder* so sick. But she's going to be all right. She's going to be all right."

"She's not," she wailed. "She's not."

Again, he held her away from her and studied her. "Why do you say that? Do we need to call an ambulance? What's wrong?"

"I don't know," she sobbed. "I'm just so scared."

"Jenny, tell me what's wrong. Now!" he said firmly.

She wiped the tears from her cheeks and took a deep breath. "She saw my grandfather tonight. She woke up and said his name."

"That doesn't mean she saw him. You remember you said she was a little disoriented that first night when she woke up here. She probably did the same thing, woke up and thought she was back in the time when he was alive. Older people get that way sometimes even when they're not sick. Is her fever up?"

She hesitated and then she shook her head. "Yes, but it wasn't like that. She was looking at the end of the bed. She acted like she could see him standing there."

Matthew ran a hand through his hair, disordering it. "*Lieb,* that doesn't mean that she saw him." He took her face in his hands and made her look at him. "It doesn't mean that she's about to die."

Tears rushed into her eyes. "You don't think so?" She could hear the desperate hope in her voice.

Shaking his head, he used his thumbs to wipe away her tears. "*Nee.* I don't. But, you need to trust God. If He wants Phoebe to be with Him, we'll have to let her go.

"Come sit here with me," he said and drew her down onto his lap. "We need to pray and then we'll go see how Phoebe is doing together, *allrecht?*"

She nodded. They bent their heads and prayed and then she got up and he followed her.

"Let me see if she's awake first," she whispered.

When she walked in, she was surprised to see Phoebe not only awake but sitting up.

"How are you feeling?"

"I've been better," Phoebe said honestly.

Jenny picked up the thermometer and held it out. "I need to check your temp. You were really hot earlier but I didn't want to wake you."

"Don't know why you're not in bed," Phoebe grumbled. "I don't need taking care of."

"I know," Jenny told her tongue-in-cheek.

Phoebe glanced at her and started to say something but Jenny waved a hand at her and pointed to the thermometer.

"Matthew would like to say hello," she said quickly, trying to forestall her grandmother arguing with her that she didn't need caring for.

Jenny took the thermometer out and checked it. Phoebe had a fever but it was 102, not something outrageous.

"I'd love to see Matthew," Phoebe said

and she leaned back against her pillows.

"Great. I'll get him."

Matthew had expected Phoebe to look ill but once he had a glimpse of her he saw why Jenny had been reacting so emotionally.

No one looked good when they were really ill but Phoebe seemed to have aged years since he'd seen her almost two days ago. Her skin was flushed with fever, her eyes glassy. Her cheeks were sunken in. She even seemed to have shrunk but maybe that was because she was lying in bed and looked smaller. A quilt was tucked around her shoulders, one that Matthew recognized as a special one Jenny had kept wrapped in a sheet on the top shelf of their closet since she returned from her last stay in the hospital.

But even though she was clearly feeling weak and sick, Phoebe's spirit was strong. She smiled when he sat in the rocking chair beside her and touched her shoulder.

"How are you feeling?"

"Like I told Jenny, I've been better," she said. "But this too shall pass."

"Jenny was worried about your temperature but it's not as bad as she feared."

"Jenny worries too much." Phoebe smiled

at her to show she meant no criticism.

When Phoebe's gaze returned to him, Matthew wondered if he was really seeing entreaty in them or if he were imagining it.

"Could you eat something?" he asked her.

"I'd rather you two went to bed than go to any trouble —"

"It's no trouble at all," Jenny insisted and rushed from the room.

"Thank you," Phoebe said. "I wanted to talk to you."

Matthew felt a trickle of alarm. "What is it?"

"You must get Jenny to go to bed. It's not good for her to sit up all night with me."

He patted her shoulder. "Now you know that no one can get Jenny to do something if she feels it's wrong. She loves you and wants to take care of you."

"She'll listen to you."

Matthew laughed. "I wish."

He felt a little guilty that she was asking him to convince Jenny to rest when he'd wanted her to do that the first night Phoebe came to stay with them. Jenny had been right to refuse to listen to him. If she felt her grandmother needed her care, if she felt she needed to watch over her to feel reassured that Phoebe wouldn't call out in vain or slip away without her loved ones close by, then he couldn't be upset that she wasn't a dutiful *fraa.* Instead, she was a dutiful granddaughter and child of God.

"Just get better quickly and she'll have to listen to you."

A fit of coughing overtook her and she raised up and grabbed some tissues from a box on the bedside table and covered her mouth. Color faded from her cheeks as she struggled for breath once the coughing stopped. Matthew helped her to sit and propped up the pillows behind her, then helped her ease back against them.

"That sounded horrible," he told her frankly. "Phoebe, do you think we should go back to the doctor? No," he said quickly when she started to object. "Don't insist you're fine. You have pneumonia and you have heart problems. We need to be very careful with you. You see, we love you very much, Phoebe. We don't want to lose you."

Tears came to her eyes. "And I don't want to lose you. I promise you that if I feel worse I'll tell you or Jenny. But I want to get better here at home."

Home. He was so glad to hear her call this part of his home hers.

"I know you sent Jenny away so we could talk," he said. "Don't pretend you didn't. But when she returns, you'll eat the soup, won't you?"

She sighed. *"Ya."*

"Gut," he said. "You know, from the first time that I met you when my *eldre* bought this place next to yours I felt like you were a *grossmudder* to me, not a neighbor. I love you, Phoebe."

She smiled. "And from the time you moved next door as a charming little boy, I've loved you, too, Matthew," she said in a low, raspy voice caused by her illness. "And now you've grown into a wonderful *mann* for my granddaughter."

Jenny walked in just then and her eyebrows rose as she saw the two of them talking low and seriously.

"Don't be jealous, *lieb,*" he told Jenny when he saw her. "Phoebe and I love each other but you're still my number one."

"Good thing," she said sweetly, putting the tray with the soup on her grandmother's lap. She grinned at him. "Otherwise you'd be wearing this soup."

But even though she joked and he'd kept his words light, they exchanged a silent message over Phoebe's head as she bent to raise a spoonful of soup.

He nodded slightly and smiled and she let out a relieved breath, obviously understanding that he was trying to let her know

Phoebe was doing okay, that she shouldn't be alarmed.

"Gut nacht," he said and he hugged Jenny and kissed her. Reaching down, he squeezed Phoebe's shoulder and tried not to frown when he realized how frail she felt, like a little bird.

He so wanted her to get well quickly — not just because Jenny worried but because he felt unsettled about Phoebe's condition. Perhaps if he hadn't had Amelia, his first wife, die young, he'd be more optimistic. While Phoebe didn't have cancer as Amelia had, in someone who was older the pneumonia and heart condition were worrisome.

God's will be done, he told himself. He went to make up his bed on the living room sofa again and before he closed his eyes, he prayed — for the highest good, not selfishly for himself because he didn't want to let Phoebe go but for whatever was best for her.

Jenny opened the front door a week later, so exhausted from caring for Phoebe that she felt she was moving in a daze.

Fannie Mae, Naomi, and Lydia stood there, smiling and holding plastic storage containers of something that smelled delicious. Well, it smelled delicious but Jenny thought she might just be too tired to eat whatever was inside.

"May we come in?" Lydia asked.

Jenny hesitated but she was too polite to refuse. "If you've come to see Phoebe, I'm afraid she's asleep."

"We didn't come to visit Phoebe," Fannie Mae said. "We know you'll tell us when she's ready for visitors."

She took the coats and shawls the others wore and went to hang them up.

Casting up a fervent prayer she wouldn't fall asleep in the middle of a visit, Jenny gestured for them to follow her into the kitchen. "Would you like some coffee? Hannah baked some cookies and sent them over."

Naomi, a young woman who was a co-owner of Stitches in Time, a quilt and craft store that Hannah taught at, made a shooing motion. "We didn't come to visit with you, either, dear one. We're here to be of some help."

That was when Jenny noticed that Naomi didn't carry a container of food but instead, wielded a plastic bucket filled with cleaning supplies.

Lydia patted Jenny's shoulder. "You look ready to fall over."

"I've been so tired lately," Jenny admitted.

Fannie Mae glanced at Lydia, then Naomi. "Maybe you're . . ." she trailed off as she glanced at Lydia, then Naomi.

"Maybe I'm what?"

"You know, maybe you're . . ."

Jenny knew she was tired and her brain felt dull but she just didn't get it.

"Maybe you're pregnant?"

Pain lanced through her heart. Having just had her period, Jenny knew for certain that she wasn't. "No," she said firmly and she shook her head.

"Taking care of someone who's sick is very tiring," Naomi said. "I remember what it was like to be up day and night taking care of Isaac, my brother, last year."

Lydia nodded. "If you'll tell us what you need done we'll be happy to do it or you can just leave it up to us what to do."

"I —" Jenny spread her hands in a helpless gesture. "I don't know what to say."

"Say you're going to go take a nap," Naomi suggested. "We'll be quiet as mice."

"But what if Phoebe wakes up?"

"We'll come get you if we need you," Naomi said firmly.

A nap sounded so good. But there was so much to do.

"Shoo, shoo," Lydia said. "I'll bring you up a nice cup of tea in a minute and I want to find you lying down. Possibly already snoring."

The women giggled like girls.

Jenny wanted to refuse but just didn't know how she was going to keep going. Matthew did what he could after his own long, hard day, as did the children after school. But Phoebe's care fell on her and sitting up at night when Phoebe was having a bad spell was wearing her down.

Smiling and laughing in spite of herself, Jenny caved. "Twist my arm," she muttered. She stifled a yawn. "Okay, okay, you win. I'll lie down for an hour. And then we'll have a nice visit and you ladies will go home. I'm sure you have enough to do for your own families without being so generous with mine."

"Now you know we all help each other out. You go on to bed before you fall down."

"Danki," she said fervently and beat it up the stairs before she could change her mind.

When she came downstairs two hours later the kitchen floor was spotless. A pot of soup simmered on the stove. The breakfast dishes had been washed and put away. And her friends sat at the big kitchen table sipping tea and chatting quietly.

"Well, you look refreshed," Lydia said with a smile.

Jenny took a seat. "That was wonderful. I didn't mean to sleep so long."

Naomi got up to fix Jenny a cup of tea and pushed the plate of cookies closer to her. "I peeked in on Phoebe and she's still asleep but she didn't feel like she had a fever. We've got the soup simmering for when she wakes up. She loves my chicken corn soup with *rivvels.*"

"There's a scalloped potato and ham casserole in the oven for supper," Lydia said. "Just warm up some canned vegetables to go with it and you're done."

The women rose in a group and left in a flurry of goodbyes and requests for Jenny to give Phoebe a hug for them.

"Remember to tell her the quilting circle is getting together in two weeks. We're contributing quilts for the auction to raise money for Haiti. You'll come too, won't you?"

"My quilting's not very good," she demurred.

"It just takes practice like anything else," Lydia assured her. "You're getting better."

"Slowly, just like my cooking," Jenny said with a self-deprecating laugh.

"You're a fine Amish *fraa,*" Fannie Mae told her. "Why, sometimes it's hard to remember that you weren't born here."

Jenny gave her an impulsive hug, then turned to do the same with Lydia and Naomi. "And sometimes it's hard for me to remember I had a life before. This is home."

Joshua answered the front door after supper and came to report that Hannah wanted Jenny to come to the door of the *dawdi haus.*

Curious, Jenny walked back there and when she opened the door, she found Hannah and Chris standing on the porch wearing big grins. Hannah held something behind her back.

"What's going on?"

"We want to see Phoebe," Hannah told her, almost dancing with excitement.

"But she's still sick —"

"We know, we know. Ask her to look out the bedroom window?"

"Okay." Jenny went into Phoebe's room.

"What's going on? Did I hear someone at the door?"

Jenny picked up the robe at the end of the bed and held it out to her grandmother. "You did. Do you think you can get up for a few minutes to look out the window?"

"*Ya.* What's going on?"

"I don't know. Hannah and Chris want to show you something."

After helping Phoebe put on the robe,

Jenny wrapped the shawl they kept on the bed around her shoulders.

"I'm not going outside," Phoebe said with a smile.

"I don't want you to catch a chill."

Jenny pulled the rocking chair over to the window and helped Phoebe sit in it.

Hannah and Chris came close to the window and waved. Phoebe waved back.

"We have something to show you," Hannah yelled through the glass. "But it's just for you. Turn around, Jenny."

Puzzled, Jenny did as they asked. When Phoebe gasped, she started to turn but Hannah called out warning her not to.

"I thought you didn't want to know if the baby was a boy or a girl," Phoebe said.

"We still don't. But the midwife I'm using was concerned about something and sent me for a sonogram. Everything's fine, but I thought you might like a preview, Phoebe."

"I want to see!" Jenny yelled.

"Too bad!" Hannah returned and she was laughing. "And you can't tell anyone, Phoebe. Not even us!"

"Can I turn around now?"

"In a minute," said Phoebe. "Hannah, it's a little hard to see. Can you bring it closer to the window?"

"I'm pressing it to the glass," Hannah

called in. "The nurse said she wrote on the side margin what the baby is."

"There — oh, my, I see what she wrote now!" Phoebe exclaimed. "What a miracle, taking a picture of what's inside your womb. It's a miracle." Her voice was soft, reverent.

"It's not fair!" Jenny yelled again, but she was laughing. This was totally ridiculous but so, so sweet it brought tears to her eyes.

Hannah was giving Phoebe something to look forward to.

"Maybe we'll let you see when you give us Phoebe back!" Chris called.

"No deal!" She had an idea. "So Chris, you must want to know if it's a boy or a girl."

"I do but I'm going along with Hannah on this one since I can't help her carry the baby."

There was a knock on the door frame. "Jenny? What's all the commotion?"

She gestured for Matthew to come in. "Hannah and Chris came over to show Phoebe a sonogram of the baby."

"I thought they didn't want to know."

"They still don't. It's just for Phoebe to know." She turned to him. "Why don't you try talking to them? You know you want to know."

"No I don't."

She pushed him toward the front door of the *dawdi haus.* "Sure you do. You want to know so I can know."

He stood firm and no amount of pushing would budge him. He turned and kissed her. "I don't know who's crazier right now — my sister or you."

"Her. C'mon, Matthew, she'll listen to you."

Laughing, he hugged her. "You're wrong."

He fell silent for a moment as they watched Phoebe. "Look at her, Jenny, just look at her," he whispered in her ear. "Look at the color in her cheeks. What Hannah's doing is as good as medicine."

"I know." She watched, love swamping her as she rested against him. Tears were running down Phoebe's cheeks and she looked like she never wanted to stir from the window.

"We better go," Chris called in. "It's getting cold out here. I don't want Hannah to get sick."

"Danki," Phoebe called. She pressed her fingers to her lips and blew them a kiss. "*Danki,* both of you. I love you!"

She turned and saw Jenny and Matthew. "What a wonderful surprise."

Pulling a tissue from the pocket of her robe, she wiped her cheeks. "I'm sorry she doesn't want me to tell you."

"I made some potato soup," Jenny said persuasively.

Phoebe laughed. "Not even for your potato soup."

"Jenny! What a surprise!" Hannah said when she opened the front door.

Then her eyes narrowed. "I'm not showing you the sonogram."

Laughing, Jenny stepped inside when Hannah moved, taking her enormous abdomen out of the way. "I came over to get some clothes for Phoebe. She said she had some more nightgowns and another robe."

"How is she doing, really?"

"The coughing's still really bad," Jenny told her honestly.

There was no point in sugarcoating anything. If she acted like Phoebe was better than she was and she unexpectedly took a turn for the worse, it would be too much of a shock.

"And she's really weak. This thing has taken so much out of her." Then she smiled and touched Hannah's arm. "But she's got so many people praying for her. I'm feeling a little better about her."

She sighed. "Some extra things for her will help with laundry. There's enough of that to do with three children. And a husband who farms."

Hannah nodded and rubbed her lower back. "Go on in and get what you need. I'm going to make another run to the bathroom. The baby stopped kicking up under my ribs and now he —" she stopped to stare meaningfully at Jenny, "or she — wants to stand on my bladder."

Chuckling, Jenny walked into her grandmother's room and went straight to the closet for a robe. She set the robe on Phoebe's bed and turned back to the closet. Maybe a sweater, too, she thought, for times when it would be warmer than a shawl when Phoebe sat up in bed or a chair.

A sweater was folded neatly on the top shelf of the closet. Jenny reached for it but as she pulled at it a button must have caught on something. She tugged and the sweater came free, bringing down with it a box filled with papers. Placing the sweater on the bed, she turned back and knelt on the floor to pick up what appeared to be old letters tied up with a ribbon. Several of them had slipped from the ribbon so she started picking them up.

And when she held one in her hand she gasped. The handwriting on the envelope looked familiar — a bold, masculine scrawl she'd seen before. She looked at the return address and saw her father's name.

She hesitated and then she found herself opening the letter.

"Dear *Mudder,*" she read. "Thank you for letting me know about Jenny's infatuation with Matthew Bontrager. You're right, I don't want her converting to the Amish faith and marrying him or any other boy. I want her to go to college the way her mother and I talked about, get an education, and have a future, not live a way of life I left."

Shocked, she tried to make sense of it all. Phoebe had contacted her father about how she and Matthew felt about each other? She'd thought that Phoebe approved . . . never thought about her disapproving or letting her father know. She'd been so in love, so enraptured with Matthew, that she hadn't even thought about what would happen if her father found out.

"Jenny? Are you finding what you need?"

Startled, Jenny got up and found herself automatically stuffing the letter into her pocket. Quickly, she scooped up the rest of the letters, put them in the box, and placed it up on the top shelf again.

"Yes! Almost done!" she managed to say.

She had the robe and sweater in her arms when Hannah poked her head in the doorway. "What about a cup of tea?"

"Can't. I left Phoebe by herself. I have to get back."

"You okay? You look pale."

"I'm fine," Jenny assured her quickly. "I'll see you later."

She hurried out, feeling as if her world had suddenly shattered.

8

"Jenny! Jenny!"

She jumped when she felt a hand on her arm and spun around.

"Chris! You scared me!"

"Where are you going in such a hurry?" He put his hands on his hips and stared at her. "You okay?"

"I'm fine," she said, clutching Phoebe's robe and sweater to her chest.

"You don't look fine. You look awful," he said bluntly. "Almost shell-shocked, like you just got bad news or something."

"Phoebe's getting better," she told him quickly. "I just got some of her clothes. And don't you know you don't tell a woman she's not looking well?"

"Okay," he said slowly, rocking back on his heels as he studied her. "Then maybe we need to get you more help."

"Some of Phoebe's friends have been coming by with food, even cleaning help.

But I need to get back now. I left Phoebe alone."

Chris pulled off his hat and wiped his forehead with a bandanna. He squinted at the sun pouring down as he scanned the fields to the rear of the farmhouse.

Jenny was reminded of how she thought he looked like the All-American boy when she first met him at the veteran's hospital. Now he seemed so at home here, fit into the community well after he'd studied to become Amish and married Hannah. He'd converted to the Amish faith when they married and even wore a beard the way all the men did here when they were married.

He returned his gaze to her. "I'd better get back to work. Tell Phoebe I miss her."

Jenny had started to move away from him but she heard the emotion in his voice.

"I'd — think a fairly newly married couple would enjoy some time without anyone else in the house," she teased him.

"You'd think wrong," he said quietly. "And we're hardly 'fairly newly married' in any case. I've grown close to Phoebe since I came here. She's —" he stopped and took a breath. "Well, I can't even think what it would be like without her."

Jenny patted his arm. "She's hanging in there. But I left her alone to get some things and I need to check on her."

He nodded. "I know Matthew's in town today. If you need anything, just holler, okay?"

"I will."

Her heart pounded as she walked into the house and she felt sick — physically sick. Once she shut the door she leaned on it and tried to think. It couldn't be true. It couldn't. She knew Phoebe loved Matthew, had always loved him like a son. And she'd seemed to approve of their budding relationship back then.

There was no doubt that her father was strict, always making her abide by a curfew when she went out with friends or on the occasional date. She understood that and appreciated it. After all, if he didn't care, he wouldn't be that way.

And while he had decided not to stay in the Amish community and join the church, he had never kept Jenny from seeing her grandmother. He'd been fine with Jenny visiting her for those two summers.

She looked at the connecting door to the *dawdi haus*. What was she going to say to Phoebe? She wanted to rush into her grandmother's room and demand to know why she'd betrayed her.

How different my life would have been if

you hadn't interfered all those years ago! she wanted to cry out. I missed out on all those years I could have had with Matthew if you hadn't interfered, if you hadn't written my father. I wouldn't have been miserable for the first year at college. I wouldn't have chosen the job I did overseas and come home shattered in body and soul.

She heard a commotion on the porch, the front door opened, and in poured Annie, Mary, and Joshua.

"*Mamm?* We're home!"

"I see," she said, trying to summon up a smile.

"Are you all right? *Mamm?*"

"Yes," she whispered and she impulsively gathered them up into a hug.

"What is it?" Mary asked and her lips began to tremble. "Did Phoebe get worse?"

"Is she dead?" Annie wanted to know. "*Mamm?*"

She shook her head but then realized that she'd been standing there feeling so miserable she hadn't checked yet. "No, she's fine. I went to get a few of her things and I'm just a little tired, that's all."

"Can I fix you some tea?" Mary asked. "I'll be careful, promise."

"And I'll get you some cookies to go with it," Annie piped up.

"You just want to sneak some for yourself," Joshua told her with the tone only an older brother could use.

Annie elbowed him in the ribs. "*Mamm?* Why don't you sit down and let us take care of you?"

"I could do something," Joshua said. He thought for a moment. "But what? What do you want me to do for you?"

Tears sprang into her eyes at their caring.

And then the thought, the most hurtful thought came into her head. These would have been my children, born of my womb. I wouldn't be asking God each month for a baby, she thought. I wouldn't cry each time I found I wasn't pregnant.

They could have been the children born of my body, not just of my heart. I could have had all those years with them. All of us could have been spared so much pain — they the pain of losing their mother. Me, the pain of my body being so badly injured and scarred.

Why, God? Why? she screamed inwardly. Why did You let Phoebe do this to me? Why?

Phoebe's room was dim when Jenny slipped inside it but Jenny could still see her grandmother sitting up in the bed, her arms wrapped around her.

And she could hear that horrible hacking cough. She rushed to her side and sat down on the bed beside her.

"Can't stop —" Phoebe gasped. "My side — oh, it hurts so much."

"Maybe we need to go see the doctor today."

"I —" Phoebe started to refuse and then she nodded. "Feels like I broke a rib coughing."

"Let me go get Matthew —" she stopped. Matthew had gone into town, she remembered.

But Chris had said to call him if she needed him. "I'll be right back. You lie down and when I come back I'll help you get dressed. Okay? Don't move until I get back. Promise me."

"Promise," Phoebe whispered, clearly out of breath. She lay back down and Jenny drew the quilt over her.

She hurried into the house, startling the children who were having an after-school snack. Stay calm, she told herself. Don't frighten the children.

"Joshua, would you please go get Chris for me?"

"*Schur.* Is it Phoebe?" His glance went to the connecting door.

"Tell Chris I think Phoebe needs to see

the doctor again, that's all," she said. "Why don't you help him hitch up the buggy to make it faster?"

He nodded and took off.

"Mary, wait here by the door and if Phoebe calls out for me, tell her I'm going out to use the phone in the shanty. But don't go in there unless you think it's an emergency, okay?"

Her eyes wide and round with concern, Mary nodded.

Jenny grabbed her shawl from the peg by the door and then realized that Annie was sitting there at the table, so still. She walked over and looked at her and then she wrapped her arms around the child and hugged her.

"Please don't be scared," she said to Annie, looking over her head at Mary. "She's just complaining that it's hurting to cough so much so I want her to see the doctor."

"But she's been sick for a long time."

"I know. I know. Now you need to be brave for me so I can go make the call to the doctor, okay?"

Annie nodded. Jenny kissed the top of her head and then she hurried on out to the shanty and called the doctor.

"Bring her right in," the nurse told her. "We'll get your grandmother in to see the doctor as soon as you get here."

Chris knocked at the *dawdi haus* door a few minutes later. "The buggy's right outside. But I see Matthew driving up."

"Good. I'll let him take us so you don't have to worry about getting sick."

"I brought the buggy as close as I could. You take it and I'll get yours put up."

"Thanks, Chris. I appreciate it."

"You're welcome, happy to do it," he said and he went off to tell Matthew.

The sheer effort of getting some clothes on was more than Phoebe could handle. By the time Jenny tucked her arms into a coat, Phoebe was coughing and wheezing.

"Sorry," Phoebe said. "I feel weak as a kitten."

Matthew hurried inside and sized up the situation. Without a word he scooped Phoebe up in his arms and carried her out to the buggy.

"No need —"

"I know, no need to carry you. You can walk. Seems like I heard that before." He grinned at Jenny. "Now I see where Jenny gets that streak of independence."

"Are you warm enough?" Jenny asked Phoebe as she tucked her shawl around her shoulders.

"Too warm," Phoebe told her. "And remember, I'm not going to the hospital."

"We're not taking you there. We're going to the doctor, remember?"

"I remember," Phoebe told her tartly. "Nothing's wrong with my memory. I'm just reminding you that I agreed to go to the doctor, maybe get some cough medicine. An X-ray if the doctor insists."

"Well, I'm sure he'll appreciate that," Jenny said dryly.

Phoebe pushed at her hair under her *kapp.* "I must look a fright."

"You look fine."

"I just want to get well," she said, leaning heavily against Jenny as they sat in the backseat of the buggy. "I'm so tired of feeling so sick."

"I know," Jenny said, patting her back, soothing her as if she were a child. "I know."

Matthew turned to look at them. "It's not much farther, Phoebe. But if you need me to, I can call for help to get us there faster."

"No need for drama, *sohn,*" she said tartly. "We had enough of that, didn't we?"

He smiled slightly and nodded before he turned his attention to the road again.

Jenny held her grandmother in her arms and her brain raced the whole ride to the doctor's office. Now wasn't the time to ask the questions she wanted to ask, the questions that burned to be asked.

The doctor's office was just up ahead. Thankfully, the peaceful clip-clop of the horse's hooves had lulled Phoebe to sleep. Or maybe it was just exhaustion. Jenny hated to wake her but had to.

"*Grossmudder?* We're here. You need to wake up."

Phoebe stirred and sat up. "Here?" She blinked in the bright sunlight.

"The doctor's office, remember?"

Matthew pulled the buggy up in front of the entrance and came around to help Phoebe out.

"You've always been such a good *sohn,*" she told him and she patted his cheek.

Jenny stepped out of the buggy and Matthew turned to look at her as he steadied Phoebe. Bright sunlight backlit his hat and his face and then as he glanced down at Phoebe it was revealed again. His expression was troubled . . . guilty, even.

The world tilted for a moment and Jenny grasped at the door of the buggy as a thought came to her.

Did Matthew know what Phoebe had done years ago to separate them?

"Jenny? Jenny?"

She jerked to attention. "What?"

"I said I'm sorry I put you both to the trouble of carting me to the doctor," Phoebe said.

"It was no trouble, Phoebe," Matthew told her. "And I'd hardly call bringing you here to find out that you probably *did* crack a rib coughing was trouble."

"Well, we don't know for sure," she grumbled.

"Because you wouldn't let him send you for an X-ray," Matthew pointed out equably.

"Well, he said it wouldn't really make any difference. It's not like he could put a cast on it."

There was silence as the horse carried them along on the road toward home. The monotonous sound should have been soothing but Jenny's mind whirled and whirled. She desperately wanted to ask her grandmother about the letter but whenever she glanced at Phoebe she just couldn't bring herself to do it.

She looked at Matthew as he sat in the front seat. Later, once she got Phoebe settled back in bed, made the family supper, and got the children to bed, she could ask him if he knew about her grandmother's actions.

But that meant that she'd be telling him that she'd violated her grandmother's privacy. She hadn't intended to. After all, she hadn't deliberately looked for the box, hadn't known it even existed. But once it fell, the letters spilled out, and she'd picked one up, opened it, and read it.

Did she want to admit that to her husband, a good man of steadfast principles? She'd never done something like this before.

She'd have to tell him.

So she leaned back against the seat and watched the passing scenery. It was nearly the season she'd returned to this community after she'd been injured. The stark, leafless trees had stood out against the blinding white, snow-covered fields, a barren landscape that reflected the way she felt. She'd been a broken shell of a woman, scarred and limping from injuries caused by a car bomber determined to silence her televised reports from a war zone.

Here, she'd healed. Here, she'd found that the feelings she'd experienced as a teenager had come rushing back, matured, and the boy next door had become her husband. They'd gotten a second chance.

He couldn't know. He couldn't. If he did, that would mean that he had stepped back from what he said he felt for her. He'd let her go and she'd been miserable for nearly a year at college.

And not long after, he'd married his first wife and had a family with her.

"Phoebe! It's so *gut* to see you out!" Mary Elizabeth called out as she slowed her buggy coming from the opposite direction.

Matthew brought the buggy to a stop.

"Went to the doctor," Phoebe told her. "Still — sick."

The effort of talking sent her into a paroxysm of coughing.

Mary Elizabeth pressed her fingers to her mouth and shook her head. "Oh, I'm so sorry. You get home and get back in bed. I'll stop by tomorrow with some soup for Jenny to give to you."

She looked at Jenny. "You take care of her and let me know how I can help, *allrecht?*"

"I will. Thank you, Mary Elizabeth," Jenny said.

Matthew called to Daisy and the buggy began rolling down the road again.

"You're awfully quiet," he stated a few minutes later.

"Is that a complaint?" She tried to make her tone light but she saw him studying her intently.

He started to say something but from the way his body straightened and his head turned she saw something had captured his attention. She looked in the direction he did and saw that a car was parked in the driveway of Phoebe's house. Chris stood beside it, gesturing as he talked to the driver.

"Looks like they have company," Matthew said.

"Chris doesn't seem happy," Jenny observed. "Who is it? Someone we know?"

Matthew shook his head. "Out-of-state plates."

As they drove past, Chris looked up and waved for them to stop.

Matthew pulled into the driveway. Chris strode over, frowning, his jaw clenched. His face cleared when he spotted Phoebe.

"Are you feeling any better?" he asked her, stroking her arm as he gazed at her in concern. "Hannah and I so want you well and back here again."

Phoebe smiled. "*Danki.* I hope it won't be much longer."

"Stop trying to steal my grandmother back," Jenny told him.

When a car door opened behind him, Chris's frown and jaw clenching returned. "Well, you won't believe who just drove up, out of the blue," he muttered.

A man who appeared in his sixties approached. There was something familiar to him but Jenny didn't think she'd ever met him. He had thinning sandy hair, what some might call a beer belly, and reminded her a little of a pug with his squared body and face.

A plump woman the same age got out of the car. "Now, William, don't start a fuss. We just got here," she said, following him.

"I drive all this way and you turn your back on me for your friends?" he griped.

With a sigh, Chris turned. "One of them has been very sick. I just wanted to make sure she's okay."

He turned back to them. "Matthew, Jenny, Phoebe, meet my father, William, and my mother, Fern."

"How nice Chris's parents came to visit," Phoebe said as she slid between the sheets of her bed.

Jenny helped her settle against extra pillows. "Does this help at all?"

"I think it does. I'll be practically sitting up but I'll try anything."

"Chris didn't act very happy about seeing them. I think he's been estranged from them for a while." Jenny took a seat in the rocking chair. It felt so good to get off her feet after a busy day.

"Estranged," mused Phoebe. "Big word for not sitting down and talking things out with each other. Not that I'm saying all families get along here. We know otherwise. But from things Chris has said I know family's very important to him."

"It's hard for some soldiers to get used to civilian life when they come back home. Especially if they've been wounded."

"You'd know."

Jenny nodded. "That's why Chris and I bonded when I met him at the veteran's hospital after my surgery."

Phoebe yawned. "The cough syrup the doctor gave me is making me sleepy. Maybe I won't hack all night."

"I hope not. I know you'll feel better if you don't."

"I hope you can get more sleep, too."

Jenny stood and leaned down to kiss her grandmother's cheek. "I'm going to go see if everyone's settled down and then I'll be back. No," she said quickly, holding up her hand. "Save your breath. I'm coming back."

Matthew was coming down the stairs when she walked into the kitchen. "Phoebe settled down?"

"Yes. Thank you for helping me take her to the doctor. The cough syrup's already making her drowsy. I think she'll sleep tonight."

"Maybe you can, too?"

Fighting a yawn, she nodded. "I'm looking forward to my bed one of these nights. Maybe I'll get rid of this crick in my neck."

He drew over a chair, sat, and pulled her down to sit on his lap. His hands began to massage the tension at the back of her neck and then moved to her shoulders. "How does that feel?"

"Like heaven," she said, trying not to moan.

Sitting there in the kitchen, warm and comforted by the feel of his hands trying to work out the stress built up in her upper body, she felt loved and cared for. She'd missed sleeping in their bed, arms wrapped around each other.

Then the events of the morning came roaring into her memory and she straightened. She remembered the ride to the doctor's and how she'd wondered if Matthew knew that Phoebe had contacted her father.

Matthew's lips caressed the nape of her neck, reassuring her that he'd missed her, too. She turned around and stared at him, pulling back when he leaned forward to kiss her.

She shook her head. It wasn't the time or place to ask him.

He looked confused. "Something's wrong."

"I'm tired," she said. "And you must be, too."

His eyes were dark with desire as he stroked the back of his hand against her cheek. "I love you."

She gave him a quick kiss on the cheek and forced herself to step away. "I love you, too." She busied herself at the sink. "Why don't you go on up to bed? It can't be doing you any good to sleep on the sofa after the way you work so hard. I don't think I'll be needing you tonight."

He frowned, obviously trying to judge her mood. "I'm going to let you twist my arm."

He touched her arm but she continued to wash the dishes and finally he let his hand fall.

"If you change your mind about coming up to bed . . ." He let his words trail off.

"Don't tempt me," she told him lightly. But she knew he couldn't tempt her until she found out what had happened and if he knew what Phoebe had done.

"Gut nacht, lieb."

"Matthew?"

He turned. *"Ya?"*

She wanted to ask him if he knew what Phoebe had done but something stopped her. What if he said yes? How would she feel? Her world had been rocked that day and her feelings were so tender. She cautioned herself to not do anything hasty. After all, it had happened so many years ago. She had Matthew and the children now. Should it matter?

"Jenny?"

She shook her head. "Nothing."

He walked back and hugged her. "Phoebe's going to be fine," he reassured her.

She told herself this was the Matthew she knew, not one who would hide something. He wasn't capable of keeping a secret.

She hugged him back and nodded.

But then, as he walked away, she thought about how she'd never have thought that Phoebe was capable of it either.

He climbed the stairs again and she listened to his steps overhead as he walked into their bedroom.

She fixed herself a cup of tea and sat at the kitchen table for a quiet moment alone. The old farmhouse creaked a little and the night was so still she could hear the ticking of the clock. She sent up a silent prayer of thanks for her family tucked up safe and warm when the weather was getting colder.

But while everything around her was serene and quiet, her mind continued to whirl with questions. She took deep breaths, willing it to stop, practicing a technique she'd learned in the hospital to alleviate anxiety. Gradually, the hamster wheel in her head slowed, then stopped.

Taking a last calming breath, she sipped her cooling tea and felt the tension that had built up again in her body ease. As it did, it was replaced by an awareness of just how tired she was. She felt her head nodding. It wouldn't hurt to put her head down for a moment, she told herself. Just for a moment. She wanted to go stay with her grandmother for another night just to be sure she wasn't needed.

A baby was crying.

She climbed out of bed and padded on bare feet down the hallway to see what was wrong. But when she walked into the nursery there was no baby, no crib. Alarmed, she rushed from the room and went into Joshua's room. It was empty. She ran down the hall and looked into Mary's room, then Annie's but there was no one there.

Sobbing, tears running down her cheeks, she ran back to the room she shared with Matthew but it was empty, too. What was happening? She was in a nightmare but she couldn't seem to wake up. Then she remembered that Phoebe was in the *dawdi haus.* She flew down the stairs, tore open the connecting door, and ran into her grandmother's bedroom. But it, too, was empty.

Jenny woke, crying out, and found herself sitting at the kitchen table. She sat there for a moment, blinking. There were footsteps on the stairs and Matthew hurried into the room.

"Matthew!" She jumped up and rushed at him, throwing herself into his arms.

He grasped her by the arms and held her back. "I heard you calling out. Is something wrong with Phoebe?"

Shaking her head, she wiped at the tears on her cheeks. "I fell asleep at the table and had such a bad dream." She took a shaky breath. "I need to go check on the kids."

"They're fine."

"I need to see them." She ran up the stairs and went from room to room, making certain for herself that they were safe in their beds. That they were *there*.

When she returned to the kitchen, Matthew was waiting for her, looking sleepy and rumpled and concerned. "You haven't had a nightmare in months. What brought it on?"

She shrugged. "Who knows? There's not always a trigger." Picking up her mug, she put it into the sink.

"But there usually is," he reminded her,

coming to stand behind her and rubbing her back. "Do you need to talk about it?"

"No, go back to bed," she told him. "I'm fine. I'm going to sit up with Phoebe for a little while and who knows, I might get to go to bed later."

He grinned and leaned down to give her a lingering kiss. "I won't kick you out if you do."

They separated, Matthew returning to bed and Jenny going to see to Phoebe. She found her grandmother sleeping peacefully. When she put the back of her hand to the older woman's forehead it was cool. No fever and no coughing. It was a very good night, she thought.

So she tiptoed out of the room and, after a glance at the stairs that led to their room, she lay down on the living room sofa. She'd told Matthew that she might go to bed but she wasn't ready for that yet and not just because she wanted to make sure Phoebe was okay.

She just wasn't sure she could pretend that everything was okay to him until she sorted out what happened today when she read that letter.

9

Jenny walked into the barn and stood, arms folded across her chest.

Not for the first time she thought if only life were easier. If only she could just push a key in an ignition and back a car out of the barn and be on her way. She didn't want to be away from Phoebe for too long even though Matthew had said he'd check on her while Jenny went into town.

Pilot snorted at her and tossed his head. Honestly, who knew that horses could express derision? she asked herself.

When she first met Pilot, Matthew had warned her that he was headstrong and that he'd tried to intimidate Hannah, too. Hannah had let Pilot know right away he wasn't going to get away with it, Matthew had told Jenny.

But Jenny wasn't Hannah who'd grown up around horses the way Jenny had cars. She'd had experience with children, too, and simply dealt with Pilot the same loving but firm way.

And horses served here — they weren't for an occasional pleasure ride. They worked in some manner here as did everyone and nearly every animal in the Amish community.

"I have to go into town and get a prescription for Phoebe," she announced as she opened the gate on the stall. Then she laughed and shook her head. Why was she explaining to a horse?

Pilot shook his great head and backed up.

"I don't have time for this," she told him. "If you give me too much trouble I'll just go get Daisy. Sweet-natured, cooperative Daisy."

He pawed the ground and shook his head again as if to tell her what he thought of that. So she gathered up her courage and walked into the stall and slipped the bridle over his head and fastened it. Don't show him you're afraid, Matthew had said. Then you'll lose control forever.

Well, there was still a cold grip of fear around her heart when she did this but Pilot hadn't ever shown any sign that he'd hurt her. If there had ever been even an inkling that could happen, Matthew wouldn't have the horse on the farm. But she couldn't help feeling a little wary as he walked outside with her and let her hitch him up to the buggy.

"Might be my lunch," she said as he began sniffing at her shoulder purse as she hitched him to the buggy. "Might be something for you."

When he nuzzled her cheek she laughed and relaxed. "You are such a handsome guy. And charming. Have I mentioned charming?"

She finished and stood back to admire her handiwork. Pilot nodded and nudged her with his nose. "Okay, okay, I'll see if I can find an apple for you for being good."

Before she could do what she said, he nosed at her purse and she laughed again.

"I swear, you can sniff out an apple like Annie can sniff out a cookie."

She pulled out the apple and handed it to him. "This is our secret, you hear? If Matthew found out I was spoiling you this way I'd never hear the end of it."

She climbed into the buggy and Pilot tossed his head and began leading them down the drive. Jenny sighed and smiled to herself. Success. She hadn't had to call Matthew as she'd had to do a few times in the beginning. He didn't mind — ever — and even showed up sometimes to hitch up Pilot when he knew she needed to go to town.

But even children knew how to do such a task here and she was determined not to be intimidated by this four-legged beast. An Amish *fraa* did such things herself and she was determined to be a good Amish *fraa.*

Driving a buggy was second nature to her now. The first few times she'd driven one after she had an accident had been hard. But like the old saying, you had to get back on the horse — or behind it! — and just do it again. Or walk. And you couldn't walk everywhere you needed to anyway.

But the accident had taught her to be more careful, to look both ways, and then get quickly onto the road. She'd hesitated when she'd approached the road that time, not given firm enough directions to Daisy. And the driver of the car had been going too fast, like so many did, heedless of the danger to buggies.

So as she approached the road, she was firm with Pilot. And former racehorse that he was, he knew not to hesitate and got them onto the road quickly.

Jenny pulled into the drive next door to see if Hannah needed anything from town. To her surprise, Hannah came hurrying out of the house before she could alight from the buggy.

"Rescue me!" she hissed. "I don't care where you're going or how long you're going to be gone. Just let me ride along."

"Do you promise to behave?" Jenny asked, tongue in cheek.

"You do *not* know what I've gone through for the last few days," Hannah told her. "Let me go get my purse and I'll tell you all about it on the way into town."

Jenny had never seen Hannah quite so rattled. She was the closest thing to a drama queen Jenny had been around since — well, she couldn't remember.

"Thank goodness you came over," Hannah said with a big sigh after Jenny helped her heave herself into the buggy.

"The visit isn't going well?"

Hannah rolled her eyes. "Everything's so tense between Chris and his father. I keep telling Chris that he needs to remember his father loves him or he wouldn't have come to visit.

"Fern says William doesn't understand why Chris came here. Or why he stayed. And Chris doesn't think he should have to explain himself."

She lifted her chin. "And he shouldn't. Chris went through a very difficult time and his father didn't seem to understand."

"It's not easy for others to understand,"

Jenny said quietly. "War isn't war. I mean, what Chris experienced — what I saw — overseas isn't like what William went through when he served. And the military wasn't the male bonding experience Chris expected, what he'd heard about from his dad growing up. His buddies turned on him when he refused to look the other way about what Malcolm did. And when Chris was injured just before coming back, well —"

"He felt God turned His back on him, too."

"Exactly."

"You understood that," Hannah told her. "Chris told me that. He said you showed up at the same hospital he was at for tests and the two of you started talking and he started getting some of the answers he'd been looking for."

"Well, I don't think I had any answers —"

"He thought so," Hannah interrupted her. "I'm glad he thought so. He came here to Paradise to talk to you some more. Just think about it. If he hadn't, he and I wouldn't have met and gotten married."

Taking a deep breath, Hannah leaned back against the seat. "William and Fern weren't expecting this." She held her hands protectively over her abdomen.

"He didn't let them know?"

Hannah shook her head. "He said they didn't come to the wedding so why bother?"

"I imagine it was quite a shock for them to have him embrace the religion and the way of life here."

"Try telling Chris that. He says his father's always been stubborn and unwilling to listen to him. Then when Chris returned home after his military service, the distance between them grew wider."

"Are you warm enough?" Jenny asked, noticing that Hannah pulled her shawl closer around her. "There's an extra blanket on the back seat."

Hannah turned for it but movement was awkward for her. Jenny took her eyes off the road and reached for the blanket. This is something I can't do in a car, she couldn't help thinking. Pilot wouldn't veer off the road if Jenny didn't pay attention.

"You're being quiet. Either that or I'm talking too much." Hannah thought about it for a minute. "I'm talking too much."

"You needed to vent."

"You look exhausted."

"Wow, such flattery."

"It's too much for you to be caring for Phoebe on top of your family and your home. And your book deadline."

"I'm managing. Really."

"Nothing else is wrong, is it?"

Jenny sighed inwardly. Hannah was far too observant and far too plainspoken. "What could be wrong?"

Hannah laughed. "Matthew's my brother, but he's far from perfect."

She sobered and put her hand on Jenny's arm. "You know if you need someone to talk to I won't say anything to anyone. Especially Matthew. I'd probably even take your side."

Jenny avoided her gaze. "Nothing's wrong."

She winced inwardly at the lie. But she didn't have any choice. This was something that was just too personal to share with anyone. She was still hoping that there was a good reason for what Phoebe had done.

And her biggest hope was that Matthew hadn't known about it.

Matthew couldn't shake the feeling that something was wrong.

Jenny was a silent shadow of herself lately. At first he'd blamed her behavior on her being exhausted. He knew what it was like to be a caretaker since his first wife had been terminally ill for so long.

His friends and family had helped. They'd brought in meals, taken the *kinner* to school, helped with farming chores, sat with Amelia when Matthew needed to grab a few hours' sleep.

But no one bore the burden of care that a loving family member who was the caretaker did.

He knew that Jenny had been so worried about Phoebe since she'd gotten sick that she'd barely slept, barely ate. But something else was going on. He felt it in the mildly uneasy way a husband did when his wife became distant for no discernable reason.

His glance went to the calendar. It wasn't her time of the month. That had happened a week ago and she'd been disappointed and a little moody as she'd been since they'd been married and she hadn't conceived. And it wasn't their anniversary. He knew better than to forget that. What husband survived forgetting an anniversary?

Just a little while ago Jenny had announced she needed to run some errands. She'd rushed out, refusing his help with Pilot. That in itself had been another signal that something was wrong.

He knew how Pilot still sometimes seemed to enjoy giving Jenny a hard time when she wanted to hitch him to the buggy. Anyone who thought horses were dumb animals should watch *that* interplay.

Restless, he checked the time and headed outside. Walking in the fields always helped him think. The earth was barren of crops, the dirt carefully turned over. Soon the weather would turn colder and snow would cover it, pristine and white. He liked to think that the earth rested, absorbing the remnants of the roots of the crops he'd harvested, using the nutrients and the rain and snow and it would be richer for the seeds he'd plant in the spring.

Lost in thought, he almost missed Chris waving to him from the fields next to his. Matthew waved back and watched Chris stride over.

"Out for a walk?" Chris asked him when they were within a few feet of each other.

Matthew nodded. "It's a good place to think."

Chris glanced back at the house he shared with Hannah and he frowned. "It's a good place to get away, too."

"Visit not going well?"

"That would be an understatement."

A chill wind blew around them. When Chris shivered, Matthew jerked his head toward his house. "I just put some *kaffe* on."

"Sounds good."

They walked into the house and both men took off their jackets and hats and hung them on pegs.

"Smells good." Chris sat at the table.

"I think there are some cookies in the jar."

"Hannah's oatmeal raisin?"

"*Ya,* I think so."

"I've had enough of those, thanks. Hannah's been doing a lot of baking. I think it takes her mind off things. Wish that's all it took for me," he muttered.

"Is there any way I can help?" Matthew brought two mugs to the table and sat.

Chris looked at him, then away.

"Oh," Matthew said suddenly. "Maybe it's personal."

Coloring, Chris glanced at him. "It is."

Where was an interruption when he needed one? Matthew wondered. He cast a desperate glance at the clock. It was at least an hour before the *kinner* got home from *schul.*

"If it's about . . . marital relations, perhaps the bishop could offer some advice. Or the counseling center in town."

Matthew tried to keep his eyes level with Chris so the man wouldn't feel badly. He was uncomfortable with the direction of their conversation but he didn't want Chris to feel sorry that he'd turned to him or feel ashamed. But his collar was suddenly feeling so tight he wanted to pull it away from his neck so he could breathe.

Chris waved a hand and began laughing. "Oh, sorry. It's not at all what you think."

Matthew looked at him warily. "No?"

"No." Chris sobered. "I'm going to tell you something but if you don't keep it to yourself I'll — I'll —" He stopped and shook his head. "Well, I don't know what I'll do but men should help each other in this, you know? Like — support each other."

"Chris, I don't understand what you're talking about."

"Childbirth! I'm scared to death of childbirth!"

Feeling a huge relief, Matthew grinned. "Well," he began. "The first thing to know is that *you're* not going to have to have the baby —" he broke off as Chris punched his arm. "Ow! I was just joking!"

"It's not funny," Chris muttered darkly. "It's easy for you to joke. After your wife had the first and you knew what to expect — well, it must gotten easier to go through it."

"Only a little," Matthew told him, sobering as he remembered. "Each time I tried to trust God and know that all would be fine but I have to admit I was always a little scared until the baby was born and both it and Amelia were okay."

"I don't know what I'd do if anything happened to Hannah." Chris swallowed hard. "I almost lost it when she got shot by a man who was trying to hurt me. I'll never forget what it felt like to see her unconscious and bleeding and wonder if I was going to lose her."

He took a shaky breath and stared at the ground.

Matthew had had trouble liking this man when he first came here. Who wouldn't have been suspicious of a man a brother found up in a hayloft in the barn? But everything had been explained and at some point Matthew had realized that he didn't need to keep an eye on this stranger in their midst — his sister kept a steely eye on him. Matthew hadn't found out until later that Hannah thought Chris came here to steal Jenny away from him.

But once she'd found out that Chris didn't have ulterior motives, it hadn't been long before the two of them had fallen in love. It seemed a strange match at first — this former warrior from the *Englisch* world and his sister, an Amish woman who'd never been outside the small community of Paradise, Pennsylvania.

Hannah loved this man and he'd come to love her as well. He was a good man who took good care of his wife, his farm, his community.

Matthew didn't like to see him so worried even if it was over his sister. So he laid a hand on his shoulder and patted it — if a bit awkwardly — and did his best to think of words that would reassure.

"Women have been having babies for thousands of years —"

"That's supposed to reassure me?"

"She's had good checkups, hasn't she? Other than the baby trying to kick its way out everything's been fine? Childbirth is much less risky than it used to be."

"Yeah, but I've been reading some of the stuff in the doctor's office while I wait for her and it's scary."

He kicked at a clump of dirt and then he glared at Matthew. "This thing about being in the delivery room. I gotta tell you, I'd rather be on the front lines."

Matthew couldn't help it. He laughed.

"It's not funny! I don't want to see Hannah in pain."

"But you're going to find a way to be there with her," Matthew said quietly. "You'll find a way to force yourself because she means too much to you."

Chris rubbed the back of his neck. "Maybe."

"And you're not going to want to miss seeing that *boppli* for the first time," Matthew continued. "There's no describing the feeling of seeing your child as it's being born. It's the closest I've ever felt to God. That and when I stood and said my wedding vows."

Emotion welled up in his throat. He hadn't ever said this to anyone but Jenny and Amelia. Well, that wasn't exactly true.

He'd never told Jenny the part about how he felt at the birth of his *kinner.* He couldn't tell her that. He was afraid saying it would just make her unhappy. If they had a baby together some time in the future, he'd tell her then.

As they turned to walk back to their houses, Matthew saw Chris's face brighten and he began walking faster. Curious, Matthew looked in the direction that Chris was and saw Hannah picking her way carefully toward them.

Then Chris lengthened his strides, closed the distance, and scooped her up in his arms. She laughed and lifted her face for his kiss.

A little embarrassed at witnessing their display of affection, Matthew mumbled a hello to his sister — who completely ignored him — and hurried past them.

And as he did, he heard Chris telling her, "I dreamed this happening once, you coming for me in the fields. It was that night we sat up with Daisy when she was sick because Malcolm had poisoned her."

"I remember that night. We talked for hours. You fell asleep because you'd been helping Matthew with the harvest."

"I was dreaming that you and I walked these fields and I was so happy, looking forward to being with you on our own land, starting a life together. You were glowing with the joy of being pregnant. We kissed —"

"And then you woke up and found that Daisy was kissing you!" she cried and their laughter floated back to Matthew as Chris carried her to their home.

Jenny was making the bed when her fingers touched the book tucked in between the mattress and the box spring.

She drew it out and set it on top of the quilt. Things had been so hectic since her grandmother fell ill that she not only hadn't been able to work on her latest book — she hadn't written in her journal.

It was hard to remember how many years she'd been writing in a journal. Definitely since she turned thirteen. Her early journals had been full of typical teenage angst as she used them to work through her feelings about school and boys and a summer doing missionary work with her father and missing her mom.

As she grew older, her entries became less angst-driven. And then, the summer she visited her grandmother here in Paradise, she'd written complaint after complaint about a place that seemed so foreign to her at first. No electricity? What, had she traveled back to the dark ages? No cars? She'd just gotten her learner's permit. And people dressed so quaintly . . . even if they were the nicest people she'd ever met. Even if everyone had welcomed her as the beloved granddaughter of one of their favorite people.

And the boy next door couldn't take his eyes off her. Or she, him. She wrote about him endlessly. His blue eyes were so intense. He had such muscles from the hard work he did . . . she'd watched him from her bedroom window whenever she could. And he listened, really listened, but didn't do so for what he could get from her like the boys she knew back home.

Why, she'd filled one journal with entries about him just from that first month's visit.

She'd always kept her journal tucked

between the mattress and box spring — not that she'd had to hide anything from her father who wasn't nosy but just because she didn't want to leave her private thoughts out and tempt him should he wander into her room.

Now, she did the same thing. Not that Matthew had never shown any curiosity about the journal but she still kept it where she did for the same reason she had at her home with her father.

She finished making the bed and picking up the journal, carried it downstairs.

The house was quiet with the children at school, Matthew off in the barn puttering around with seed catalogs and cleaning equipment and whatever else he did in the winter and Phoebe was taking a nap. It seemed like the perfect time to journal.

A cup of tea at her side, she sat at the table and began the conversation with her thoughts. The minute she started, it seemed like her pen flew across the page. Everything that had been troubling her heart spilled onto the page: her grandmother's illness, her fear of losing her, the feeling of betrayal when she'd discovered the letter. Her dilemma of wanting so desperately to know if Matthew knew and yet experiencing anxiety about how she'd been guilty of reading the letter.

A slight sound made her look up and she saw that her grandmother stood in the doorway that connected the main house with the *dawdi haus.*

But Phoebe wasn't looking at Jenny . . . she was staring at the journal on the table in front of her.

"I didn't mean to disturb you."

"You're not," Jenny said. "Come sit down and I'll make you something to eat."

She closed the journal and laid her pen down next to it. Getting up, she helped her grandmother to a chair. "Did you have a good nap?"

Phoebe nodded and wrapped her shawl more closely around her shoulders. "*Ya.* But it seems all I do is sleep."

"Rest is the best medicine. That's what everyone says, isn't it?"

She put the tea kettle on and then rummaged around in the refrigerator. "Fannie Mae brought over some split pea soup with ham. Would you like that? Or are you tired of soup?"

"Soup is fine. I've been enough trouble."

"You haven't been any trouble at all."

Jenny turned around with the plastic container of soup in her hand and paused for a moment. Her grandmother was still staring at the journal and she wore a troubled expression.

Going to the cabinet near the stove, Jenny found a saucepan and set it on the stove. She dumped the soup into it, started the gas flame beneath it, then turned to set soup bowls on the table. All the while she kept an eye on her grandmother — as much wondering why the older woman was focusing her attention on the journal as assessing how she was feeling. Each day she seemed a little stronger but the pneumonia wasn't giving up easily or quickly.

Jenny sliced some bread, set out butter, and stirred the soup several times while she debated calling Matthew in for lunch. She glanced at the kitchen clock and decided it was still a little early for him.

Once the soup was warm, Jenny ladled it into bowls and joined Phoebe at the table.

After saying a blessing over the meal, they began eating. But before long, Jenny noticed that Phoebe was just stirring her soup with her spoon.

She glanced up and saw that Jenny was watching her. She shrugged. "I'm sorry, I'm not very hungry after all."

Jenny wasn't hungry either. Split pea soup had never been her favorite, either, and besides, she kept thinking about how she wanted to talk to her grandmother about the letter. But it just wasn't time.

She set her spoon down. "Maybe you're just tired of soup."

Phoebe shrugged and stared down into the pea-green depths. She sighed. "Maybe."

"Tell me what you'd like and I'll fix it."

"No, you have too much to do." Phoebe stirred the contents of her bowl again and lifted a spoon of soup to her lips. "This is fine."

But Jenny saw the faint look of distaste flash across her grandmother's face. She glanced down into her own bowl and thought — not for the first time — that split pea soup was a disgusting color — that yellowish-green called chartreuse. Stringy pieces of ham popped up here and there, floating on the thick soup. *Erk,* she thought as she let the spoonful of green sludge drip from the spoon to land with a plop into her own bowl.

And here she got teased about *her* cooking. Obviously split pea wasn't Fannie Mae's specialty.

She rose, picked up the two bowls, and set them in the sink. Turning, she folded her arms across her chest. "Now tell me what you'd like to eat. You've been sick.

Maybe your appetite needs tempting."

"Oatmeal," Phoebe said suddenly.

She could make that. Annie wanted oatmeal every morning.

"Not oatmeal," Phoebe said as Jenny got the box out of the cupboard. "Oatmeal cookies."

"You want oatmeal cookies for lunch," Jenny repeated slowly.

"Why not? Oatmeal's eaten for breakfast, isn't it? And oatmeal cookies are just baked oatmeal. With some good things in them like the oatmeal and eggs, right? I remember you said Hannah brought some over but I wasn't hungry for them before."

Jenny nodded. "Yes, she did. Lots of them, as a matter of fact. But I'm not sure there are any left." Saying a quick prayer that there were, she looked in the cookie jar. Sure enough there were half a dozen left. "I guess there's no harm in eating dessert first."

"I want cookies for lunch," Phoebe said decisively. "And ice cream. We have some ice cream, don't we?"

"Sure." There was no harm in humoring her, thought Jenny, but before she went to get it, she put the back of her hand against her grandmother's forehead. It was cool.

"What flavor? We have vanilla, chocolate

chip, and strawberry."

"Vanilla," Phoebe said promptly.

Jenny lifted the carton of ice cream from the freezer and then, just as she started to turn, the chocolate chip spoke to her. With a sigh, she picked it up as well and took it to the table.

"I guess we eat healthy enough we can have dessert first," Jenny said as she scooped out vanilla ice cream.

"Dessert first? This is all I want," Phoebe said with satisfaction as she accepted the bowl. She picked up one of the cookies on the plate before her and placed a spoonful of ice cream on the cookie, then topped it with another cookie. "See, I'm having a sandwich. Happy now?"

Jenny laughed. "An ice cream sandwich isn't the kind of sandwich I should be getting you to eat."

Phoebe bit into one and sighed. "Wonderful. I'll eat extra vegetables later, okay?" She looked over as Jenny put several scoops of chocolate chip into her bowl.

"It was calling my name," Jenny said, putting a spoon of ice cream into her mouth. "Whatever you do, don't let the children know we did this. I'd never hear the end of it."

They sat there enjoying their ice cream

and Jenny noticed that Phoebe was looking like she'd perked up a little. Maybe letting her eat the ice cream had been a good idea.

She'd been thinking a lot about how she was going to ask her grandmother about her discovery of the letter. Her emotions had gone all over the place from feeling betrayed to being angry to feeling disappointed and then distrustful and back and forth again. But she wasn't sure whether her grandmother was well enough . . . what if she caused a relapse?

Before she could open her mouth, they heard the door open and shut and Matthew strode in. His eyebrows went up as he took in the scene.

"I didn't realize we were having a party," he said. "What's the occasion?"

"*Grossmudder* is tired of soup. Especially split pea soup."

Matthew glanced at the stove with anticipation. "We have split pea soup?"

"Fannie Mae made it. I didn't call you for dinner because I thought it was too early."

"It's never too early for dinner." He went over and took a taste with the big wooden spoon Jenny had used to stir it. Turning, he grinned. "Mmm. More for me if you two aren't going to eat it."

Jenny laughed. "You remind me of Mikey.

He'd eat anything."

"Mikey?"

She rose. "Old television commercial. Go wash your hands and I'll fix you a bowl."

Phoebe nearly made it through the second ice cream sandwich. She set the uneaten portion down on the plate and yawned. "I'm going to go lie down for a while," she told them and shook her head when Matthew asked if she wanted help getting back to bed.

"Shall I bring you a cup of tea? And please don't say 'don't go to any trouble.' "

With a tired smile, Phoebe nodded. "That would be *wunderbaar, danki.*"

While the water for the tea heated Jenny rejoined Matthew at the table. Maybe she was going about this wrong, she thought. Maybe instead of waiting for Phoebe to get better she should be asking Matthew if he knew anything. There was just that small matter of her reading the letter, though.

She sighed. What a mess.

"Anything wrong?" Matthew asked her.

"No, why?" Another lie.

"You just seem . . . distracted."

"I'm just off my schedule." She fixed the tea, poured him a cup of coffee and set it before him, and then started out of the kitchen.

At the doorway she suddenly realized

she'd left her journal and she glanced back. Matthew was looking at it thoughtfully as he reached for his coffee. Then he looked up and their eyes met. She'd left it out a couple of times and always felt safe and yet today she didn't feel comfortable doing so. But if she walked over and picked it up, wasn't she telling him she didn't trust him?

10

She didn't trust him.

Shocked, Matthew stared at the journal. He'd never had any desire to look at it or any other personal papers of hers. He'd always trusted her and thought she trusted him. What had happened to change that?

It didn't take her long to return.

"That was quick." He watched color rise in her cheeks.

"She was already asleep." She put the teacup in the sink, picked up the journal, and left the room.

He listened to her steps in their room overhead, and then heard her descending the stairs. When she returned, she pulled her coat from the peg by the door.

"Where are you going?"

"I promised *Grossmudder* I'd get her the quilt she was working on."

"Jenny, we need to talk," he said, pushing back from the table.

"I'll be home soon," she said.

She was out the door before he could respond.

He got up from the table and stood at the kitchen window, watching her hurry to the house next door.

The distance between them felt like it was growing by the moment and he didn't know how to fix it. Here he'd told himself it was because she was tired, overwhelmed by the responsibility of caring for her grandmother. He'd blamed it on her being a little depressed around her time of the month when she found out that once again she hadn't conceived.

But now he didn't know what was wrong or how to fix it. He was a simple man, a farmer who didn't have a lot of words, who relied on action to show how he felt. He'd thought he'd shown her he loved her, thought everything was fine, that she was happy here.

But maybe everything he'd thought was wrong. He was usually a pretty calm person, taking things as they came, secure in the belief that even when life looked confusing and a little worrisome that his God was in charge, that His will was in force, and all was well.

The split pea soup he'd eaten began

churning in his gut. Turning, he picked up the bowl and set it in the sink. He poured another cup of coffee, glanced at the clock, and sat down. How long did it take to fetch a quilt?

Fifteen minutes later, he was still sitting there waiting for his wife to return. Sighing, he got up, put his cup in the sink, and reached for his jacket. He reasoned that if he was going to wait he might as well get something done in the barn.

He glanced over as he walked to the barn, wondering if Jenny saw that he was going there if she'd come home. No, he shouldn't think that way. That was just plain ridiculous. Things between them couldn't have gotten that bad that quickly.

Could they?

Jenny knocked on the front door, then opened it as she always did.

"It's Jenny," she called out.

She stepped inside, then stopped when she heard raised voices coming from the kitchen.

"When were you going to let us know? When the kid went off to college?"

"Lower your voice," Chris said. "Hannah needs her rest."

"I asked you a question," Chris's father

said in a quieter voice.

"And I answered you. If you didn't come to the wedding who knew you'd be interested in a grandchild?"

"I explained why we didn't come."

"You hurt my wife's feelings!"

Feeling she was eavesdropping, Jenny turned to leave and ran into Chris's mom, Fern.

"They at it again?" she asked, smiling as she set her packages down on a table by the door. "They've been like this since Chris learned to talk. Come on," she said, slipping her arm through Jenny's, "Let's go in the kitchen and warm up with a cup of tea. Maybe they've woken up my daughter-in-law and she'll join us. How's your grandma?"

"Getting better," Jenny told her, surprised at the easy friendliness of the woman. William had been a little standoffish with her.

The men looked surprised when Jenny and Fern entered the kitchen.

"I knocked," Jenny said apologetically.

"I didn't hear you," Chris told her and he gave his father a meaningful look.

"What's all the fuss?" Hannah asked, yawning as she walked in. "I could hear you all the way upstairs." She turned to Jenny and hugged her. "I wasn't expecting you."

"I came over to get the quilt *Grossmudder* was sewing before she got sick."

"I'll get it for you in a minute," Hannah said. "Sit down, let's have a cup of tea."

"Exactly what I suggested," Fern told her, rubbing her hands together for warmth.

Jenny wanted to suggest that she would get the quilt but it was in her grandmother's room and that was where Chris's parents were staying. She supposed she shouldn't go in there now.

"How is she doing?" Chris wanted to know.

"Better. When she said she was missing her quilting I thought I'd get it to occupy her. Otherwise, before we know it she'll be trying to do housework."

Chris held out his hand to Hannah and she took it and let him lead her to a chair. "Did you get any rest at all?" he asked. "You weren't up there long."

She sat and sighed. "The baby doesn't let me get much these days."

Fern took the teakettle to the kitchen faucet and filled it. "Taking after his father, I imagine. Chris was a bundle of energy from the very beginning."

She turned to look quizzically at Hannah. "You two really don't want to know the sex of the baby until it arrives?"

"That's when we knew," William said, accepting a cup of coffee from his wife. "It was good enough for us back then."

"It just seems like such a nice surprise to find out when it's born," Hannah said, her smile dreamy as she looked up at Chris. "It's one thing to say that you don't care if it's a boy or girl as long as it's healthy but not knowing means you really do."

"Makes a lot of sense," William said gruffly, smiling slightly at Hannah.

Surprised at his softening toward his daughter-in-law, Jenny glanced at Chris and saw that he was looking askance at his father.

"Could I cook supper tonight to help out?" Fern asked as she sat next to Hannah.

"Oh, I'm fine. It wouldn't be right to have you cooking while you're visiting."

"We're family," Fern insisted gently. "When you come to our home, you can cook a meal for us."

She looked at her son. "I hope you'll bring Hannah for a visit there one day. Watch your son or daughter play in the fields where you played."

"Don't you remember, your son doesn't want any part of us or our farm?" William stood and stomped out of the room.

"He never changes, does he?" Chris asked his mother.

Sighing, Fern stood and patted her son's cheek. "Neither of you do," she said simply. "Neither of you do."

Bending, she kissed Hannah's cheek. "Don't you let it worry you," she told her. "Both of them have a bigger bark than they have a bite."

Hannah smiled. "I know they love each other."

She turned to Chris and held out her hand. "Here, help the whale up. I'm going to get that quilt for Jenny so she can get back to Phoebe."

And Matthew, thought Jenny suddenly, wishing she could find a way to delay going home.

Chris hoisted Hannah up out of the chair and kissed her cheek.

"You know," Fern said pensively as she stared at Hannah. "I'm going to go out on a limb here and say I think you're going to have a girl."

Hannah stared at her abdomen then at her mother-in-law. "Really? Why do you think that?"

"Because you're carrying high. If you carry high, you're having a girl and if you carry low, it's a boy."

When Hannah looked at her, Jenny lifted her shoulders and let them fall.

"I thought it was the opposite. I don't really know."

And I don't want to talk about this, Jenny wanted to say. But she didn't. Hannah had every right to talk twenty-four hours a day about her pregnancy if she wanted to. It was selfish of Jenny to want to avoid the subject.

"You could ask Leah. She says she's got a good prediction rate."

"I think it's a girl," Hannah said. "Chris says he doesn't care as long as it's healthy. If it's a girl, we're going to call her Lydia after his grandmother. If it's a boy, we'll call him Jonah, after my father."

Hannah started down the hall to Phoebe's bedroom and Jenny would have followed. But then she heard sniffling.

"You'd name the baby after my mother?" Fern whispered as her eyes filled.

Chris grinned. "As long as it's a girl."

Fern turned to look after Hannah. "Chris? When did you say she's due?"

"Not for another month. Why?"

"She's waddling."

"Ssh!" he hissed. "She could hear you. You heard her say she feels big as a whale."

"You don't understand. That's how you know a woman's getting near to delivery.

The bones in her pelvis soften so she can have the baby easier."

Chris paled and sat down. "Really, Mom. Too much information."

But she didn't hear him. "I'm going to go talk to your father. We can stay at a motel if you can't put us up here. But I'm not leaving and missing out on my seeing my first grandchild when it's born."

She hurried out of the room.

"Another month of my father? I can't live through that, Jenny."

Then he brightened. "Wait a minute. Phoebe'll be well by then and she'll need her room back."

She wanted to argue with him but she wasn't so sure how she'd be getting along with her grandmother after they talked about the letter.

"Here's the quilt," Hannah said as she brought it to Jenny. "And her basket of supplies. Do you want Chris to help you carry it to your house?"

Jenny lifted it all. "No, I'm fine. Listen, you're looking really tired. Let your mother-in-law cook supper. I think she really wants to help."

Glancing over Jenny's shoulder, Hannah smiled. "They're nice people. I know they were a little worried about what Chris was getting himself into by staying here. I know we look quaint and old-fashioned to the *Englisch.* But I think it's helping that they're seeing everything for themselves."

She sighed. "Now if we can just keep William and Chris from killing each other."

Matthew watched Chris pace around the barn.

"If you keep doing this you're going to exhaust yourself by the time the baby comes," he said.

"I know." Chris blew out a breath. "I've done everything I can think of. Planned the crops for spring. Ordered the seed. Repaired the tack."

Matthew hid his grin as he bent over the dresser he was sanding.

"I need a hobby."

"A hobby? What's that?"

Chris stared at him and then he laughed. "Yeah, guess that's a strange word here."

"I know what a hobby is," Matthew told him dryly. He stood back and studied the dresser, then ran his hand over the sanded surface. "What did you used to do in your spare time?"

"I had this Mustang."

"Really? You could have brought him." Matthew looked up from his task when

Chris laughed. "What?"

"It's a car. You haven't heard of a *Mustang?*"

Matthew shook his head. "We don't exactly keep up on things like that."

"No, right." He looked thoughtful for a moment. "Man, what a honey that car was. Midnight blue. Sleek lines. V-8 engine. Lotta horsepower under the hood. She could go from zero to —" he stopped. "Sorry."

"It's *allrecht.* I think I understand. I've seen how *Englischers* feel about their cars. It's different but I feel some fondness for Pilot when he takes me somewhere in the buggy. Pilot doesn't have as much horsepower but he shows me a lot of affection."

Chris grinned. "I understand."

Matthew stared at his brother-in-law. He'd never thought to ask this question but suddenly it seemed important to him. "Chris, are you happy here?"

The other man stared at him. "Of course. Why do you ask?"

Shrugging, suddenly unable to look at him, Matthew pretended a need to focus his attention on the front drawer of the dresser.

"Are you afraid I'll go back with my parents?"

Matthew glanced up. "Well, I wondered . . ." he trailed off.

"You don't think Hannah thinks that, do you?" Chris ran a hand through his hair, making it stand on end. "She can't think that. She has to know I love her."

"You don't miss anything about your old life?"

"Are you crazy? My life's here, with her and the baby coming." He stopped and stared into the distance. "Oh geez," he said.

With a sigh, he sank down on a nearby bale of hay and appeared lost in thought.

"Chris. Chris!" he repeated.

"What?" He shook his head, as if to clear it.

"I didn't mean to upset you."

"I'm just trying to think about whether I said or did anything that would make Hannah concerned I'd go back home with my parents. She doesn't deserve any stress right now."

Matthew threw down the sandpaper and walked over to crouch down in front of Chris. "I'm sorry I asked the question. I meant no harm. You and Hannah look so much in love. It's just that things are so different here. It's not the life for everyone."

"I know that. It's taken some adjustment. But nothing I wasn't expecting. You forget, too, that I had a pretty structured life in the military. I don't have any problem with rules."

He stood and Matthew did as well. But this time, when Chris paced around the barn, his steps were less frenetic, his expression more thoughtful than stressed. "Talking with Jenny helped a lot. That and talking with the bishop."

"Jenny?"

"You know she's the reason I came here to begin with. The way she talked about this place, you and the children. The way she seemed to glow when she described how she felt about her new life — the one she'd have after she finished studying to join the church and marry you and the children." He stopped and laughed. "Well, she didn't marry the children. You know what I mean."

"She did marry the children in a way," Matthew said. "We became a family the day we married."

The memory of how he and Jenny had walked, she with her arm in his, to be married was so precious. Jenny had worked so hard with her physical therapy to do it without depending on her cane.

What could have happened to cause this distance between them? he wondered. They barely talked lately, only went through the motions.

"Are you okay?"

Matthew realized that Chris stared at him, his expression concerned.

"Shur," he said but he must have been too quick for Chris frowned even harder.

"You've been quiet lately," Chris said.

"When we're all together there's so much talking." Even to his own ears it sounded lame. Matthew walked around to the side of the dresser and looked for flaws.

"Everything okay between you and Jenny?"

"Of course."

"Okay." Chris drew out the word. He walked over to the smaller dresser that Matthew had made for Annie's room. "Matthew?"

"Hmm?"

"Have you ever made a cradle?"

Matthew turned to look at him. "*Ya.* Each of the *kinner* slept in it beside our bed until we moved them to a crib in their own room. Did you want to borrow it?"

"I want you to teach me how to make one. I think it might be something good to keep me occupied until the baby comes."

"A hobby?"

Chris laughed. "Yes. And I think Hannah would like it."

Matthew clapped him on the back. "I

think she would love it."

"Can we go into town for some wood tomorrow?"

"Shur."

Chris surprised him by hugging him. "Thanks, man," he said.

When he stepped back, he looked away, as if embarrassed by what he'd done. But not before Matthew saw him blinking back tears. Matthew found himself doing the same.

"Guess I'd better get back home. If I know my father he'll be eating my share. He does love Hannah's cooking."

"Ya," Matthew agreed. He needed to get inside for supper, too.

And he'd do his best to talk with his wife that night, find out what was causing the distance between them.

11

A few days later, Jenny found a message waiting for her on the phone in the shanty.

Her friend Joy's voice came through bright and friendly on the voicemail, making it seem as if she stood with Jenny in the small space, filling it with her energy and spirit.

"Hey, hope everyone's doing well! Just calling to see if we could come visit for a few days. Not going to impose on you for a place to stay. Just want to see you and the family, get a room at the B & B we love near you. If it's not a good time you better say or I'll be upset with you. Call me back when you can."

Torn, Jenny clutched the phone. A visit with Joy and her husband, David, and Sam, their little boy, would be wonderful. They'd been pretty much Jenny's only friends in her old life in New York City — whenever Jenny was in the country and not reporting overseas. She'd played matchmaker, introducing network *wunderkind* David to Joy, a marketing specialist Jenny had met in the building elevator one day. They'd attended each other's weddings and the "city mice" as Joy referred to them visited the "country mice" here in Paradise once or twice a year.

Jenny thought about what fun they'd all had the last visit and wanted so much to return the call and say, "Yes! How soon can you be here?"

But this meant that there would be more people she had to pretend around and act like nothing was wrong. She wasn't sure just how much more she could do that.

She wondered if she should think about it for a few hours. No, she decided. Joy and David hadn't been here for ages and she missed them so. Sam, too. They wouldn't be any trouble — they always insisted on staying at the B & B not far from the farm. Impulsively, she picked up the phone to call Joy back to confirm the visit.

Maybe she'd have to pretend that things were okay when her friends visited. But maybe she'd have figured out what to do before then. She had to, she told herself. The tension was proving too much.

When she walked outside, she saw Fern coming up the drive.

"I've been thinking," the woman said in

that no nonsense way of hers. "I think us girls should go shopping."

"Shopping?"

Fern nodded. "We've been looking over her baby things everyone's been making but I'd sure like to buy some things as well. And she wants to pick up some fabric for a quilt. One for the baby. Well, another one. Said she'd already made two." Her eyes filled and she blinked rapidly. "Such an emotional time. We came here to see what was what with Chris and found us such a happy situation."

Jenny patted her arm. "It's wonderful to see, isn't it? They love each other very, very much. And I know they're so happy about having a baby."

She hesitated. "I'm running a little behind on my deadline —"

"Pish tosh, can't work every minute. Why don't you go tell your man we're going into town for a few hours?"

Jenny nodded and sighed. "Okay. Are we taking Hannah's buggy?"

"Honey, we're paying through the nose for those wheels we rented," she said, gesturing to the car in the other driveway. "Let's use them."

She turned and strode back to Hannah's house, turning to yell, "We'll pick you up in fifteen minutes."

When Jenny opened the barn door, the two men inside jumped and Chris quickly grabbed a tarp and dragged it over something.

"Close the door, quick!" Chris ordered.

Jenny did as he asked. "What's up?"

"Hannah's not right behind you, is she?"

Jenny shook her head. "Why?"

Chris pulled the cover off and revealed a baby cradle.

He and Matthew were working on a baby cradle. Jenny felt a lump rise in her throat.

"It's for Hannah. For the baby."

"Yes, I guessed."

"It's a surprise."

She nodded. "I won't tell." Her glance slid to Matthew then quickly away.

Caught up in his excitement, Chris didn't notice that Jenny and Matthew were avoiding looking at each other.

Chris walked around the cradle and studied it. "Matthew's showing me how to make it. He said he carved one for the kids when they were babies."

His unexpected words hit her in the chest. Matthew had made a cradle for his children? She told herself she shouldn't have been surprised. After all, Matthew was a very good furniture builder. Of course he would have made his children a cradle.

Well, she couldn't get upset about something like that. It had been years ago. It had nothing to with her.

But oh, if only he were hiding in the barn, working on a cradle for a child of their own right now. She wasn't an envious person. She wasn't.

She wasn't!

But she so wanted Matthew to be building a cradle for their child. She wanted him making a surprise like that for her. She swallowed at the lump. Her heart fairly ached thinking about it.

A horn honked outside.

Thank heavens, she thought. "Fern wants me to go with her and Hannah to get some things for the baby. We'll be back in a couple of hours."

Matthew nodded.

"She just came over. I didn't have time to fix your dinner. There's leftover roast beef —"

"I'm sure we can fix a sandwich," Chris told her with a grin. "If Matthew doesn't know how I can show him."

Jenny stared at Chris for a moment. He looked so happy, so carefree. She thought he looked like he might burst from it. How different he appeared compared to the haunted man who'd come here suffering from post-traumatic stress syndrome and a bone-deep disappointment in his fellow soldiers who'd turned their back on him after he'd testified against one of his own. Then he'd nearly died when he'd been hurt in a car bombing.

He'd talked about how every soldier — whether he was an atheist or agnostic — believed in God on the battlefield. But he'd stopped believing in Him and come here. And everything had changed. Just as it had for her.

The car horn honking again made her jump. She jerked her head to look at Matthew again, at his still, silent form. He watched her, unsmiling.

The difference between the two men couldn't have been more dramatic.

"I'll be back soon."

"Jenny?"

She turned back.

Matthew had his wallet in his hand. "Do you need money?"

She shook her head. "I have some. Thanks."

"Then have a *gut* time."

She nodded. "Thanks."

■ ■ ■ ■

Jenny stirred her iced tea and then took a sip.

"You're awfully quiet," Hannah remarked as she set her fork down.

After taking a quick look at Fern standing at the buffet line, she smiled. "Fern enjoys talking. I enjoy listening to her."

"She's sweet, isn't she? Wish I could have stopped her from buying so much at the baby store."

"It makes her happy to think about having her first grandchild."

Hannah set her fork down and leaned back in her chair. "Yes, it does, doesn't it?"

"You're not eating much."

"I'm not very hungry." Hannah frowned as she shifted in her chair.

"You okay?"

"Yes. Just a little cramping." In a motion that had become habitual, Hannah rubbed at her abdomen.

"No foot under the ribs?"

"Not lately."

"What's this about ribs?" Fern asked as she stopped beside the table. She hesitated, glanced at the buffet and frowned. "I didn't see any ribs on it. I do like some good ribs."

Hannah laughed and explained how the baby had made her so uncomfortable a few weeks ago.

"You aren't finished, are you?" Fern said, waving her fork at Hannah's plate. "Why, you didn't eat enough for a bird."

"I sure did."

"Back in my day —"

"I know, the doctor told you to eat for two." Hannah smiled. "They don't want you to do that these days."

"Looking at you, you barely look pregnant the way you just adjust your clothes with pins instead of wearing maternity smocks and things."

Hannah burst out laughing. When she stopped she wiped at her streaming eyes. "Oh, that's a good one. I look huge right now and I know it."

Fern made quick work of her second helping from the buffet while Jenny finished her meal and Hannah sipped at a glass of water. Before long, Fern was getting up to take a look at the dessert buffet.

"Never had shoofly pie," she said. "Gotta go take a look at it." Off she went.

"What are you doing here?" a woman said loudly as she stood beside a booth near them.

Jenny and Hannah looked up.

"It's Officer Lang," Hannah said. "You remember, you met her at the hospital after I got shot."

Jenny didn't think she'd ever forget anything having to do with that day. "Who's she talking to?"

"Can't see. But she doesn't sound happy."

"Since when can't a man have a meal in a restaurant?"

"The deal was that you stayed away from Mrs. Matlock."

Hannah and Jenny glanced at each other at the mention of Hannah's name.

A man stuck his head out of the booth and looked in their direction. "Oh, sorry, didn't see you when I came in," he said.

"No, don't do that, Malcolm," Hannah said firmly. "We'll be leaving in a minute. Surely he can stay and finish his food, can't he, officer?"

Officer Lang hesitated, resting one hand on the utility belt on her hip. "You remember your husband insisted on the restraining order, Mrs. Matlock."

Hannah sighed. "Yes, I remember."

Tilting her head to one side, she studied the officer. "Did someone call you here or were you stopping for coffee or dinner?"

The officer's eyes narrowed. "I was going to eat. Why?"

"Well, then, maybe you could join us and the whole problem is solved."

"I thought you said you were about to leave."

"Or you could join me," Malcolm offered.

Jenny could see that the statement surprised the woman for she turned and looked at him, wary.

"And why would I want to do that?"

"Serve and protect, right? Be a lot easier to glare at me from close proximity."

"I can do that from her table just fine."

"No doubt," he said, picking up a French fry and dunking it into a puddle of ketchup on his plate. He chewed it and washed it down with a big soft drink. "We can talk about my AA meetings and how I'm becoming a model citizen."

The officer straightened and Jenny, who'd learned about body language from years of being in danger zones overseas, saw that the woman had tensed.

Malcolm must have realized he'd overstepped, for his smile faded and he gestured at the seat opposite him. "Sorry, I have a lousy sense of humor. Why don't you let me buy you lunch and make it up to you."

"I'm not sure —"

He said something in a low voice that Jenny couldn't hear. Hannah either, apparently, for she looked at Jenny with her eyebrows raised in question.

Officer Lang slid into the booth.

"Well," Hannah whispered to Jenny. "That's interesting. What do you suppose he said to her?"

"Please," Jenny whispered back.

"Please?"

Jenny nodded.

"You don't suppose . . ."

"What?"

Hannah smiled as she watched them. "You don't suppose that he might be interested in her?"

Sneaking a look, Jenny shook her head. "A cop and a convicted felon? I think you're just seeing the world with rose colored glasses, sister-in-law. I'm sure he was just trying to be nice to her. I mean, would you mess with someone with a gun?" she asked.

Then she clapped a hand over her mouth. Tactless, tactless, tactless, she chided herself. Hannah had gotten in the way of Malcolm when he'd tried to shoot Chris not so long ago. "Oh, no, I'm sorry, what am I saying?"

"It's okay," Hannah told her. "It's history now. I'm fine and Malcolm is on the right path to making a success of his life."

She looked up and grinned. "Speaking of

paths. Someone we know sure has been beating a path to the buffet. I can see where Chris gets his love of food from."

Turning to Jenny, Hannah giggled. "Oh, I'm so awful talking like that. You must think I'm terrible."

Jenny smiled into her coffee cup. "I already know you are. I'm just hanging around with you trying to reform you."

Fern set her plate on the table. "What was all that commotion?" she asked, jerking her head at Malcolm and Officer Lang.

Hannah hesitated. "Did Chris tell you about Malcolm?"

"Name doesn't sound familiar," Fern said as she sat down.

"You know how Chris testified against a fellow officer when they were serving overseas?"

"Sure. We heard about it. Chris didn't let us know but it was in our paper." Fern put a forkful of shoofly pie in her mouth and chewed with obvious enjoyment.

"Malcolm's the man Chris testified against."

Fern swallowed and glanced over. "He's the one who tried to rape one of the Afghan women?"

Hannah nodded. "He was drunk and he'd done some drugs."

"No excuse," Fern said bluntly. "Chris was right to step up and speak out against him."

"It's not our way to judge," Hannah said quietly. "Anyway, you know that Chris's fellow officers didn't agree and they made things difficult for him. Then he was hurt and returned home. When Malcolm's sentence was overturned, he came here to have his revenge, to hurt Chris for all he felt he'd done to him."

Fern's eyes grew big. "He didn't hurt Chris?"

"No, he hurt Hannah," Jenny told her. "She stepped in front of the gun when Malcolm aimed it at Chris and got shot."

"Why, you could have been killed!" Fern cried.

"Jenny's making it sound worse than it was," Hannah said lightly, "The bullet hit me in the arm. It wasn't that bad."

Jenny started to speak, to tell Fern that Hannah could have bled to death from the bullet hitting an artery but Hannah sent her a warning glance.

Fern's eyes filled with tears and she reached across the table to grasp Hannah's hands. "I'm so glad you're all right."

Sighing, Hannah shook her head and looked at Jenny. "I shouldn't have told her."

"So did he go to prison and he's already out?" Fern demanded.

"You have a wonderful daughter-in-law, Fern. She forgave him and saw that he got parole."

Fern looked dumbstruck for a long moment and then she shook her head. "I've heard of the Amish and how they forgive. I couldn't have done that. I have to tell you, I'm not feeling so charitable about him right now."

"He's gone to counseling and he doesn't drink or do drugs any more," Hannah said simply. "He's a wonderful man. He's even volunteering at the veteran's counseling center a couple of days a week around his construction job."

"And you'd know all this because?" Jenny asked her.

Hannah blushed. "We talked some last time I came to town."

"Ignoring the restraining order Chris insisted on," Jenny muttered.

She held up her hands when Hannah gave her a look. "Don't worry, I'm not going to tell Chris." She looked at Fern. "He's turned his life around. He gets to see his son now because of Hannah."

Fern patted Hannah's hand. "You're a saint, my dear. I'm a God-fearing woman and I know we're supposed to forgive and all, but I couldn't have done it."

"I'm not a saint," Hannah told her. "Really, don't even say such a thing. Malcolm was a good man who made some mistakes. It's not our way to judge," she said, repeating her earlier words.

The waitress came to take away plates. Fern handed her the plate with half of the serving of shoofly pie.

"I want to save room for some of your pie later, Hannah."

She peered at Hannah over her glasses. "I *did* see one of your pumpkin pies in the kitchen before we left, didn't I?"

Hannah tried to beat Jenny to the check when the waitress dropped it on the table, leaning forward and grabbing for it.

She won. Smiling, she turned to her mother-in-law.

"You did see a pumpkin pie. On the other hand, William and Chris are at the house."

"And Matthew's close by," Jenny inserted. "You know how he loves your pumpkin pie."

Fern took a last sip of coffee and wiped her mouth with the napkin. "Ladies, I think we need to get moving."

Picking up her purse that looked the size of a small suitcase, she deftly plucked the check from Hannah's fingers and sailed toward the cashier.

Jenny and Hannah stared at each other and then they laughed.

"I love that woman," Hannah said.

They followed Fern to the cashier.

Sometimes Jenny wondered why she didn't just buy ten thimbles for her fingers.

It surely would save her fingertips from all the pricking they got at a quilting. She'd never been particularly interested in the activity; she didn't seem to have the patience for it even though there were a lot of parallels to writing. Both took quite an attention to detail, piecing together random bits to make up a whole, focusing on something for an extended period of time.

But while writing was necessarily solitary, quilt-making was quite a social activity and she willingly threw herself into it so that she could be with other women and chat about the important things — children, home, the community.

A fire blazed in the fireplace, creating a warm, cozy atmosphere. Cups of tea and plates of cookies had been passed around along with stories and news and yes, even a little gossip.

Young and old mixed, friends and family. Today, even *Englisch* and Amish.

"Reminds me of quilting circles back on the farm in Kansas," Fern remarked as she cut up pieces of material she'd bought yesterday at *Stitches in Time.*

Hannah wore a dreamy expression as she stitched on a crib quilt, one with a tumbling block pattern of many colors — not exclusively pink or blue since she didn't want to know the sex of the baby.

A crib quilt. Did she know that Chris labored over a cradle for their baby? Jenny wondered. No, she couldn't. Of course, she sewed on a crib quilt. What woman expecting a baby here wouldn't?

And Phoebe stitched on one, too. Jenny couldn't help feeling a little pang in her heart at that. She wished that Phoebe was making it for her.

Determined to focus on something besides herself and a little self-pity, Jenny took a deep breath and looked around the room. There were more women than usual today. It was all in honor of the extra quilts being sewn and donated for the Haiti auction held in Sarasota, Florida, each year.

Jenny had innocently asked why they were sending quilts to a country she thought was too warm to need such and the ladies had all giggled at her. Leah had quickly explained that it was one way for the Amish to contribute to an auction where the quilts were sold and the money sent to help the people in Haiti.

So she sat like the others and tried to make a contribution to the cause. What she got were pricked fingers and crooked stitching she had to keep pulling out and redoing.

She knew more of the names of the patterns the other women stitched. One sewed a Grandmother's Fan. Another pinned the patches that formed a Trip around the World quilt. Jenny wondered how far the quilt would travel to a new home.

The Crazy Quilt with its random pattern and bright fabrics was the one she'd chosen. Mistakes didn't show as much and she felt she wouldn't get as frustrated trying to make order of the more complicated patterns the other women were used to after sewing them for years. She loved the one that Lydia worked on with patches from pieces of clothes she'd made for her children.

Fannie Mae's little girl, Lizzie, was lying under the quilt frame where her mother and several other women were stitching a really big Sunshine and Shadow quilt, a popular design. Jenny remembered how Hannah had made such a quilt for Chris before they got married. Little legs stuck out from beneath the quilt. When she didn't move for the longest time, Jenny became curious about what was so fascinating.

She got up and tiptoed over, holding her finger over her mouth to warn the others not to say anything, and got down on the floor beside Lizzie. When she peered underneath, she saw that Lizzie was lying there looking up at the needles busily going in and out, in and out, of the quilt overhead. Lizzie glanced at Jenny, her eyes wide, her thumb in her mouth, and Jenny lay beside her, watching them, too, enjoying the rhythmic motion for a few minutes until she crawled out, straightened her dress, and went back to her seat.

"Was it fun?" Fannie Mae inquired, grinning at Jenny.

"Fascinating," Jenny told her, picking up her needle. "You see things from a whole new perspective."

She told Fannie Mae how Lizzie had watched the needles and touched the fabric scraps on the floor, holding them up to study with her blonde eyebrows drawn together.

Fannie Mae nodded. "That's my Lizzie. She seems to look at life differently than my other *kinner.*"

"That's my Annie, too," Jenny told her, and they were off discussing children like mothers do.

Like mothers do, thought Jenny, and tears stung the backs of her lids. But it wasn't pity this time, she thought. She was a mother. Matthew's children had embraced her as one and she knew it was the greatest blessing along with his love that she'd ever received.

She sighed. No, she wasn't a saint, she thought, watching as Lizzie got out from under the quilt and climbed up into her mother's lap to nurse. She'd told herself that some time ago as she watched Hannah looking so blissful at being pregnant. She loved her sister-in-law and wanted her to be happy. Hannah not only had been thrilled when her brother married Jenny, she'd done everything she could to make her feel welcome and adapt to the community. She'd even helped her at every opportunity when Jenny needed to go into New York City for meetings with her editor.

And things could have turned out so differently for her beloved sister-in-law when Malcolm had come after Chris and tried to hurt him. She'd been lucky to only be wounded, the bullet missing vital organs. Hannah had been so worried she might not be able to have children. Jenny had reassured her otherwise. And now Hannah sat here so happy. So pregnant.

But Jenny had had to deal with the knowledge that her injuries from the car bombing had likely scarred her inside and rendered her infertile.

That word. It made her throat close up. Suddenly the room felt like it was getting smaller, the walls closing in like special effects in horror movies she'd seen years ago.

She must have gotten to her feet too quickly, for some of the other women looked up and gave her curious stares.

"Just remembered something I need to do," she told them and hurried from the room.

In the kitchen she stood at the sink, clutching the cold porcelain in her hands, and stared, unseeing, through the window. The sky was darkening and rain began to fall, matching her gray mood.

"Jenny?"

She spun around at the familiar voice. Phoebe stood in the doorway.

"Yes?"

"Anything wrong?"

She shook her head. "I just needed a drink of water."

As Phoebe continued to watch her, Jenny

realized that she hadn't moved to get a drink. She got a glass out of the cupboard and filled it with water from the tap. It took little effort to drink it — her throat was dry, so dry.

Phoebe moved into the room. "Jenny, I've been wanting to talk with you. Something's wrong. You've been acting strangely."

Jenny turned and refilled the glass so she wouldn't have to meet Phoebe's eyes. They always saw so much.

"Nothing's wrong."

"You're sure?"

"Yes. I've just been tired. It's been a busy time."

"Not helped by me being sick for so long."

"It wasn't your fault." It took a big effort but Jenny forced herself to turn and meet Phoebe's eyes. She hadn't minded taking care of her grandmother. It had been an act of love.

Even after seeing evidence of her betrayal.

There had to be a good reason for her going to her son and telling him that his daughter was in love with the boy next door. There had to be.

Lydia walked into the room and smiled brightly at them, not noticing the stiff way Jenny and Phoebe were behaving toward each other.

"I thought I'd make some more coffee."

"*Gut* idea," Phoebe said. "Let me help you."

The two women worked in tandem preparing the coffee, an ease between them that came of years of performing such a task together.

Jenny used the opportunity to slip from the room but not before glancing back and seeing that Phoebe watched her, a worried expression in her eyes.

Yes, they needed to talk, thought Jenny. But now wasn't the time.

She wasn't sure when it would be.

Matthew found Jenny sitting at the kitchen table, scribbling on a big yellow pad of paper.

"Are you coming to bed soon?"

Jenny glanced up, blinking at Matthew. "In a little while."

"You're working on the book?"

She nodded, meeting his eyes but with a faraway, unfocused expression. She was in what she called "the zone" — the place where she was so fully into what she was writing, so into the words that were flowing, that she wasn't aware of her surroundings. Sometimes she could sit and write with so much noise from the *kinner* that he wondered how she could do it. But she'd explained they were little distraction after writing in a war zone with bombs exploding in the near distance.

"Where's your laptop?"

"Battery ran down. Janie stopped by on her way home to charge it for me. I just had a few ideas I wanted to jot down so I didn't forget them."

"So you'll be coming to bed soon?" he repeated.

"Soon," she promised.

"Promise? You said that last night and didn't come up for hours."

He didn't say that he suspected that she'd waited until she was sure he was asleep before she crept up the stairs and into their bed.

He touched her shoulder and then his hand dropped when she stiffened.

"It's just that I'm so behind on my deadline. You know that, what with Phoebe getting sick and all."

"I know." He sighed. "Don't wear yourself out or you'll get sick, too. I'll take the *kinner* for an outing after *schul* tomorrow so you can get some writing in."

"Thanks."

He kissed the top of her head and made the lonely walk up the stairs. Suddenly the memory of the first night they'd walked up them, side by side, as a newly married couple, flitted through his mind. The memory came so suddenly, so vivid and precious, that his throat tightened and he blinked rapidly when his eyes filled.

Turning, he glanced back at her, bent over her writing at the kitchen table. He felt so alone, so lonely, and wondered if she did. He'd left her alone to write other times and not felt this way.

Oh, he'd been selfish enough to want her to come upstairs with him for their time together, but those other times she'd been sitting there with her laptop, her fingers flying across the keyboard, looking as if she were playing a silent word music on it that only she could hear. He'd loved how blissful she looked and when he read what she wrote later, he'd been so proud of what she created.

But now, when she looked so tired, it seemed to him that it just looked like drudgery, almost a penance she was doing instead of joyful creating.

As if she felt his gaze on her — or maybe she just heard his steps falter on the stairs — she glanced up and saw him.

"Soon," she said.

He hoped she meant it. Turning, he began

the solitary climb again.

Jenny kept looking for the children, for Matthew, as she climbed the grassy hill. It seemed so strange to be alone. Surely they were just ahead, too impatient to explore to wait for her.

But when she got the top of the hill, she found her father sitting on a big rock.

He turned when he heard her indrawn breath of surprise.

"There you are, Jenny Rebecca," he said and he grinned and held out his arms.

"What are you doing here?"

He frowned and his hands fell to his sides. "That doesn't sound very friendly."

"It isn't," she admitted and she felt terrible about it. "What did you expect? I found the letter you wrote Grandmother."

His face sagged and he turned to look at a tree in the distance. "Wish she'd torn up that letter."

"Did you think I'd never find out?"

When he didn't answer, she shook her head and sank down on the grass a few feet away from him. "You wish she'd torn up the letter. Not you wish you hadn't written it."

Turning back, he shook his head. "I'm not sorry."

Jenny felt her heart pounding. She leaped to her feet, feeling anger rising in her. "You're not sorry? I lost years with Matthew. Years! I got hurt, almost died, and I'll probably never have children, and you're not sorry you kept Matthew and me apart?"

"You have children now," he said reasonably. "And you have Matthew."

"They could have been my children —"

"They *are* your children."

"But I want one of my own." Even to her ears it sounded whiny. But she couldn't stop herself. "I lost all those years!"

"Did you? Are you sorry you went to college? Helped people know what's happening to children in war zones? Probably have a better relationship with Matthew now than you might have had as a teenager getting married too young back then? He loves you despite your scars. He loves you whether you can have a baby —"

"But I want a baby —"

"You didn't use to only think of what you don't have instead of what you have," he said as he stood and regarded her sadly.

Jenny sat, watching him walk away, and didn't call him back. Okay, she wasn't a saint. She knew that. But his disapproval stung. Didn't she have every right to be upset with him?

She woke and found she'd fallen asleep at the kitchen table. Her cheeks were wet with tears.

12

The dream hung over Jenny the next morning like a dark cloud.

Falling asleep over her writing had given her a crick in her neck too. Jenny winced as she lifted a skillet at breakfast.

Matthew laid a hand on her shoulder. "Are you *allrecht?*"

"Yes." She met his concerned gaze. "I fell asleep at the table. Got a crick in my neck. I'll be fine."

His fingers drifted to it.

"The children," she whispered and indicated with a jerk of her head their watchful eyes.

Mary smiled at her parents as she set the table. She remained as shy and quiet as she had been the day Jenny met her, often excusing herself to curl up on her bed and write in the journal Jenny gave her. Annie looked up from the notebook she was scribbling the words she constantly collected and grinned. Joshua hung his jacket and hat on a peg and, though he appeared casual, Jenny saw that he took everything in. He'd always been that way, so much like his father: serious, steady, a boy of few words but always curious about everything.

Funny, they weren't her biological children but they were surprisingly much like her.

This was her family, Matthew and the children. She remembered what her father had said in the dream, that she had Matthew and the children *now* and yet all she could think about was what she didn't have. He'd said she didn't use to be like that.

He didn't understand!

The crick in her neck turned to a cramp and she moaned and rubbed at it.

Joshua stood.

"That's not all you're eating, is it?" Jenny asked him. "You can't get by on that amount of food until you have lunch at school."

"*Nee.* I'll be right back."

He grabbed his jacket and left the house.

Jenny looked at Matthew. "Where's he going?"

"I don't know. More coffee?"

"Yes, thanks. It might help me wake up."

"Maybe you can get some rest after they go to *schul.*"

Without saying anything, he sent her a message that he'd join her if she let him know she'd welcome him. Jenny felt her cheeks heat at the intense look, the intimate message he sent her. Even now, after they'd been married for several years, his desire for her came as a surprise.

The connecting door to the *dawdi haus* opened and Phoebe walked in.

"Phoebe!" Annie jumped up and ran over to wrap her arms around the woman's waist.

Phoebe smiled and kissed the top of Annie's head.

"Guder mariye," she said. "How is everyone this beautiful morning?"

She said it to everyone but her gaze went straight to Jenny.

"Good," said Jenny. She poured a cup of coffee for her grandmother and set it at her usual place at the table.

Joshua came back in, shed his jacket, and pulled out Jenny's chair at the table. "Sit down and I'll rub your neck with this. It'll help."

Jenny looked at the bottle he held in his hand. "Horse liniment? You want to rub horse liniment on my neck?"

"*Ya.* It really helps Pilot when he gets a neck cramp."

She looked at her husband and saw his

lips twitching. "He's right, Jenny."

Her son loved horses so much. He obviously felt that if it was good for horses, it was good enough for people, not the other way around.

Joshua poured a small amount of the stuff into his hands. "Come on, it'll make your neck feel better."

Jenny bent to sniff at it and wrinkled her nose, then saw the look of eagerness on his face fade.

"Oh, all right. If you're sure it'll help," she said and sat down in the chair.

Joshua rubbed the liniment into her neck muscles, working at the cramping. Although her son's hands weren't big, they were strong from working on the farm with his father. She felt the cramping in her neck begin to subside. If it wasn't for the pungent smell, Jenny would have really enjoyed the massage.

Annie made a face and closed her book. She picked up her bowl of oatmeal and moved down the bench to sit closer to Mary.

Jenny sneezed.

"How did you hurt your neck?" Phoebe asked sympathetically.

"Fell asleep writing at the table last night."

"I need to help out more. You shouldn't be up so late." Phoebe put her fork down on her plate. "I'll start with making supper tonight."

"Maybe your pot roast?" Matthew glanced up from his breakfast, his expression interested. "With the potatoes and carrots? And do you think you could make that apple cranberry pie? It's my favorite of the ones you make."

"Matthew! She needs to take it easy for a while longer. Now you have her fixing a big meal?"

She wished she could call back the words when she saw Phoebe's face fall.

"I've rested enough. I'm tired of being cooped up."

"Jenny's right. It's selfish of me." Matthew patted Phoebe's hand. "Give yourself a little more time."

"How is it feeling?" Joshua asked her as he withdrew his hands.

"Much better," she told him, rolling her neck. "I just wish it didn't smell like . . . horse liniment."

He grinned at her. There was probably nothing he liked better than being around horses. She hugged him and got up.

"Everyone, hurry up. Don't want to be late for school."

She made quick work of packing lunches. Matthew had told her that his favorite school lunches were those he ate during the winter when the students placed their sandwiches on the radiator to warm them. So she sliced bread, cheese, and ham left over from last night's dinner. The cheese would melt on the sandwiches when placed on the radiator, she thought. Melted cheese sounded so good, she thought, going to get an apple for each of them from the bowl on the counter. Joshua might even eat his if he didn't save it as an after-school treat for Pilot, she mused.

"Cookies or whoopie pies?" she asked them.

"Whoopie pies!" they chorused.

Smiling, she added them to the lunch boxes. After a glance over her shoulder to make sure she wasn't being watched, she withdrew several folded notes from a drawer and tucked them in with the food.

She hugged the children as they left and gave Joshua an extra squeeze. He grinned at her and reminded her even more of his father.

"Hope you feel better," he told her.

"Thank you. Love you all. Be careful walking to school."

Matthew followed them out the door, off to work in the barn.

Which left Jenny alone with her grandmother.

"I'd like to talk to you."

"I need to —" Jenny began.

"It's important," Phoebe interrupted her with some firmness.

Inwardly sighing, Jenny sat.

"I'm going to ask Lydia if I can stay with her until Chris's parents leave."

Jenny couldn't have been more shocked. "Why would you do that? You're not comfortable in the *dawdi haus?*"

Phoebe sat there with her eyes focused on her hands folded on top of the table. Then she looked up at Jenny. "I feel like I'm causing tension here."

"You're not causing tension." Jenny's stomach churned.

"You've been unhappy for some time now. You won't talk to me about it. You can barely look at me."

She'd noticed. Jenny didn't know what to say.

"Jenny, look at me."

Then Jenny didn't have to find the words. They just spilled out of her. "I can't help it. I found the letter."

"Letter?" Phoebe looked confused.

"The letter from my dad, thanking you for letting him know I'd fallen for Matthew.

That's why he came early for me that summer before college."

Phoebe went white. "You found the letter? You read it?"

Jenny jumped to her feet and paced the kitchen. "I didn't mean to. It fell off the shelf when I got your sweater for you."

She stopped in front of her grandmother. "I didn't mean to read it. I just saw that it was in his handwriting and I was opening it. And then I couldn't believe what I saw."

Jenny pressed her hand over lips that trembled. "I loved Matthew. I loved him so much and you helped break us up. I thought you loved me. I thought you loved *Matthew.*"

"I did. I do. Both of you." Phoebe's eyes filled with tears. "But I loved your father, too, and I couldn't see him hurt. I lost him when he couldn't live this life. He had a right to know that you were choosing it."

Phoebe closed her eyes and then opened them. "I know what it's like to not see your child. How could I do that if you embraced this life and then chose to separate yourself here?"

"I would have still seen Dad."

"But you were so young. You weren't ready to make that decision. And your father wanted more for you. It was your mother's wish as well."

"It was *my* life. *My* choice to make!"
"Are you sorry you went to college?"
"No. But look what happened afterward. Look where I went and what happened."
"But everything turned out well. You have Matthew now. You have the *kinner.*"
"I lost so many years," Jenny whispered, her voice shaking. "I'm scarred and I'll probably never have children of my own."
Phoebe stood and reached out a hand to her. "But you *do.* You have *kinner* of your own."
"You don't understand. If you hadn't interfered, they could have been mine."
"But they are —"
"No! I could have given birth to them!"
"What's going on?" Matthew asked.
Jenny blinked. She'd been so wrapped up in her pain she hadn't heard the door open.

Matthew looked at his wife, then at Phoebe. He hadn't believed his ears when he'd walked in and found them in a bitter scene.
"Jenny? What's going on?"
"Grandmother was telling me that she's thinking of moving out."
"But Chris's parents are staying until the baby's born."
"She says she wants to move in with Lydia until they leave."

Matthew took off his hat and scratched his head. "I don't understand."

"I don't either," Jenny told him. "I don't understand how someone I thought loved me could have betrayed me to my father," she blurted out. "My own grandmother betrayed me."

Phoebe began coughing. Her face grew red. Before Jenny could react, Matthew pressed her into a chair and got a glass of water for her.

"Danki," she said, sipping the water. The hectic color in her cheeks faded and the coughing ceased.

"Perhaps you should go lie down," he suggested gently.

Without waiting for her to respond, he took her arm and helped her to her feet, then walked her to her part of the house.

When he returned, Jenny was sitting with her elbows on the table, her face in her hands. She looked up when she heard his footsteps. "Is she okay?"

"Ya."

She gave him a sharp glance. "Did you know that she told my dad about how we felt about each other?"

"I wondered when he came to talk to me —"

"You never told me he talked to you." She

sank rubbed her temples. "You just mentioned once that you met him. What did he say?" When he hesitated, she dropped her hands into her lap. "Matthew, what did he say to you?"

"Jenny, what point is there in discussing this?" he asked, reaching for her hand, frowning when she kept it in her lap. "All it can do is create bad feelings."

She felt herself tensing. "Did he tell you to stay away from me?"

He nodded heavily. *"Ya."*

"I thought we loved each other. Why didn't you come tell me what he said?"

"He told me he didn't want me to see you anymore. He said he wouldn't give me permission to marry you."

"We didn't need his permission. I was eighteen."

Too agitated to stay seated, she got up and paced the room again. "I don't understand why you didn't tell me."

"He said he wouldn't give —"

She threw up her hands. "I don't care!"

"But Jenny, I wouldn't come between a father and his child. It's not done. The wishes of a parent are respected here."

Tears sprang into her eyes. "Maybe you just didn't want to marry me!"

"How can you say that? I love you. I loved

you then. I love you now."

"I don't know what to think." She swiped at the tears on her cheeks. "The people I love, the people I thought loved me — all of you betrayed me!"

She spun on her heel and started for the door. "I have to — I have to get out of here for a while."

"Jenny! Don't go! Wait, at least take your jacket! It's getting cold outside!"

"Where's Jenny?"

Phoebe appeared beside him, coughing again.

Distracted, Matthew turned and was alarmed by her color again. "Phoebe! You need to lie down."

"I heard Jenny. She sounded so upset." She glanced around. "Where did she go?"

"She said she needed to go for a walk."

"A walk?" Phoebe walked to the window and glanced outside.

"I need to go after her. She didn't take her jacket."

But by the time Matthew got outside, he saw Jenny in front of the other farmhouse, talking with Chris.

The two of them started walking.

He'd lost his chance.

When he returned to the house, he found Phoebe waiting with an expectant expression in the kitchen. Her shoulders slumped when she saw the jacket in his hand.

"I couldn't catch her."

"Maybe she just needs to cool off," she told him.

"I don't want her catching a cold."

"Perhaps she'll come back quickly. It's not like her to become so upset and walk off like that."

"I don't blame her." He hung her jacket on a peg. "I should have told her. Maybe not back then. But when she came back here, I should have told her."

Phoebe straightened. "We did what we thought was best."

"I'm not so sure about that any more." He poured himself a mug of coffee. "Are you?"

"*Allrecht,* I had my doubts sometimes. But when she came back and the two of you looked at each other again, I thought, well, God's giving them a second chance. It's all worked out. There was no need to make her upset at her father. She had enough upsetting her being so injured, so despairing."

She walked over to the refrigerator, opened it, and pulled out a plate with a defrosting roast on it. "I'll start supper," she said.

He'd been so happy to hear that she

wanted to cook earlier. Now the thought didn't give him any pleasure.

"Gut," he said and tried to appear enthusiastic. "I'm going out to the barn."

"Jenny!"

Chris. She walked faster and pretended not to hear him but when she felt his hand on her arm, she stopped.

"Something wrong?"

"I just wanted to go for a walk."

She tried to surreptitiously wipe the tears from her cheeks but he turned her around to face him and frowned when he saw she'd been crying.

"What's wrong? Are you hurt?"

She shook her head. "Listen, I just want to go for a walk."

"You're cold," he said, mistaking her trembling for being chilled. He took off his jacket and slipped it over her shoulders.

"I'm fine. Really." But she was grateful for the warmth and slipped her arms into the sleeves.

"Okay," he said, drawing out the word as he studied her. "Can I walk with you?"

"Hannah —"

"Will be fine with my parents. Mom's telling her all about how I was growing up. And Dad? Well, save me from Dad. Please." He frowned as he fell into step beside her.

"Still not getting along?"

"Still? Ever, you mean. Stubborn old codger."

"We could never use that word to describe you, could we?"

"Codger? You better not."

She suppressed a smile. "I meant stubborn."

He slanted a look at her. "Me? Stubborn? Absolutely not."

"It seems I remember your discussions with the bishop about some of the *Ordnung* rules before you joined the church."

"You can't say you agree with all of them. Even though I learned respect for authority in the military, you can't be passive."

"And then there was the way you persisted in planting certain crops against the advice of others."

"Worked, didn't it?" His grin was cocky.

"And then —"

"Hey, is this a list?"

"No." She smiled.

She bent to pick up a brightly colored leaf from the side of the road. Looking up, she scanned the gray sky. She'd come here when it was a bleak and bitter winter years ago. The ground had been covered with snow. Soon it would be again.

"Just saying maybe the apple doesn't fall far from the tree."

"Better watch it if you say I'm like my dad," he said, his voice a low growl.

But she saw the teasing glint in his eyes before his expression became thoughtful.

"I guess we get some of both parents, don't we?" he asked. "I know I can be stubborn. If I wasn't, there'd never be an argument with Dad. I'd just say, 'yessir' and that would be the end of it."

"You'd probably give him a stroke if you did that now," she warned. "He'd think you were just trying to get him upset."

He laughed. "Right."

"I think you got your work ethic from both of them. Your dad hasn't rested since he came here. He's always looking for something to do."

"Tell me about it. He doesn't understand that we need a little bit of a break after harvesting the old-fashioned way, without all the modern machinery."

"What do you think you got from your mother?"

"I'm not sure. I don't cook much. Thank goodness that's not encouraged in males so much here as in the *Englisch* world."

"I think you got some of her thoughtfulness, her sweetness."

"Hey, watch it. You're talking to a former military guy here. I'm a manly man."

"Uh huh. I see how you act around Hannah. You do so many sweet things for her. Like the cradle."

"You didn't —"

"No, I didn't tell her. She still thinks she's going to use the one Matthew made for the children."

She felt tears sting her eyes again and furiously blinked them back.

"What is it?" he asked suddenly. "Why were you crying earlier?"

They heard the car behind them at the same time. He moved to the other side of her, forcing her to walk closer to the grass, and shot a sharp look at the car passing them. The driver gave them a wide berth and drove on.

"It's nothing."

"Matthew doesn't strike me as the type of man who would hurt a woman," he said slowly, carefully. "But I've heard of several men in the community —"

"Oh, it's not that," she said quickly, horrified. "Matthew would never hurt me."

"There's hurting and hurting. Words can hurt more than a hand."

She nodded. "No, if anything, I've hurt him by —" she stopped and shook her head.

"I don't believe you've done or said anything to deliberately hurt him."

"You'd be surprised." She sighed. "No, what I'm really upset about — I can't talk about right now. But I handled something badly. Really badly."

"When you're ready to talk, let me know." He glanced up at the sky. "I think we should be heading back. Looks like rain."

She turned back as he suggested. "You're quite the farmer, aren't you?"

"Ya," he said, chuckling.

They were silent as they walked back toward the farms. She thought about what they'd been talking about — what Chris got from his parents and what she had from her own.

Her mother had encouraged her in education, always stressing that Jenny had to be a good student. She'd have learned more from her if she hadn't died when Jenny was young. She knew she'd gotten her sense of helping others from the missionary work her father had done during two summers — and dragged her along to do as well.

But what kind of lesson had she learned from a father who had taken her from the man she loved and given her no choice in the decision?

They were back at the farmhouses. Dusk

was falling and light shone from the battery and kerosene lamps inside. Family dwelled inside both, with all the joys and problems that came with family.

And with all the love.

She took a deep breath and told herself that Chris was right. She'd start with prayer — the best place — and ask God for guidance.

"Thanks for walking with me," she told him, handing him back his jacket.

He hugged her. "It'll work out, whatever it is that's bothering you. I'll pray for you." He sniffed, then set her away from him. "Interesting perfume you have on today."

"Perfume? I don't wear perfume."

"Smells like 'Eau de Filly' to me," he said. "You been out in the barn with the horses?"

The liniment. She thought she'd washed off the smell. "Very funny!"

He grinned. "*Gut nacht,* Jenny."

Whistling, he began the short walk home.

Matthew watched Chris hug Jenny and felt an unaccustomed tug of jealousy.

She'd turned to another man for comfort.

He wasn't jealous. No, he knew Chris too well to feel that he'd behave less than honorably with Jenny.

But he'd wanted to comfort Jenny and

instead, Chris had been the one to do so. He hurried away from the front window as she climbed the steps and walked into the kitchen. Somehow he didn't think she'd appreciate that he'd been watching.

And she deserved her privacy.

But he had to find a way to talk to her. There was no place for distance between them.

13

Jenny walked into the house and immediately, the familiar, delicious aroma of pot roast enveloped her.

Phoebe looked up from the bowl of apples she was peeling. Her expression could be described no other way than wary.

"You look cold," Matthew said.

Rubbing her arms, Jenny nodded. "A little."

She turned to Phoebe. "You didn't have to start supper. I wasn't gone long."

"I wanted to. I can let you finish —"

"No, you go ahead. I've got a headache. I'm going to go upstairs and lie down for a little while." She glanced at the clock. "The children will be home soon."

Opening a cupboard, she found the bottle of ibuprofen and shook out several, taking them with a glass of water.

Phoebe started to say something and then she caught herself and nodded. "Why don't you take a cup of tea up with you? The water's hot."

"No, thanks. Maybe later."

"Jenny, we need to talk —"

Jenny shook her head which just made it pound more. "Not now. Please. I need to lie down."

She ran up the stairs, closed the door, unpinned her *kapp,* and then threw herself on the bed. The headache wasn't an excuse. Her head really pounded now after all the emotion, after the suppressed tears. The tension of wanting an explanation after finding the letter.

Yet as she lay on the bed staring up at the ceiling she felt even more conflicted. She'd told Chris she'd handled something badly and her eyes filled again with tears as she thought about how the hurtful words had spilled out. Her heart ached. She didn't know how to fix what had happened.

She couldn't think. Closing her eyes, she tried to still her racing thoughts. Gradually, the medicine began to work and she felt herself relax.

When sleep came, it came with restless dreams she couldn't remember when she woke.

Jenny paused with her hand on the doorknob and took a deep breath. With all that had been happening, she found she needed to compose herself before she opened the door.

"Jenny Banana!" Sam cried and grabbed her around the knees.

"Sam the Ham!" she said and reached down to hug him. "You're getting so big."

"I'm seven now," he told her proudly.

She straightened and hugged his father, David, and then turned to Joy. But when she started to put her arms around Joy, she realized that Joy had some kind of backpack thing on.

"We wanted to show you our newest addition to the family," Joy said, grinning.

She turned around, revealing a baby of about six months tucked in some sort of carrier.

Jenny clutched at the door frame for support. "Oh — my! What — when did this happen?"

"About a month ago," Joy told her.

"I'm confused! You never said you were expecting a baby! And this baby looks like she's more than a month old."

"We 'dopted," Sam told her.

Then she realized they were still standing in the doorway and it was chilly outside. "Come in, come in."

Once inside, David lifted the child out of the carrier and bounced her in his arms.

Jenny couldn't help it — she kept staring at the baby.

Sam tugged on Jenny's skirt. "I got to name her. Guess what her name is?"

"Betty? Betty Betty Bo Betty banana banna bo berry?"

"No, silly!" Sam chortled. "It's Emily Ann. I picked out her name."

"A baby." Stunned, she tried to take it in. Her eyes went back and forth, back and forth, from Joy to David. Tears threatened and she tried to blink them away. "You adopted?"

"We got to thinking about what we could do to make a difference and adopting our next child just seemed right. You want to hold her so I can take my jacket off?" David held the baby out.

She felt a momentary panic and used her fingers to wipe away the tears she hadn't been able to hold back. "I haven't held a baby in years!"

"It's easy," he assured her, and thrust her into Jenny's arms.

"She's so tiny." Jenny cradled the child in her arms and breathed in the scent of baby soap and powder. She stroked her cheek. "So soft."

David helped Sam take off his jacket, took Joy's, and then went to hang them all on a peg in the kitchen.

Walking over to the sofa, Jenny sat and began carefully taking off the fleecy one-piece garment the baby wore. Joy joined her on the sofa and dangled a set of plastic keys to entertain the baby.

"I didn't know you were adopting." She looked up at Joy, then David. "You never told me."

"We weren't sure how long it would take. Or even if they'd let us have a baby. So we didn't tell anyone until we brought her home."

She reached up and took David's hand as he stood near them. "We've made a lot of changes this past year. We can't wait to tell you about them."

Sam glanced around. "Where are the kids?"

"They'll be home in a few minutes."

Out of the corner of her mouth, she asked Joy if it was okay for Sam to have some cookies. When she nodded, Jenny turned to Sam and told him there was a plate of his favorites — oatmeal raisin — in the kitchen.

"There's some for you, too," she told David.

"And milk?"

"Of course. I just started some coffee so it's fresh. Maybe you can put the kettle on so Joy and I can have some tea?"

"Sure thing." David followed his son into the kitchen.

"And don't eat all the cookies, you guys!" Joy called after them.

Jenny couldn't take her eyes off the baby. She had the big blue eyes so many babies had, plump cheeks, and little snub nose. When Jenny pulled off the baby's cap she found a mass of fine blond hair.

"Oh my goodness, it looks like chicken feathers," she said with a laugh. "Fluffy chicken feathers."

Then she looked at Joy. "Oh, I didn't mean —"

Joy laughed. "It's okay. It does look like chicken feathers, doesn't it?"

Loud voices and a banging on the door announced the children were home. Annie was first inside and she skidded to a stop as she caught sight of the baby. Her eyes went round with surprise.

"Is that yours?" she asked Joy, dropping her lunch box to the floor with a clang.

The baby startled at the sudden noise, throwing her hands in the air and squalling.

Annie clapped her hands over her mouth, then glanced at Joy. "I'm sorry! I didn't mean to scare her!"

Sam raced out of the kitchen. "What happened?"

He saw the lunch box on the floor, then looked at the baby. "Oh, it's okay, baby." He turned to Annie. "She doesn't like loud noises."

"So Sam never makes them at our house," Joy said, rolling her eyes as if to indicate otherwise.

Sam held out a cookie to Annie. "Want one?"

"Sure. Hi."

Mary and Joshua were more reserved, coming to stand close and look at the baby. But while Mary cooed at her and admired her pink outfit, Joshua was quick to tell Joy she was pretty and take off to the kitchen.

"Sorry, she's not a foal," Jenny told Joy. "If she were, he wouldn't be able to tear himself away."

Joy laughed. "I understand. I was pretty much into horses at that age."

"Jenny, where do you keep the tea?" David called from the kitchen.

"I'll show him," Mary told them.

"Would you get your father after you do? He's in the barn."

Mary gave the baby one last look, smiled at Joy, and then left them.

"I think she'd like to have a little baby sister or brother."

"No luck yet?" Joy's eyes were kind.

Jenny shook her head.

"It took my sister five years to conceive," Joy told her.

Baby Emily started fussing and sucking on a finger. Joy dug a bottle out of the diaper bag and headed for the kitchen to warm it.

"But —"

Joy turned. "It's okay, I'll be right back. You'll be fine."

Jenny and Emily stared at each other. "What would happen if I did get pregnant?" she asked the baby. "I don't know the first thing about babies."

"Joy said there was a surprise in here —" Matthew stopped. "Well, well, a *boppli!* That's quite a surprise!"

She smiled. "Isn't she beautiful?"

He leaned down and studied the baby. "*Ya.* Beautiful."

Then he looked at her and frowned. "Why are you crying?"

"They're happy tears, aren't they, *Mamm?*" Mary said. She'd come into the room so quietly they hadn't heard her.

Jenny nodded. "She's amazing."

She touched one of the baby's hands and Emily's curled around it. "It's funny but she looks a little like Sam did when he was a baby."

Mary came to sit beside Jenny and her arm crept around Jenny's shoulders as they gazed at the baby together.

"She's so sweet. I wish —" she stopped and sighed. "Sorry, *Mamm. Daedi* says if it's God's will I'll have another brother or sister."

She glanced at her father. "I hope it's God's will for me to have a baby sister. Joshua spends so much time with the horses I barely see him." She kissed Jenny's cheek and then walked back into the kitchen.

"She's never said anything about a baby before." Jenny's throat was so tight she barely got the words out. "I — I didn't know she wanted another sister or brother. Did you know?"

Matthew took her place on the sofa beside Jenny. "*Ya.* We talked one night. I think she was afraid to say anything to you. She's old enough to know that sometimes . . . it doesn't happen. She asked if we hadn't a *boppli* yet because you'd been hurt."

If she'd thought her heart ached after the quarrel with her grandmother and Matthew, well, that pain paled beside this.

The baby whimpered so Jenny took the pacifier that hung on a ribbon fastened on her sleeper and tucked it into her rosebud mouth.

"I had no idea."

His arm slipped around her waist. She stiffened, then forced herself to accept his comfort. She'd been so consumed by her own pain she hadn't thought of how the children might feel about a baby. The Amish loved children and believed they were a gift of God. Large families were the rule, not the exception here. Why hadn't she thought that the children might be wondering when — *if* — a baby would join the family?

Matthew had reassured her so often that it was God's will if they had more children, and she'd believed him. His faith, grown and nurtured over a lifetime in the Amish faith, had sustained her until recently.

She'd backslid in her own faith journey for spiritual, as well as mind and body, healing and true peace.

"I love you," he said quietly. "It pained me to hear you doubt that. We need to talk and work through this. God brought us together for a reason, Jenny. You must know that."

She didn't know what she believed at that moment but it wasn't the time to talk about it with friends visiting and just in the next room.

"I'm praying for us to understand, to heal, and to gain some peace, Jenny." He searched her eyes. "I'm hoping you are, too."

"Hey, look what I have," Joy called as she walked into the room holding up a bottle of formula.

She stopped when she saw them. "Oh — is something wrong?" She hurried to look at the baby, then Jenny. "Nothing's wrong with her, is it? She's been spitting up a lot."

"No!" Jenny quickly assured her. "She's perfect. Matthew and I were just talking about something else."

Joy sighed. "David's always telling me that I'm a little paranoid about her. But I think every mother's that way about a baby."

She slipped the bottle into the pocket of her sweater and reached for her child. "Come on, precious, bottle time."

"There's a rocking chair in Annie's room if you'd like to have some quiet and feed her."

"Good idea," Joy said, turning and walking toward the stairs.

Jenny slipped out from under Matthew's arm as she stood and faced him. "Let's go see what everyone's up to in the kitchen."

She hurried away from him, escaping into

the kitchen.

"Something's wrong."

"With Emily?" Jenny leaned down and tickled the baby's bare tummy. "I think you're worrying too much. Spitting up's normal for a baby."

Joy glanced at her over her shoulder, then back at Jenny. "Not with her. With you and Matthew."

Jenny froze but tried to act natural. "I don't know what you mean."

Turning, Joy handed Jenny the baby, who regarded her with solemn eyes. "Sure you do," Joy said. "Something's wrong. You and Matthew are behaving differently with each other than the last time we came."

"I don't know what you're talking about," Jenny said quickly. "We're fine." She nuzzled her nose in the chicken feather hair and the baby kicked and waved her hands.

Joy tucked a discarded diaper into a plastic bag then wiped her hands on an antiseptic towelette. She pulled a clean terry sleeper the color of sunshine from the diaper bag and drew it up over Emily's legs.

"Wiggleworm," she said and Emily cooed and waved her arms and legs even more.

"All done," Joy said as she fastened the last snap. She turned and held the baby to

Jenny. "Here you go."

Once again Jenny was nonplussed, staring at a new little person who stared owlishly back at her. She walked over to the rocking chair and sat down, using her foot to put the chair into motion.

Joy sat on the corner of the bed. "Do you want to talk about it?"

"There's nothing to talk about."

"We've known each for a long time. You can tell me anything, Jenny. Is it that you're not happy living here in Paradise? Is it too different for you to be Amish?"

Jenny shook her head.

"Is it Matthew? Are you unhappy with him?"

There had never been another time when Jenny wanted to talk to someone more than this and yet she was so conflicted she didn't know what to say. And it wasn't just Matthew. Her feelings about what her grandmother and her father had done were a heavy weight on her heart and emotions. She knew bottling it up wasn't good for her.

But she was afraid that once she opened her mouth the anger and betrayal and maybe even fear would spill out and she wouldn't be able to contain herself. She'd just splinter and fall apart in a million pieces.

Blinking hard against the tears that burned against the backs of her eyelids, she tried to focus on the baby. She knew babies picked up on emotions and she didn't want to upset Emily. And she didn't want to upset Joy and ruin the visit from cherished friends.

"Maybe I should tell you why there's so much change in our lives right now," Joy began. "David and I had a really difficult time last year. You know how consumed he is by his job. What a workaholic he is. If it wasn't staying late or the cell phone ringing at all hours or him on the computer . . . well, Sam and I weren't getting any of his time and attention."

She sighed. "And the more money he made, the more things it seemed we needed. A bigger house, a fancier car. Investments. Lavish vacations where we never got to relax because work would interrupt. We'd planned a second honeymoon in Hawaii and got called back for a big news event two days after we flew there."

She sighed. "I was afraid we were headed for divorce."

Jenny realized she'd stopped rocking but when she glanced down she saw that Emily had fallen asleep.

Joy got up and carefully lifted the baby from Jenny's arms. "Do you mind if I put her here on the bed?"

"No, of course not." Jenny pulled the pillows from the top of the bed and placed them on either side of the baby.

Joy sank down on the bed again and patted the place beside her. Jenny hesitated and then she sat and Joy slipped her arm around her waist.

"What happened? What did you do?"

"We talked," Joy said after a moment. "I made him shut everything off and we talked. For hours. He finally got how unhappy I was. He understood he was missing out not just on our marriage and all that we'd meant to each other but also that he was missing out on Sam."

"Oh, Joy, why didn't you call me? Why didn't you tell me?"

Joy squeezed her waist. "It was just overwhelming for a time. And David's your friend, too. I didn't want you to feel put in the middle."

She sighed. "And one day I started to call and I just couldn't do it. You've been through enough bad stuff. It's time you had some peace in your life."

If only, thought Jenny. If only. "I wish I'd known. I wish I could have helped."

"I know. But it was okay. David's a good man. I felt if I could really get his attention it would be okay."

Joy was silent for a long moment. "Jenny, Matthew's a good man, too. Are you talking about whatever it is that's wrong?"

"It won't do any good," Jenny said.

Just then she heard a noise, a sound like an indrawn breath. Matthew stood in the doorway.

Then he turned and was gone.

Matthew nearly ran David down as he hurried down the stairs.

"Hey, where are you going in such a hurry?" David asked, stopping him by laying a hand on his arm. "Did they ask you to change a diaper or something?"

"Don't go up there," Matthew said tersely. "They're talking about something personal."

David's grin faded and his hand fell to his side. "I guess Joy's sharing with Jenny some problems we've had this past year."

He had Matthew's attention. "Problems?" Maybe listening to what this *Englisch* friend was experiencing might help him to understand what was happening in his own marriage.

Then he shook his head. David might not like to talk about it.

He thought wrong.

"I made the biggest mistake of my life," David blurted out. "I almost lost everything that was important to me."

Phoebe glanced up when they entered the kitchen. "Want to join us for a game of Dutch Blitz?"

Matthew turned to David. "I need to go out to the barn for a minute. Want to join me?"

"Sure." David tousled his son's hair. "You having fun?"

"I'm winning," Sam told him, giving him a gap-toothed grin. "And we're about to have whoops."

"Whoops?"

Phoebe laughed. "Whoopie pies. I made some for Sam when I heard you were coming. Don't worry, I'll save you one."

David grinned at her. "You know me so well."

Matthew grabbed his jacket and handed David his. "Ready?"

They walked outside and hunched their shoulders against the chill.

"Did you lose the television job?"

David shook his head and his laugh sounded rueful. "No. If anything I was getting more work and opportunities from them. I was working too much, enjoying the money too much. Joy let me know our marriage was in trouble."

Matthew opened the barn door and they stepped inside. "Are you saying she wanted a divorce?"

"No one wants one," David said, pulling his collar up to protect his ears from the cold. "But she thought we might be headed that way."

Matthew listened as David described how he'd spent more hours at the office, caught up in the pursuit of success, something called ratings, and accumulation of a bigger house, a better car.

It sounded nothing like the kind of problems he and Jenny had been experiencing. Jenny had walked away from the *Englisch* life and didn't seem to mind not having the things that were important to it.

But trust. That was important to her and he didn't know how to get past how she felt he'd betrayed her trust in him.

"You okay?"

Matthew glanced up from unwrapping the bandage around Pilot's foreleg. "*Ya,* fine."

"You and Jenny okay?"

Taken aback, Matthew stared at him. "Why would you ask that?"

David shrugged and looked uncomfortable. "I dunno. Seemed like there was this . . . tension between the two of you that reminded me of how Joy and I were getting along for a while there."

"Did you ask Joy's father for permission to marry her?"

"Whoa, what?"

"You know, before you asked her to marry you, did you talk to her father?"

David shook his head. "We don't do that so much anymore. Kind of old-fashioned. Not that I'm saying it's bad, you understand," he said quickly, as if afraid he would offend. "It's Joy's life. She's the one who makes the decisions."

Matthew pulled out the kit filled with first-aid items for the horses and rummaged for what he needed. They were silent for several minutes as he cleaned the wound on the foreleg, applied some medicine, then wrapped a bandage around it.

David watched from a safe distance, looking skittish every time Pilot moved or tossed his mane.

"He likes to play games with people who act afraid of him," Matthew told David. "Don't let him intimidate you."

"It's okay," David said. "I can watch from over here." He glanced around. "I swear, this barn's as neat as some people's houses."

"This time of year it's a little easier to keep it this way."

"It's been this way every time we've visited." David picked up a level from a tool bench and examined it. "So why'd you want to know about asking a father for permission to marry his daughter?"

Matthew hesitated.

"I understand you don't share personal information as easily as we do," David said quietly. "But sometimes it helps to talk."

Before Jenny returned from being injured overseas, Matthew hadn't had any *Englisch* friends and to be honest, David was Jenny's friend first. Matthew wasn't sure how to talk to him about this. And it wouldn't be fair for him to say anything about Phoebe.

Silence stretched between them, the only sounds the shifting of horses in the stalls, the wind blowing around the barn.

"Jenny's upset that she just found out her father came to get her early back when she was here that last summer," Matthew said finally. "He didn't approve of me being interested in his daughter and so he took her away."

"I see."

But David was frowning as he took it all in. "Why would she be upset if you got together in the end?"

The barn door opened and their children spilled inside, a noisy jumble of movement and voices.

"Sam wants to see the kittens," Annie said. "Phoebe says we can show him then we have to come right back for whoopie pies and hot choc-lit."

"Don't get any ideas," David told Sam. "We're not taking any kittens home."

Sam nodded but he glanced at Annie and grinned.

Annie led the way to a stall and opened it. "Look, they're awake! Here, you can hold this one, just be careful."

David looked at Matthew who was watching the interaction of their children with the mama cat and her litter. "You're together now but Jenny's regretting those lost years, isn't she?"

"How is it you understood that when I didn't?" Matthew asked him. "At least, I didn't until we talked."

"I know the way Jenny thinks," David told him. "I've known her longer. That's all."

He sighed. "She loves children — especially yours. But I'd imagine she'd keep thinking these children could have been hers."

"They are hers," Matthew told him and he heard the passion in his voice. "It wasn't God's will for us to be together then. But it is now."

"Tough concept for someone not raised in your faith."

Matthew stared at the man before him who moved in such a different world than he did. But David had put his finger so neatly on the crux of the problem.

"Sometimes it seems like Jenny's so much a part of this place that she's been here forever. I forget she hasn't grown up here."

"It doesn't seem strange seeing her dressed in Plain clothes anymore," David mused as they watched the children play with the kittens.

Then he held up his hands. "Sorry, I didn't mean to sound like it's strange the way you're dressed here."

Matthew grinned. "It's *allrecht.* I know what you mean. It's not what you're used to."

Sam walked over and held a kitten up to show to his father. "Please, Daddy, can we take this one home? She's so soft and she likes me. See, she's kissing me," he said when the kitten licked his cheek.

David held up his hands. "No, no, we can't have a kitten!"

Sam tilted his head and studied his father. "Maybe I should ask Mommy."

Kneeling, David patted the kitten on the head. "Son, I know the kitten is special. But

Mommy has a lot on her hands right now taking care of you and the new baby."

"Maybe we could have the kitten instead of the baby if it's too much trouble for her to do both," Sam said slyly.

David tickled Sam on the stomach. "Now you know you don't mean that. You love the baby. You're her big brother and you're going to look out for her."

"Like Joshua does for us," Mary said. "Right, Annie?"

"Right," she said, wrapping her arms around her brother's waist. "He's a good *bruder.*"

Joshua rolled his eyes but when he looked over at him, Matthew could tell his sisters' words meant a lot.

14

Jenny breathed in the scent of baby Emily's hair and thought about how rich someone was going to be one day when they bottled clean baby smell.

"I can take her now," Joy whispered.

"I don't mind holding her."

Joy smiled. "I can see that." Her smile faded and she studied Jenny. "Have you thought about adopting?"

"Yes." She traced a finger over Emily's rose-petal-soft cheek. "I haven't talked to Matthew about it much. I so wanted —" she stopped. "They talk a lot about God's will here."

"Couldn't it be God's will to adopt if you haven't conceived? I mean, if you apply and you get a baby, that's what was supposed to happen, right?"

"I guess," Jenny said slowly, thinking it over.

"So maybe if you want a baby as badly as

you do then you should think about it. Talk to Matthew about applying."

Looking up, Jenny nodded. "Maybe I will. If he'll talk to me. Everything is such a mess."

They jumped when they heard a girl scream and brakes squeal.

Joy and Jenny stared at each other, eyes filled with horror. Then they jumped to their feet and ran.

"Sam!" Joy screamed as she ran for the stairs, forgetting that Jenny still held the baby.

Jenny would have screamed a name but she didn't know which to choose. Annie? Mary? Joshua? Annie was the youngest and impulsive but she knew to stay away from the road, just as Mary and Joshua did.

Like Joy, she could only think it could be Sam.

Phoebe was already running out the door ahead of them. Mary stood beside the road, holding Annie's hand. A car sat sideways in front of them, as if it had swerved and slid.

A boy's body lay on the pavement, dressed in Plain clothing.

"Joshua!" Jenny screamed.

He lay in the road, blood pooling around his head, as a man bent over him, talking on a cell phone.

"I'll get Matthew," Phoebe said and she took off for the barn.

Jenny felt her knees weaken and she sagged against the porch railing. Her hands tightened on the baby and then she turned and pushed her into Joy's arms before running to kneel beside Joshua.

She forced herself to touch her fingers to the pulse in his neck and felt it — faint but there, thank God.

"Sam!" Joy cried when she reached them. "Where's Sam?"

"In the barn with his *daedi,*" Mary said.

"I didn't hit the boy," the driver rushed to say. "Yes, we need an ambulance," he yelled into his cell phone. "A child's lying in the road."

He glanced at the address on the home and read it to the 9-1-1 dispatcher. "Hurry, he's hurt his head and he's unconscious."

"I always drive slow through here because of the buggies," the man told Jenny. He pulled a handkerchief from his pocket and handed it to her. "Here, press this on his head to help stop the bleeding."

"He ran after the kitty," Annie was sobbing. "He told me to stay out of the road and he'd get it. Then he tripped and fell and hurt his head right in front of the car. The man just — just —"

"The man stopped the car in time," Mary finished for her.

Matthew and David came running, Sam tucked securely in David's arms.

Jenny watched the color drain from Matthew's face. "Joshua?"

He joined her on the pavement while the man stood and walked down the road a little to look out for the emergency vehicles.

"Joshua, wake up, *sohn,*" he said urgently.

"Don't move him," Jenny warned. "An ambulance is coming."

"*Sohn,* please, wake up," Matthew pleaded as he knelt beside Jenny.

Joshua's lashes fluttered and he muttered something that had his parents exchanging a look of puzzlement.

"What language is that?" Matthew asked her.

"I don't understand it, either."

And then, to Jenny's amazement, Joshua opened his eyes and looked at them. *"Mamm? Daed?"*

Nearly speechless with joy, Jenny nodded. "We're right here," she said. "No, don't sit up," she said when he tried.

But Joshua pushed against her hands and did so anyway. He said something she couldn't understand.

"What is it, *sohn?*" Matthew asked him,

wiping at the blood on Joshua's forehead.

Joshua repeated what he'd said and it still didn't make sense. It wasn't Pennsylvania *Deitsch* or German . . . no, it sounded more like gobbledygook.

And then he turned his head and threw up.

They were so occupied with soothing him and wiping his face they almost didn't notice when the police car pulled up and the officer got out.

Joshua stiffened and then his body began jerking, convulsing, and he fell against Matthew.

The officer hurried up and knelt beside Joshua. "He's having a seizure," he said tersely. "It happens a lot after head injuries. Here, let's carefully lay him down on his side. We don't want to move him too much since we don't know if he has any other injuries. But we don't want him to choke, either."

"Now what do we do?" Matthew asked him after Joshua was carefully laid on his side.

Jenny could hear the fear in his voice. She felt it, too.

"We just keep a watch on him and make sure he doesn't hurt himself," the officer told him. "The ambulance is right behind me."

Jenny's heart caught in her throat as she helplessly watched Joshua convulse. When the ambulance pulled up and the paramedics came running toward them, she thought she'd never been so grateful for them.

The first responders asked Jenny and Matthew to move a few feet away so they could work. They complied reluctantly and stood with their arms around each other, watching as the medics spent several minutes examining Joshua, conveying his condition to the hospital, and administering some medication in an IV. The seizure stopped but Joshua didn't open his eyes again.

That frightened Jenny more than the seizure. Maybe Matthew as well. She couldn't tell who trembled more.

Finally, Joshua was carried into the ambulance and one of the paramedics turned to Matthew and Jenny.

"We've got room for one of you," they were told. "Which will it be?"

There was no choice as far as Jenny was concerned. Joshua was the child of her heart but he'd been Matthew's son since birth.

"You go," she told Matthew.

He gave her a quick hug and then he

rushed to climb inside the ambulance.

The doors were closed, the police officer banged on them to signal all was clear, and the vehicle began racing down the road, siren wailing.

The driver of the car walked over and started talking. Jenny could barely understand him. She couldn't focus.

"It wasn't your fault," she said. "Mary said so." She tried not to think of what might have happened if his reflexes hadn't been good and he'd avoided hitting Joshua as he lay in the road.

He handed her a business card. "If there's anything you need, let me know."

She managed to thank him and shoved the card into her pocket, forgetting him as soon as he drove off.

"Joshua's hurt?"

Sam's clear childish voice carried over to Jenny. David murmured something to him that she couldn't hear.

Joy came over to pull Jenny out of the road. She slipped her arm around Jenny's waist. "Come on, let's get the children inside. David'll drive you to the hospital and I'll stay with the children."

Numb, Jenny nodded.

Joy rubbed her arm and guided her into the house. "I know it's scary but I've heard that people sometimes have seizures after they hurt their heads. But they do just fine."

"The police officer said something like that," Jenny admitted.

"Joshua's going to be okay. It was a good thing that he woke up so quickly. You have to remember that."

But he hadn't woken up again. Jenny tried telling herself that it was probably the medication that had done that. Still, she couldn't help thinking that he might not wake up again. He might have permanent brain damage. Even if he didn't, he might have sustained the kind of brain injury she had from the car bombing overseas.

She shuddered when she remembered how she'd been so frustrated trying to talk and the wrong word had popped out, how she'd had to work with therapists for months on her speech. Would he have more seizures? What if he had other injuries that were serious?

Phoebe ushered a sobbing Annie and Mary into the house and spoke with them quietly. David followed them, with the baby in one arm, Sam in the other. The baby was crying and Sam was crying. Everyone in the room was crying.

Jenny pressed her hands to her temples, then wiped at the tears running down her cheeks. She turned to her grandmother. "I think we should say a prayer for Joshua before I go."

Phoebe nodded and then she moved to wrap Jenny in her arms. "Joshua will be *all-recht,* dear one. You must believe that."

Jenny nodded and then she stepped back. Annie stood there with her thumb in her mouth — something she'd done in the past when she was stressed. Sitting down on the sofa, she held out her arms to the girls and gathered them onto her lap.

"He told me not to go into the road," Annie said, repeating what she'd said earlier. "He said he'd get her. But he got hurt. It's my fault."

"No, it's not," Jenny assured.

Mary was silent, too silent.

Joy and David sat, too, comforting their children. But they clasped each other's hands and made a prayer chain with Jenny and the girls and Phoebe led them in praying for Joshua.

When it was over, David stood and set Sam down on the sofa beside Joy. "Jenny, get your jacket and purse and I'll take you to the hospital now."

"Can we go with?" Mary asked.

Jenny looked at her, then Annie, and saw the tears drying on their cheeks and the worry in their eyes but shook her head. "It's best if I go there first and find out what's going on."

"I'll come right back for you and Phoebe if he can have visitors," David promised.

Mary wrapped her arms around his waist and hugged him and then took Annie's hand. "*Kumm,* let's make a card for Joshua."

"With glitter?"

"Of course. Lots of glitter."

"I'll make you that hot chocolate," Phoebe said. She turned. "Sam? Are you ready for some?"

He looked at his mother and she nodded.

"Joy? Some *kaffe* or tea?"

"Sounds wonderful." She got to her feet, carrying baby Emily in the crook of her arm. "I think it's time for another bottle for the kidlet here, too." She hugged Jenny. "Let me know about Joshua the minute you find out. I'll be praying for him. For all of you."

David drove them to the hospital, one hand on the steering wheel, one hand clasping Jenny's. He didn't say anything. He didn't have to. The warmth of his hand, the reassuring look he sent her occasionally meant more than words.

The hospital was a place she'd been to several times since she'd returned here from overseas. She'd been a patient in the ER after she'd been hurt in Phoebe's buggy by a driver going too fast. The children had been in for the usual minor accidents.

But Matthew had been forced to confront bad memories of the place where he'd had to say goodbye to his first wife when he visited Jenny here. She knew it was going to be hard on Matthew if the news wasn't good when he talked to the doctors about Joshua.

David let her out at the ER entrance. "Do you have a cell? I didn't think to ask."

"I think Matthew has the one he uses for business with him. Everything happened so fast, I don't know."

"If he doesn't, call me on the hospital phone and I'll bring you one of ours. But either way, call us the minute you know something. If you want Joy to come sit with you, let me know. I'll bring her."

She reached for the door handle and then leaned her forehead on the window.

"Jenny?"

"I'm so scared, David," she whispered. "You remember what a head injury did to me."

He pulled over to a visitor parking place, turned off the car, and hugged her. "Come on, you can't think like that." He set her from him. "Do you want us to pray before you go in?"

Her eyes widened. They'd prayed earlier as a group with Joy and Phoebe and their children. But he'd never offered to pray with her one-on-one even though he and Joy were her deepest and best friends.

He shrugged. "I don't make a big deal of it but I prayed a lot for you since you were hurt overseas."

"I — never knew."

He shrugged. "Maybe a person never knows everyone who's praying for them."

She was afraid she was going to cry. Instead, she took a deep breath. "Thank you. I think I can go in now."

Turning, she started to open the door. Then she looked back. "If you could pray some more for Joshua, I'd appreciate it."

"Without ceasing and never ending."

Surprised at David quoting Scripture, Jenny kissed his cheek, got out, and went to find Matthew.

Waiting in a room at the hospital made Matthew feel even more helpless than sitting in the ambulance had — while it was upsetting to see Joshua lying motionless after the seizure, at least he'd had him in view and watched the medical professionals working on him.

Here, he was politely told that the doctors

and nurses needed him to sit in the waiting room while they examined his son. There were tests to perform, people to consult. They promised gently but firmly that they'd come out and talk to him as soon as they knew something.

He trusted them. It was a good hospital and the staff had treated his family well in the past. After all, it hadn't been their fault he'd lost Amelia. The cancer, His will, had been stronger, her time to meet with God at hand.

And all the other times he'd come here, to see Jenny after the buggy accident and the various minor accidents *kinner* got involved in — everything had turned out *allrecht.*

But his heart was still beating fast and his hands shook.

"Matthew?"

He looked up as Jenny came rushing toward him. He stood and was relieved when she embraced him and didn't let go. Something lifted and settled inside him as she pressed her cheek against his and held on. He absorbed her love and support. Whatever their problems, he needed this now.

Everything else — the hurt, the hard words, the distance — fell away with the human contact.

Finally, Jenny stood back. "What have they said about Joshua?"

"They haven't told me anything yet, just that he's stable and he's having tests and a CAT scan."

Without speaking they clasped hands, bent their heads, and prayed for their son. And then they sat and kept holding hands and tried not to watch the clock.

Finally, Jenny could bear it no longer.

"Five minutes," she said. "If they don't come out in five minutes and tell us something, I'm going in."

He smiled as he touched her cheek. "The doors are locked."

"How do you know?"

"I watched another parent try them when anxiety got to her."

Jenny lifted her chin. "Well, they can't keep me away from my son. I need to see my son."

Matthew knew his wife. He figured she'd beat the door down if necessary.

Fortunately, he didn't have to worry about that. A nurse came out and called to them a few minutes later.

"They heard me," Jenny muttered beneath her breath.

Knowing was best, Matthew told himself. Whatever the news, it was better than waiting outside, feeling helpless.

The walk down the hallway, then past the cubicles, felt endless. Cries of pain, murmurs of comfort came from behind some of the curtains. There was a flurry of movement as nurses rushed past them to a cubicle where Matthew feared something really serious was happening.

A nurse stood beside Joshua's gurney. She smiled when they walked in. "The doctor stepped out for a minute but he'll be right back."

Joshua lay with his eyes closed, his face pale against the paper pillow. A bandage wound around his head. An IV was hooked up and fluids were being pumped into him. Machines blinked and beeped at his side.

Matthew and Jenny moved to each side of his bed. She carefully stroked Joshua's hair. He could see that part of his son's head had been shaved and several black stitches had been sewn on his scalp. A small cast covered one even smaller wrist.

"Has he woken up yet?" Matthew barely recognized his voice. It sounded old and rusty as if he hadn't used it much.

"Not yet," the nurse told him gently. She looked tired but she had kind eyes and from her age, Matthew guessed she had years of experience with frantic parents.

The doctor stepped inside. He shook their hands and then slapped the X-rays up on a lighted box.

"He took quite a blow to his head," the man said without preamble. "Looks like a bit of concussion but I think he'll be fine. He's also got a simple fracture of the wrist."

Matthew felt Jenny slump with relief at the news. "What about the seizure?" Jenny asked before Matthew could.

"It's fairly common after a head injury."

The police officer had said that. Matthew had wanted to believe him.

"We have some blood tests being analyzed to see how bad the seizure was. It dumps a chemical into the bloodstream. Sometimes a head injury will cause epilepsy but if he has no more seizures there'll be no need for meds."

"When will he wake up?"

The doctor smiled. "Soon. Try to relax."

He left and they stood there with the nurse, watching for a sign of awakening from Joshua, listening to the beep of the machines.

"We had to cut off his clothes to make it easier to examine him," said the nurse whose nameplate announced her as Susan. "I thought you might want this." She handed Jenny a folded up piece of paper.

Curious, Jenny opened it and then she burst into tears. "It's a note I wrote him," she told Matthew. "I put one in his lunch-box every morning. He kept the one from today. Why would he do that?"

Feeling the sting of tears in his own eyes, Matthew tried to smile at her. "He loves his *mamm.*"

An hour passed, then another. The nurse brought chairs for them to sit beside Joshua's bed.

"Talk to him," the nurse invited.

Matthew stared at her. "He can hear us even when he looks like he's sleeping?"

"I've found it to be true," she said, nodding. "I know it was scary to watch him having a seizure, but some children never have another after a head injury."

"I just want him to wake up," Matthew said.

She patted his arm. "He will." She straightened the sheets on the bed. "What were you doing before the accident? Had you had supper?"

Matthew nodded. "We were visiting with friends who came from New York to see us," he said, struggling to remember what had happened before the accident. "Joshua ran into the road to catch a kitten that got out of the barn. He did it so his younger sister wouldn't. He fell and hit his head."

"Ah, a good big brother, huh?"

Matthew nodded. *"Ya."*

"So he's not going to get into trouble?"

The nurse was staring hard at him, looking like she was trying to send a message.

"Nee," Matthew told him. "It was a mistake he'll not likely make again."

"So what's Joshua's favorite dinner?"

"Pizza," Jenny told her. "He loves pizza."

"Maybe that's where you'll go as soon as you get out of here," the nurse said and she winked at Matthew and jerked her head at Joshua. "I bet that'd perk him right up. What's he like on his pizza?"

"Lots of pepperoni."

"I just took my kids to this place where they have games the children can play. You know, like Whack-a-Mole and old fashioned tabletop games. I'll tell you where it is if you like."

Then she frowned. "I'm sorry, I think the games are nothing your faith would object to but —"

Matthew held up a hand. Had he seen Joshua's lashes flutter? He gestured to Jenny to join him at his side and held her close.

"No, I'm sure they're *allrecht,*" he said, not sure of that at all. But at the very least, they were going there as soon as they could for pizza.

"The pizza sounds like a very good idea," he said. "Don't you think, Jenny?"

She looked at him, confused, and then when he gestured at Joshua, her face brightened. "And root beer. Joshua and the other children really love root beer."

Joshua stirred and he slowly opened his eyes. "Games? Pizza?"

Matthew felt his heart rise in his throat. He cleared it. "Games. And lots of pepperoni."

Thank you, God, he said silently and he looked at Jenny who was crying.

"That sound good, *sohn?*"

"Yeah." He turned his head slightly and winced. "Hi, *Mamm.*"

"Hi."

"You're crying." He turned back to his *daed.* "You, too."

"Your *mamm* calls them happy tears. We were worried about you."

"Head hurts," he complained. "And I'm sleepy. I want to —" he stopped and closed his eyes, then blinked and opened them again. "I want to sleep a little while. Is that okay?"

"We'll be right here when you wake up," Jenny promised him.

"Pizza. We're going for pizza, right?"

Matthew met the nurse's eyes. *"Schur."*

The nurse glanced at Joshua and then she smiled at them. "I should buy stock in that place. Every time I mention it to one of my pediatric patients, they perk right up."

Jenny tucked Joshua's blanket around him and wished she had his quilt to put around him instead. She sighed. Maybe tomorrow he'd be home and she could do it then.

There was a noise at the door and she looked up to see Hannah and Chris.

"How is he?" Hannah whispered as she hurried forward to hug Jenny.

Something pushed at Jenny and, startled, she stepped back.

"Sorry, the baby's been kicking a lot today."

"Can I touch?"

Hannah took her hand and placed it on her abdomen. The kick was instantaneous, as if the baby were trying to connect to her. "Wow."

"I think maybe he's more active because of me rushing."

"He?" She smiled at Chris and accepted his hearty hug.

"Just a term. We still don't know if it's a he or she."

"Not fair — Phoebe knows."

"Tough," Hannah said without rancor and sank into the chair Chris pushed closer to Joshua's bed for her. "How's he doing?"

"He's been sleeping a little while but he's doing fine. No more seizures. And his speech —" she broke off as it all just became too much. "His speech seems fine. We got lucky."

Hannah tried to lever herself out of the chair but Jenny waved her back and dug in her pocket for a handkerchief. "No, stay there. I'm sorry, it's just — it's just —"

"Been really stressful," Chris said and he gave her a big hug again. He patted her back. "I know it must have brought up bad memories of what happened to you."

He glanced around. "Where's Matthew? I thought he was here with you."

Jenny stifled a yawn with her hand. "He went for coffee and some sandwiches. But he's been gone a long time."

"I'll go find him." He turned to Hannah. "Want anything?"

"Coffee," she said, pouting. "But I can't have it."

"Maybe some chocolate milk?"

She grinned. "It sounds babyish but yes." After he left, she looked at Jenny. "He knows me so well."

Joshua stirred and opened his eyes. He

focused for a moment and then grinned. "*Aenti* Hannah."

"Hi, Joshua. How are you feeling?"

"Okay," he said.

But both of them saw him wince at even the slightest movement of his head on the pillow.

Jenny checked the clock on the wall. "Let me go ask the nurse if you can have something for the pain."

"*Nee,* it's okay."

"But you're hurting." Jenny frowned as she stroked his hair visible above the bandage around his head.

He avoided her eyes. "I made enough trouble." His mouth trembled when he looked up.

"Ssh," Jenny said, her heart breaking. "Oh, son, you didn't cause us any trouble. It was an accident!"

"I shouldn't have been out in the street running after the kitten," he said staunchly, looking older than his years. "I'll pay you back for the hospital. I'll work this summer —"

"Work? What's this about work?" Matthew asked as he walked into the room with their coffee.

"He thinks he caused us trouble and he should pay for the hospital," Jenny said. "I was trying to tell him he didn't."

"I disobeyed the rules," Joshua insisted and he began crying. "Forgive me, *Daed, Mamm?*"

Matthew set the cardboard carrier with the coffee down on the bedside table. "Everyone makes mistakes, *sohn.* And you kept your sisters out of the road."

He bent down to hug Joshua. "I know you won't do something like that again. Mary told me Annie wanted to run after the kitten but you wouldn't let her." He patted his son's shoulder. "I ran into the doctor on the way back and he said he thinks you can go home tomorrow."

"And have pizza on the way home at that place the nurse said?" Joshua looked hopeful as he shifted to get more comfortable in the bed.

"Pizza on the way home. We'll bring your sisters tomorrow when we come get you."

He looked at Jenny and she nodded. "We'll bring plenty of quarters for the games," she told him. "You can Whack-a-Mole as much as you want. Although Annie may not approve of a game where you're hitting an animal, even a fake one."

Suddenly her stomach roiled and she pushed the cup of coffee in Matthew's hand and bolted for the bathroom. She slammed the door behind her and barely made it to the toilet to throw up.

15

"Mamm! Mamm!"

Jenny flew down the stairs when she heard Annie calling for her.

"What is it?" Breathless, panting at the exertion, she halted in front of Annie. "What's wrong?"

"Josiah just brought this box!"

Annie set it carefully on the kitchen table.

Frowning, Jenny approached it and then jumped back when the box moved.

"What's in it?"

"I don't know. Can we open it?"

There was a muffled noise and the box moved several inches on the table.

"No! Leave it alone! Let me think." Jenny searched her memory for what Chris had done in the military. Had he been in the bomb squad? Maybe they should go get him . . .

A bit unnerved, she pushed Annie behind her and tried to think what to do. Surely

Josiah wouldn't bring them something bad, would he? He'd gotten over his attitude about her, seemed brusque sometimes but wasn't actively unfriendly as he'd been when she first came here and he thought she should go back to New York City. As a matter of fact, he'd almost cracked a smile at her at worship services last month.

Phoebe walked into the room. Seeing them standing there looking at the box, she moved closer. "What's up?"

"Josiah gave this box to Annie."

"What's in it?"

Jenny exchanged a look with Annie who was peeking from behind her. "We don't know. We're afraid to look."

"I'm not afraid to look!" Annie piped up.

Annie started to move around from behind her but Jenny held her back. "Well, I am. So stay where you are."

"This is just silly!" Phoebe put her hands on her hips and stared at them. "Why would you be afraid of anything Josiah brought?"

The box jumped.

Muttering under her breath about people with active imaginations, Phoebe quickly folded back the flaps and out popped an orange-colored kitten.

"Pumpkin!" Annie cried, rushing forward.

The cat hissed and jumped off the table,

racing into the other room where it scaled the living room curtains.

Annie ran after it but she couldn't reach it. Jenny hurried over and almost had the kitten in her grasp when Pumpkin decided to jump down.

Onto Jenny's back.

"Ow!" she screeched, dancing and batting her hands at the kitten as its claws sank into her shoulders despite her clothing. "Get it off! Get it off!"

"What's going on?" Mary asked as she entered the living room. "I could hear you yelling all the way upstairs. Oh! Pumpkin!"

Laughing, shaking her head, Phoebe grasped the kitten and wrapped it in a dishcloth she carried. She made shushing noises and finally the kitten settled down so that she could hand it to Annie.

"Here, go take her out to her mother," she told the girl. "But if she gets like that again, let her go and do not chase her into the road. Promise me."

"I won't," Annie said soberly. "I promise." She looked at her mother. "I do."

"I'll go with her to make sure," Mary told them.

"How can one tiny kitten create such chaos?" Jenny asked Phoebe. "And have such sharp claws?"

"Let's take a look at those scratches. They can get infected."

"I can do it," Jenny said as she started toward the stairs.

"You cannot reach your back," Phoebe told her quietly. "Will you not let me take care of them for you?"

Jenny stopped. She was right. And it was time to start bridging the gap that had grown between them.

"Thank you," she said, nodding.

"*Kumm,* I have what we need in my rooms."

Following her, Jenny stepped into the *dawdi haus,* a place she hadn't entered since her grandmother had been ill.

Phoebe drew the shades over the window and then turned to help Jenny draw down the top of her dress.

"That looks painful," Phoebe said as she looked at the scratches.

Turning, she took a first-aid box from a kitchen cabinet. "Sit down and we'll take care of it," she invited.

As she did, Jenny found herself glancing around. A pot of herbs basked in the sunlight filtering into the kitchen window. An earthenware vase of bittersweet Annie had picked sat in the center of the table.

But it was more than that. Some of

Phoebe's things Jenny couldn't remember bringing from her house to this one were here: the teakettle a good friend had given Phoebe, some decorations and books and the quilt that lay across the back of the sofa.

Little touches that showed that Phoebe had begun making a home here instead of next door, even though when they'd been so upset with each other she'd said that maybe she should go live with a friend because she was getting in the way.

Jenny wanted to ask her grandmother about them but wasn't sure of this new way they were treating each other, a reaching out as tenuous as a strand of spider web.

"This might sting a bit," Phoebe warned.

The stuff she was using to clean the wounds smelled herbal, something naturopathic that Jenny knew people in the community favored over fancy, expensive *Englisch* medicine from pharmacies.

"I remember my mother using iodine years ago and blowing on it to keep it from stinging," Jenny said. "It was so long ago."

She fell silent for a long moment. "It's funny the way the smell of things brings people back. That face lotion, I think it's called Oil of Olay. Lemon muffins. And when I smell lilacs in the spring I remember the night we sneaked into the vacant property down the street from the house where we lived. They were going to cut the trees down the next day to build the new junior high school.

"So Mom and I went and cut armloads of them and brought them home and stuck them into every vase and jar we could find. When I think of lilacs now I can smell them warm and soft in my arms."

She glanced up at her grandmother. "And you. There's always this scent of lavender about you. And I never smell cinnamon buns without thinking of you. How you always baked them for me when I came here, even though it was summer and the house got warm early."

Phoebe smiled slightly and set the cloth down that she'd used to clean the scratches.

Jenny felt her grandmother's fingers dab on something cool and soothing and then she helped Jenny pull her dress back up over her shoulders.

"Dad always wore this aftershave I bought him," Jenny continued. "I don't know that he liked it but I'd given it to him for Father's Day when I was ten and he kept buying it after he used it up."

She took a deep breath and then found herself blurting out, "I had a dream about him last week."

Phoebe sat in the chair beside Jenny. "You did?"

Jenny studied the vase of bittersweet. Life felt like that right now. "He and I argued about how I felt he was high-handed taking me away from here that last summer."

"Jenny —"

She held up a hand. "No, please, let me finish. I don't want to fight with you, too. I still think it should have been handled differently. I had a right to make my own decisions. People get married at that age all the time."

"But he and your mother wanted you to have an education. You wouldn't have had that here."

Jenny shrugged. "Maybe. Maybe not. And maybe I wouldn't have cared." She glanced around the room. "I was so lonely sometimes, *Grossmudder.* Especially when I went overseas."

She fell silent, wondering if her grandmother would ever understand the pain she'd been through. It had been worse than when she'd sustained physical injuries from the bombing.

"I loved Matthew so much. I know I seemed young then but I really did love him. And when he didn't answer my letters . . . and I heard later that he got married — well, it broke my heart.

"And now . . ." she trailed off and when she looked at her grandmother, she couldn't help blinking away her tears. "I told Daddy it hurts so much that I missed out on having children, that I might never have them."

"But —"

"No, I know what you're going to say," she interrupted. "Daddy said the same thing I think you're about to say — that I *have* children. And I don't even have to say he's right. I know he is."

She wiped away a tear with her hand and her grandmother reached over for a box of tissues and handed them to her.

"I love these children I have. I did from almost the minute I met them. They *are* my children now. And Joshua's accident . . . wow, what clarity you get from something like that."

She broke down then and Phoebe gathered her into her arms.

"Shh," Phoebe said, patting her back.

"One minute I'm holding that little baby of David and Joy's and wanting one like her so badly it's like a pain here —" she sobbed, gesturing at her heart. "The next I'm hearing Mary scream and running out to find Joshua lying in the street. And when he started seizing —"

"Ssh," Phoebe whispered. "Everything's *allrecht* now. He's coming home soon. Don't cry, dear one. You'll just make yourself sick again."

Jenny wiped her eyes and pulled away from the comfort. "I know. David will be here any minute," she said, glancing at the clock. "I'm going to go wash my face."

"Maybe I should call my friend and cancel our plans."

"No, you go ahead. Like I said before, I imagine the pizza place will be kind of noisy and all with children. If you cook Joshua's favorite supper for him tomorrow and make a fuss, he'll be happy."

"I'll do that, then."

There was a knock on the door. "*Mamm,* David's here," Mary said.

"Perfect timing," Jenny told her. "Tell him I'll be right there."

"Here, use my bathroom," Phoebe said. "I'll go keep everyone occupied until you come out."

Nodding, Jenny watched Phoebe stride toward the connecting door. "My bathroom," Phoebe had said. She was referring to this addition to the main house as hers.

It was a step, she thought, to bridging the gap that had stretched between them. She hoped that somehow they'd find a way to close it.

"I can get dressed myself. I'm not a *boppli.*"

"No, *sohn,* you're not. But it's hard with your wrist, isn't it?" Matthew responded reasonably.

"Ya," Joshua admitted as he struggled with the buttons on his shirt and then gave up. "You can help. But just this one time. I'm so hungry for pizza."

Matthew tried to hide his smile as he fastened the buttons. "Just this one time," he agreed.

The wrist wasn't going to heal in a day. Few things were accomplished in a day. Especially getting his and Jenny's relationship back on track even though they'd made some strides toward it while their son was injured.

Jenny didn't understand how things were here, even though she'd seemed to adapt so well. A young man had to listen to a young woman's father. He held the authority and he was to be respected. And while Matthew felt he'd have been a good husband to Jenny and provided for her well even at that young age, he'd been trained to give that respect even if he didn't want to.

Somehow he had to make Jenny understand that.

He handed his son the dark pants Jenny had brought him. Joshua held his arms as Matthew slipped them over his legs and after they were fastened, Matthew's eyes widened. The hems were two inches from his son's feet.

"Well, look what we have here," he said. "Did you grow that much in the hospital in one day?"

Joshua grinned. "I'll be taller than you soon."

Matthew nodded as Joshua sat and he put socks on his feet and then shoes. He felt more than heard Joshua make a noise and looked up to see his son wince. "What is it?"

"Nothing."

He didn't think it was nothing. "Stand up," he said and when Joshua did, he knelt and pushed his thumb down on the toe box to see if there was any room, the way every parent did when he bought shoes for his *kinner.* He didn't need to see Joshua's face to find that the shoes were too small. "You've outgrown the shoes, too?"

"They're fine."

Matthew stood and laid a hand on his shoulder. "They're not. And I don't want you to tell me that when it isn't true. We don't want you walking around hurting because you've outgrown your shoes. Your *mamm* and I will take you shopping in a few days when you're feeling better."

"But —"

"And just think," he said, taking out a comb to gently unsnarl Joshua's fair hair above his bandage. "The way you're going, you might grow taller than me. But you're going to have bigger feet."

Joshua laughed then and hugged him. They stood there for a long moment and Matthew silently thanked God for not taking this gawky boy home. Joshua squirmed when he must have thought that his father was holding him too long, too tightly. But he settled and simply held on, too.

And then Annie was knocking impatiently at the door and sticking her head inside, wanting to know what was taking so long, and everything was back to normal.

"*Mamm,* look! They have macaroni and cheese pizza!" Annie exclaimed.

Jenny turned away from talking with Joy to study Annie's plate. "I see."

"Can you ask for the recipe so we can make it at home sometime?"

"I'll do that," Jenny promised with a smile.

"It's a gourmet delight," Joy said with a grin when Annie ran off to show her dad what she'd found.

"Imagine, it's the best possible pizza — two favorite foods on one pie!" Jenny shuddered at the thought. "Look at Joshua," she said. "That's his third serving."

Joy patted her arm. "Kids bounce back so quickly. We forget that sometimes."

"I know." She was silent for a time. "But I think I better tell him that's his last. It might be too much for him too quickly, you know?"

"You worry too much." But Joy smiled. "We mothers do, huh?" She stroked Emily's cheek. "Look at this. At home we tiptoe around so she can sleep and she's out like a light in the middle of mayhem."

Jenny walked over to Joshua sitting at a separate table with his sisters and Sam. The pizza place was a riot of light and noise from the many games and kids yelling and having fun with them. All the adults wore slightly pained expressions from the chaos.

And Joshua did, too.

"Hey, sweetheart, I think maybe that should be your last piece, don't you? I don't want you to have a tummy ache tonight."

"Okay."

"How about we get a pizza to go and put it in the refrigerator for later or for tomorrow?"

"That'd be good. Phoebe might want a piece, too."

Jenny didn't tell him she doubted that Phoebe would want pizza, not when it was too sweet that he remembered her. "Is your head hurting you?"

"Not much," he said.

But she could see the pain in his eyes. "Let's leave in a few minutes. Maybe we can come back sometime."

He brightened. "My birthday?"

She smiled. "Maybe."

Before she returned to the table where she'd sat with Joy, Jenny went to order a pizza to go — one half pepperoni, one half macaroni and cheese. That would please the adults and the kids.

She told Matthew what she did on her way back to sit with Joy. "This place can't be making any money off us tonight. They probably would have shut their doors if they knew the Bontrager kids were coming."

"Hey, they didn't eat any more than the other kids here tonight."

"I didn't see anyone else's kids go back for four servings."

Matthew considered that. "You're right. Leave some money in the tip jar."

David came to join them. "Had to stop playing Whack-A-Mole," he complained.

"Your Annie says, 'it's mean to play a game where it's funny to hit a little animal.' "

Annie walked up. "*Mamm, Daed,* will you tell those boys over there that they shouldn't play that mean game?"

Jenny looked at Matthew. "Time to go."

Matthew held Jenny's hand as they went from bedroom to bedroom checking on their children. It was his favorite time of the day, when they were about to have their alone time.

Even though tension still stretched between them, he held onto the hope that tonight might be different.

A quick peek into Annie's room showed that she slept with her doll under her arm. Mary had to be told just a few more pages and it was bedtime. And Joshua was already asleep, one foot hanging free of the covers like always.

Jenny wanted to go tuck it back in. Matthew shook his head and pulled her along. "You know five minutes from now it'd be sticking out again. He's slept like that since he was a baby."

He wished he'd watched his tongue the minute he said that. *Baby.* He felt her instant withdrawal.

They undressed with their backs to each

other. It was as if they had never been intimate as husband and wife. Jenny drew on a nightgown. Matthew pulled on pajamas. They climbed into bed, not touching, both staring at the ceiling lit by dim moonlight.

The space between them seemed huge.

He touched her hand lying on top of the covers and she stiffened so he withdrew it. Just when he decided to say something, Jenny turned on her side and he thought she was going to go to sleep. But he heard a slight noise and when he rolled over to face her back, he thought he saw it shaking.

"Jenny? What is it? Are you crying?" He reached for her and made her turn toward him. Her cheeks were wet with tears.

"I hate this distance between us," she whispered miserably.

"It doesn't have to be there. I told you why I —"

She shook her head. "If you loved me —"

"I did! I do! Don't you see? It's because I loved you that I let you go. You don't understand me *or* the Amish if you don't understand that it's not about what we want. I had to respect your father's wishes."

"And don't you understand that I had the right to know, the right to decide? I wasn't eight. I was eighteen."

He watched her sit up, then swing her legs to get out of bed. "Don't go. Please."

She sat with her back to him and he waited. Then, just when he thought she'd get up, she turned.

"How do we get past what happened?" she whispered. "How?"

"I can't undo it. Either you accept it and we move on or it'll end up destroying what we have *now,* Jenny. Do you want that?"

"Of course not."

"And there's something you're not considering, either. I don't believe that it was just your grandmother and your father and me, Jenny. I don't think we were supposed to be together then."

"How can you say that?" she demanded, her voice rising. "We loved each other!"

He took her hand. "I don't think we were supposed to be together yet, Jenny. I don't know why, but I think we were supposed to come together later. No, think about it," he said when she opened her mouth to protest. "Because if we were, nothing could have stopped us."

"So now I'm supposed to blame God?"

"Not blame Him. We're supposed to believe in His will, His time."

She flopped back against her pillow and appeared to think about that. "I spent enough time not being happy with Him when I was hurt overseas," she said. "I think He heard enough about that. And lately . . ."

He leaned over. "Lately what?"

"Lately I've been talking to Him about how I want a baby."

"I know you want one, Jenny." His eyes gleamed in the moonlight and his mouth curved into a smile. "I'm ready to do everything I can to make that happen."

She punched his arm and grinned when he yelped in pain. It was worth it to see her smile. And when he draped his arm across her waist and she didn't stiffen, didn't move it, he felt hope rise inside him.

She yawned. "Why is it we have some prayers answered and others not?" she asked him drowsily.

"I don't know. Only He knows. We have to trust Him."

"I know. I really do. It's just hard sometimes."

He watched her eyelids drifting shut. "So tired," she whispered.

"It's been a long day."

"And a long one before it. So stressed."

Her words were coming slower, softer. He wondered if she had fallen asleep.

"Matthew?"

"Yes, love."

"Maybe we should adopt."

Surprised, he stared at her. "Adopt?"

She opened her eyes. "Yes. You and I talked about it last year and said we'd think about it. Well, I don't want to think about it. I don't want to wait any longer. I don't want to go on being unhappy every month when I'm not pregnant."

She turned her head on the pillow. "I think we need to face the fact that I'm not going to get pregnant. I want us to have more children, Matthew. I want to adopt."

"Adopt," he repeated.

"Maybe that's what we're supposed to do. I keep thinking how Joy and David didn't need to. They'd had Sam and there wasn't any reason they couldn't conceive. But they gave a child who needed a home a chance. Maybe that's what we're supposed to do. Maybe that's what He wants."

"Then that's what we'll do. We'll adopt."

She lifted herself up on one elbow then and kissed him. "Thank you."

He kissed her and his hand lingered on her cheek. "Jenny?"

"Hmm?" Then she clapped her hand over her mouth as she yawned. "Sorry. So tired."

He moved his arm in open invitation for her to put her head on his shoulder and sighed when she did.

"What were you going to say?"

He heard the exhaustion in her voice and shook his head. "Nothing."

As he listened to her breathing slow and become even, as he savored the closeness, even though she slept, he thought about how he'd wanted to ask, "That doesn't mean we can't keep trying though, does it?"

"What would you like for breakfast?" Jenny asked.

Joshua shrugged. "Doesn't matter."

"Is your head still hurting?"

"A little. It's okay."

"Want some oatmeal?" Annie asked him.

Jenny watched him shake his head and then wince. She walked over to the cupboard and took out the bottle of pain medication. Handing him a pill, she pushed his glass of milk toward him and when he reached for it she noticed that his hand missed it the first time.

She glanced at Matthew and he nodded, showing he understood her concern. Their son wouldn't admit it but he'd obviously just had another episode of double vision. The doctor had warned them about this and said they were to keep him calm and at home until it went away.

"Are you going to *schul* today?" Mary

asked him.

"Sure," he said but Jenny shook her head.

"Sorry, sweetheart. You can't go yet."

"But I'm so tired of hanging around the house. It's been days and *days,*" he moaned.

Jenny glanced at the clock, gathered up the school lunches, and passed them to Mary and Annie. "Have a good day at school."

"We will," they chorused.

And then Annie turned to Joshua and hugged him. "We'll be home before you know it. If your head isn't hurting later, maybe we can play a game. Or I'll read one of my stories to you."

He smiled. "*Danki.* Do good on your spelling test."

"I will," she told him confidently.

They got goodbye kisses and hugs from their parents and then ran for the door.

Matthew stood and reached for his jacket. "I'm going out to the barn." He glanced at Jenny and she nodded.

"Can I —" Joshua started to ask but Matthew shook his head.

"It's too dangerous out there with your vision problem," he said. "Maybe tomorrow."

Jenny hurried after Matthew, catching him as he was about to step outside. She whispered to him, keeping her eyes on Joshua, and Matthew nodded.

Joshua went back to moping and couldn't be tempted with any of his breakfast favorites. Finally, Jenny plucked his jacket from the hook on the wall and handed it to him.

"I thought I couldn't go out to the barn."

"You can't. Here." She plucked an apple from the bowl of fruit in the center of the table and handed it to him.

"What's this for?"

"Breakfast. Go sit on the front porch. Maybe you'll get in a better mood."

"Sorry," he said, hanging his head.

"I understand," she told him. "But all the same, go outside and get some fresh air. Maybe it'll improve your mood." She took another apple from the bowl and handed it to him. "Take two."

He looked at her like she'd lost her mind — wow, he was already good at that and he wasn't yet a teenager, she thought — but he did as she asked and trudged off with his shoulders slumped. She heard the front door open and then shut and smiled.

Then she walked to the door and peeked out through the curtain. Joshua was sitting in a chair, his head propped in his hand, and looked the picture of misery. He was so into his pity party that he didn't hear Pilot approaching. The horse leaned his head in over the porch railing and nudged the boy's shoulder.

Joshua turned and cried, "Pilot!"

Jenny watched the two embrace for a long moment and then Pilot nudged Joshua's hand for the apple. Joshua fed it to him happily.

There were footsteps behind her. Jenny turned to see Matthew had come into the room. He looked over her shoulder at the scene on the porch.

"Good medicine, huh?" he asked.

Jenny nodded, remembering how Hannah and Chris had brought the sonogram over to show Phoebe when she'd been ill. It had taken her mind off being ill and really helped her heal. "The best."

He laid a hand on her shoulder. "You're such a good *mamm,* Jenny."

With that he turned and left her staring after him.

16

"He's okay."

Jenny glanced at Hannah. "Who?"

"You know who. Joshua."

"I'm not sure he was ready to go back to school yet. What if he has a headache?"

"The teacher will send him home," Hannah told her.

"But I won't be there."

"Matthew will be. And Chris. And Chris's dad."

Fern glanced back over the seat. "Every mom worries."

Jenny smoothed her skirt. "I guess. I just remember what awful headaches I had when I had a concussion."

"But Joshua told you he hasn't had one in several days," Hannah reminded her. "And Mary's there to keep an eye on things."

"We're going to have a nice lunch out," Fern said as she drove. "Hannah should be popping out that baby this week and then we girls won't have time for lunch or shopping for some time."

"Popping out, huh?" Hannah muttered.

Fern took her hand off the steering wheel and patted Hannah's hand as she sat beside her in the passenger seat. "Nothing to it, dumpling. You'll be fine."

Laughing, Hannah shook her head. "Dumpling? Yup, I guess I look like one."

"Term of endearment, honey," her mother-in-law told her with a chuckle. "But I guess it's not far from the truth, huh?"

She glanced in the rearview mirror. "You okay back there, Jenny? You're being kind of quiet."

Jenny pressed a hand to her mouth. "I'm — I'm afraid I'm not feeling too well. I —" Suddenly, Jenny had to get out of the car and quickly! "Fern, pull over, please!"

"I never knew you to get car sick before," Hannah said as she exchanged seats with Jenny.

"I've never been car sick before." Jenny sank down miserably in the seat. "Are you sure you can fit back there? I don't want you to squash the baby."

"I'm fine," Hannah said.

They went on to town — Jenny insisted she was fine now — and had lunch. Well, Fern had lunch, eating for two while Hannah pushed food around on her plate and Jenny sipped from a glass of water.

"I know you're under a lot of stress," Hannah said as she refused dessert. "But I've never known you to get car sick," she repeated.

"First time for everything," Fern said cheerfully and shared a story about how Chris had once thrown up in the family car on a trip.

Jenny felt even less like eating after that.

"I think I'll go get another piece of that pie," Fern said. "You sure you girls don't want something from the dessert buffet?"

Hannah shook her head and pushed her plate away. "No, thanks."

The minute Fern was out of hearing range Jenny turned to Hannah. "What's wrong? Something's wrong."

"It's nothing," Hannah told her.

Jenny frowned but Fern was already back with her pie. Talk returned to shopping for the baby. They explored a baby store and visited Stitches in Time where Fern bought adorable knitted "cupcake" hats for the baby in pink *and* blue, just in case.

And Jenny saw that Hannah was flagging and finding places to sit wherever they went.

So Jenny went to Fern and quietly suggested that they return home. "If you say anything to Hannah about cutting our shopping short she'll insist she's fine," she whispered.

"She does look a little peaked," Fern agreed. She pronounced the last word with the emphasis on the first syllable.

A few minutes later, Fern announced that her feet hurt and asked if anyone minded if they returned home. Jenny said she was tired and after looking at each of them, Hannah quickly agreed.

Halfway home, Hannah suddenly screamed and bent over in the car.

Startled, Fern swerved onto the shoulder of the road and the car stopped in the soft dirt. "Oh, my! Is everyone all right? Hannah? Jenny?"

Hannah lay back in her seat. "Fine," she said weakly.

Jenny unhooked her safety belt, climbed out of the front seat, and got into the back with Hannah. She placed her hand on Hannah's abdomen. "Are you in pain?"

"I — yes," Hannah gasped. "I just had the most horrible pain. And my back — it's been hurting all day." Her eyes were filled with fear.

Fern turned to look at Hannah. "Honey, why didn't you tell us? You might be in labor. It starts sometimes in the back."

"No, I'm all right, I —" she stopped and cried out again.

"Jenny, put your seat belt on," Fern directed. "I'm driving us to the hospital to have her checked out."

But the car had become stuck and it refused to move. Jenny unhooked her seat belt and leaned over to do the same to Hannah's so she could be comfortable while they waited for help.

"Oh no," Hannah whispered. She turned to Jenny. "I think I just had an accident."

"Don't blame you," Fern said as she rummaged in her enormous purse. "I about went in my pants when you screamed like that. Listen, don't worry about it, car's a rental. Now, where *is* that cell phone?"

Jenny glanced down at the floorboard and that's when she saw the trickle of blood running down Hannah's leg. Before she could think what to say, Hannah grabbed her arm and her fingers bit into it as she went into another convulsion of pain.

"Fern!" Jenny hissed.

The woman turned and raised her brows.

"Do you think you have a blanket in the trunk? I'd like to keep Hannah warm."

Fern started to say something but then she sensed Jenny's urgency. "Sure, hon, I'll get it."

"Hannah, let me help Fern find that blanket," Jenny said, prying Hannah's fingers off her arm.

"She can't find it herself?" Hannah responded irritably and then she apologized.

"It's okay, sweetie, I'll be right back."

Jenny scrambled out of the car and ran to the rear of it to find Fern pulling the cell out of her purse. "Call 9-1-1," she said, pulling a blanket from the trunk. "Tell them Hannah's not just in labor, she's bleeding. Then call Chris. Try not to panic him but tell him to get here fast."

Fern dropped the phone and when she picked it up, they saw that the back had come off and the battery landed in the dirt. Jenny picked it up, brushed it off, then tried to push it back into the phone.

"Here, see if you can do it," she said, thrusting the phone into Fern's hands. "I'm going to go back to Hannah. We have to keep her calm and warm."

Just then a car pulled off the road and a woman got out. "You need help?"

"Kate!" Jenny said, recognizing the female police officer. "Have you got a cell phone?"

"Sure," she said, pulling it out. "Who do you need to call? Road service?"

The passenger door opened and Malcolm stepped out. "Hey, can I help?"

"We're trying to call 9-1-1. Hannah's in labor and she's bleeding."

Kate made the call, identifying herself and stressing the urgency for an ambulance. Then she gave the cell to Fern, telling her to call Chris.

Fern yelled into the cell the moment it appeared it was answered, telling Chris that Hannah was in trouble and to come quick.

A car whizzed past, too close for comfort, as Fern hung up.

"She doesn't know she's bleeding," Jenny warned Kate as they rounded the car.

"Malcolm, do a little traffic control and motion to drivers to slow down and go well around us," she directed.

"I'd be better off helping," he said. "I was a medic, remember?"

Kate paused, then nodded. "Okay, let's see what we can do until the paramedics get here."

She glanced at Fern. "Maybe you can do the traffic control, make sure some dummy doesn't run into us. Just stay safe."

"I'm on it," Fern said, folding her arms over her chest and watching the road.

They opened the car door on the side opposite the road. "Hey, Hannah, I hear the baby's decided to come," Kate said in a calm tone.

"Oh, please, help me! I don't want to lose this baby!"

"We're not going to let that happen," Kate assured her. "Listen, Hannah, you remember Malcolm?"

Hannah nodded as he stuck his head in the space next to Kate.

"He was a medic in the military. Can he help me with you?"

Before she could respond, Hannah stiffened and then she was crying out as another contraction seized her. Malcolm took her hand and let her squeeze it, wincing at the strength of her grip.

"Breathe through it," he said calmly. "Don't fight it. We'll see what's going on in a minute." When it eased, he smiled. "Good. Have you gone to childbirth classes?"

"Yes." Tears began rolling down her cheeks. "I don't want to have my baby here."

"The ambulance will be here and you'll be in the hospital before you know it. Now, let's get you more comfortable, okay?"

Together, he and Kate eased her down on the backseat while Jenny went around to the other side so that she could sit with Hannah's head and shoulders in her lap and hold her hand.

Kate began to tear away the blood-soaked skirt of Hannah's dress.

Fern appeared at the door and paled when she saw what was going on. She thrust the plastic bottle of hand sanitizer she kept in her purse at Malcolm.

"Good thinking," he said, squirting some of the stuff into his hands, then Kate's.

Jenny felt a wave of nausea wash over her when she saw the blood running down Hannah's leg but she forced herself to look at Hannah and keep her attention. "Well, this is an exciting end to a day of lunch and shopping, don't you think?"

When Hannah lifted her head to see what was going on, Jenny leaned closer so that her sister-in-law would have to focus on her face. "What are the names you're thinking of using again?"

"I know you're trying to distract me and it isn't working," Hannah told her. But she lay back against Jenny. "Chris. I want Chris."

"We called him. He'll be here as soon as he can."

"He better be. I'm not having this baby without him."

Jenny glanced at Malcolm. He looked grim as he checked Hannah.

"The baby's coming, Hannah," he told her tersely. "There's nothing we can do to stop it. Just keep breathing through the contractions, okay?"

He muttered something over his shoulder and Kate went to the rear of the car. Jenny watched her speak into her cell and their eyes met through the rear window. Kate held up her thumb to indicate that everything was going to be all right. Jenny prayed that it would be.

"So are you expecting a boy or a girl?" Malcolm asked them.

"We don't know," Hannah said. "Chris and I want to be surprised. Well, it wasn't his idea but he went along with it when I said I wanted to be surprised."

"Then I guess we'll all be surprised," Malcolm said. "And sooner than you think. Hannah, the baby's head is crowning. Hey, Kate, come here! I can use your help!"

Jenny held Hannah's shoulders and coached her to breathe through the contractions and it seemed just seconds later when Malcolm yelled, "Yes, I've got him!" and the cries of a newborn filled the interior of the car.

He handed the baby to Kate who'd pulled off her sweater to tuck around him to keep him warm.

"A boy!" Jenny called out to Fern. "You have a grandson!"

"Is he all right?" Fern asked, sticking her

head in the open window on Jenny's side. "Please, Jesus, tell me he's okay?"

"He looks fine," Jenny told her.

"Look at him, Jenny," Hannah whispered as Kate handed her the baby. "Isn't he a wonder?"

Jenny nodded and said a silent, heartfelt prayer to God for his safe arrival. Neither of them could take their eyes off the baby, its little face scrunched up as it cried and waved its little hands.

"Oh!" Hannah cried as another contraction rolled over her. "Am I having another?"

"Afterbirth," Malcolm told her tersely. "You're fine."

But he and Kate wore expressions of concern as it was delivered and they were pressing the soaked blanket on Hannah.

A siren wailed, growing louder as it approached. Jenny said another prayer as the fire engine parked and first responders jumped out. They got their gear and ran up and Malcolm and Kate stepped aside.

"Don't go," Hannah pleaded with Jenny.

"I'm not going anywhere," she told her.

"We need to check the baby out," one paramedic told them and reluctantly Hannah gave him up.

Then Jenny had to get out of the car when another paramedic needed to help move

Hannah onto a stretcher.

She stood with Fern at the rear of the car, and Malcolm and Kate joined them.

"She's bleeding more than she should be, isn't she?" Jenny asked him bluntly.

Malcolm met her eyes and he hesitated. Then he finally nodded. "Yeah. But she's got help now."

"I don't know what we'd have done if you two hadn't stopped," she told them and hugged him.

He held out his arms so the blood that coated them wouldn't get on her clothes and shrugged and bent his head. "I didn't do any more than anyone else would have. And it's kind of the least I could do, considering, wouldn't you say?"

"There's nothing 'least' about it," she told him fervently.

A horse galloped toward them, a man on its back.

"Here comes Chris now," Jenny exclaimed as he neared them.

Jenny frowned. Chris looked murderous as he rode the horse right up to him.

"Maybe I should go sit in the car," Malcolm said, backing up.

Chris jerked on the reins and the horse reared, then settled. He jumped off its back and ran toward Malcolm and Jenny saw him look at the blood on his hands and shirt. Grabbing Malcolm's shirt, he shook him violently.

"Where's Hannah? What have you done to her?"

"I —" Malcolm began but Chris didn't give him a chance. He smashed his fist into his face.

Jenny screamed and rushed at him, pulling him away from Malcolm who'd landed on the ground. "No, you don't understand! He didn't hurt Hannah! Kate! Help!"

Kate came running.

Jenny watched her quickly assess the situation. "Chris! Hannah's right over here!" she called. "Come on, you don't want to do anything foolish. Malcolm just delivered your baby."

Chris struggled to rein in his fear and anger, his chest heaving as he stood looking at the blood on the other man's arms. Malcolm shook his head as if to clear it and started to get to his feet, then stayed where he was when Chris continued to stand over him.

Kate held out her hand as she approached Chris. "Please, Chris, your wife needs you right now. She's bleeding heavily and they're loading her and the baby into the ambulance. You need to come with me now. Right now."

Her calm words finally reached Chris. He bounded toward the ambulance without looking back at any of them.

He climbed inside and the ambulance doors closed behind him. It took off and the siren blared.

Kate reached down to grasp Malcolm's hand and help him up. She touched his cheek and he winced. "I bet that's pretty painful."

"Yeah," he acknowledged but he shrugged. "I'll live. Can't blame the guy for coming to the conclusion that I'd hurt Hannah again."

"I'm so sorry," Fern rushed to apologize but he shook his head. "I just told him to come quick, she was in trouble."

"I'd have come to the same conclusion. I mean, look." He gestured at the blood that covered his hands and shirt.

Fern rushed off to find the hand sanitizer and returned with it and a towel she got from one of the paramedics. She insisted on helping him clean up, telling him over and over how grateful she was for him helping Hannah deliver safely.

"Here comes Matthew," Jenny said as he approached driving the buggy.

Malcolm cast a wary look at Matthew.

"Hannah's brother? Should I run for the car?"

Jenny patted his arm and shook her head. "Matthew's not like that." But she remembered seeing him do just that when he met Chris for the first time.

"I know," he said, touching his jaw and wincing again. "He could have pressed charges against me for setting fire to his barn and he didn't. I got pretty lucky with the Bontragers when I was messed up and blamed Chris for everything wrong with my life."

"Well, I'd say the Bontragers are feeling pretty thankful they practiced forgiveness, wouldn't you? And Chris will be thanking you once he finds out what you did," she told him. She hugged him, then Kate. "Thank you both again."

"So you have transportation to the hospital?" Kate asked them.

"Yes, thanks," Jenny said and she turned and slipped her arms around Matthew. "Oh, I'm so glad you're here. Wait 'til you hear what happened."

She heard Kate telling Malcolm they were going to follow them as she and Matthew walked to the buggy.

Matthew watched Jenny cradling her new

nephew and thought about the strange turn of events of the past week.

Who would ever have thought that they all owed so much to the man who had come here to hurt Chris years ago after they both got out of the military and then had hurt Hannah instead?

His sister sat tucked up on the sofa in her house, safe if a little pale and tired looking. She'd been rushed into surgery after the birth, given a transfusion after losing so much blood, and spent two days in the hospital. But the doctors had told Chris that she'd be fine with some rest.

She watched, smiling indulgently as one relative after another tried to cajole Jenny into letting them hold the baby. Grandpa William and Grandma Fern and Phoebe — told she was an honorary great-grandma while she was at Matthew and Jenny's house — had had turns first and now sat drinking coffee and eating apple spice cake that Phoebe had baked that afternoon.

Matthew thought Grandma Fern looked impatient to hold the baby again. Once she'd found out that Hannah was expecting, she'd firmly told her husband she wasn't going back home until her daughter-in-law delivered. Now it didn't look like she intended on being budged home anytime soon.

Jenny glanced up from the baby and smiled at Matthew. He thought about how she wanted to adopt. He'd promised to think about it and he had. He wanted nothing more to make Jenny happy and if a *boppli* would do that, he hoped that God would clear the path to having one this way if He hadn't the traditional way.

Besides, he loved children, so more would be a fine thing. The *kinner* would even be happy because they'd always wanted another *bruder* or *schwesder.*

"You're looking smug," she said as she walked over to him and they looked at the baby together. "Does it feel pretty good to be an uncle?"

Wrapping his arm around her waist, he bent to study the baby. "*Schur* does. The *kinner* like having a cousin to fuss over, too," he said. "I didn't think I'd get them to go off to *schul* this morning. I promised they could come straight here and see the *boppli* again afterward."

Just at that moment, there was a commotion at the door.

"It's the Bontrager gang," she murmured and they shared a smile.

The children tried to pass through the

door at the same time. Much not-so-gentle pushing ensued until Annie won out and ran toward them.

"I get to hold him first."

"Go wash your hands," her parents said at the same time.

Phoebe supervised the hand washing and then the children sat on the sofa and each got their turn to hold the baby, starting with Annie.

"I wish we could have —" she began and then she stopped, looked at her father, and bit her lip.

Matthew tensed but when he glanced at Jenny, she didn't look stricken as she'd done when one of the *kinner* had expressed a desire for a sibling. He took Jenny's hand and he smiled when she squeezed it. Maybe she had gained some peace from making the decision to talk to him about adoption, he mused.

The baby having been transferred to each of his three cousins, Hannah held out her arms in hopes of getting her son for some cuddling. Joshua held the baby out to Chris. As he passed his father, he stopped and bent slightly to show off his son to his grandpa.

"Well, Dad, did I finally do something right?"

William bristled at that. "What a thing to

say! I never said you didn't do anything right."

"Here we go," Fern muttered and she rolled her eyes at Hannah.

Chris straightened. "All we've done all our lives is butt heads."

Fern stood and took the baby from Chris. "Well, that's just because the two of you are so alike. Both of you are stubborn as mules."

"I'm not stubborn," Chris protested. Hands on his hips, he turned to his father. "It's him who's stubborn."

William harrumphed.

Hannah held out her hand to her husband. "Your mother's right. But we love both of you." She smiled up at him. "And your father told me the other day he's proud of what you've accomplished in such a short time here on the farm."

Surprised, Chris stared at his father. "You did?"

Reddening, his father nodded grudgingly. "Sure. I give credit where credit is due."

Chris started to say something but then, after a glance at Hannah, subsided. "Thanks."

"You've had a big hand in things, too," his father said, bending to kiss the top of Hannah's head. "Chris seems a lot more peaceful here and I have to think that's due to you."

Matthew watched tears well up in his sister's eyes. "Why, thank you. *Grossdaedi.*"

William looked a little misty-eyed. "Grandfather," he said. "I'm a grandfather." He harrumphed and patted Hannah's shoulder.

"I love my son but I really love the woman he chose," he said. And then, as if embarrassed, he left the room, muttering something under his breath about getting them all more coffee.

Chris settled his son in the cradle Matthew had taught him how to make. He stroked his son's cheek and then the wood he'd spent hours carving by hand, sanding, then staining and rubbing. A nudge of his hand sent the rocker moving and the baby closed its eyes and slept.

"Here I thought the two of you were looking at seed catalogs all those evenings you were in the barn," Hannah told Chris.

He grinned. "It's not bad for a first attempt, do you think?"

She patted the sofa cushion next to her and when he joined her, she leaned over to kiss his cheek. "I think it's pretty spectacular."

There was a knock on the door. Joshua

ran to answer it and Kate Lang walked in carrying a big Mylar balloon bouquet and a box wrapped in glossy blue paper. "I hope you don't mind me stopping by for a minute," she told Hannah. "I heard you were home from the hospital and just wanted to drop by and see how you're doing."

Annie jumped up and took the balloon bouquet to set on a nearby table. She stood tapping the balloons and watching the way they bobbed and glittered.

Kate oohed and ahhed over the baby while Hannah opened the present to reveal a hand-knitted blanket.

"You made this?" Hannah said, stroking it reverently. "It's so beautiful."

"Yeah, well, it's just something I do to relax in the evenings after work," Kate said. "I don't let the guys at the station know about it. They'd tease me to death."

Joshua tugged at Matthew's sleeve. "*Daedi,* there's someone in a car outside."

"I better go," Kate said. "Someone's waiting for me."

"Is it Malcolm?" Chris asked her.

Kate nodded. "He didn't feel he should come in."

Without hesitating, Chris strode out the door, returning with a wary-looking Malcolm. Then Chris took his son and placed him in Malcolm's arms.

"We might not have him right now if not for you," he said, his voice sounding like it was thick with unshed tears. "Malcolm, meet Jonah Malcolm."

Visibly moved, Malcolm stared at the baby. "You didn't have to do that."

"I think we did." Chris said quietly. "Maybe one day our sons can play together."

Malcolm nodded. "The ex is letting me have him every other weekend now." He glanced at Hannah and smiled. "Things have really turned around for me since Hannah decided I was worth another chance."

Hannah stood and hugged him. "You were." She glanced at Kate. "Looks like someone else believes in you, too."

He glanced at Kate and grinned. "Yeah. Go figure, huh?"

Matthew saw Hannah sway but before he could react, Chris swooped her up and carried her back to the sofa where he sternly warned she was to stay or she'd be banished to their bedroom.

Kate and Malcolm left a few minutes later and after glancing at the time, Matthew shepherded his own brood back to their house to do chores.

"I'll be right there," Jenny promised as she helped Phoebe gather up the coffee cups and cake plates.

"I should be helping," Fern said but she managed to get Jonah in her arms again and was settling into a wooden rocker.

"Mother, the least you could do is let me hold that young 'un again for a few minutes," Matthew heard William complain as he left.

"Wait your turn," she said with a laugh. "Hey, young man, let's talk about how soon you can get your Mommy and Daddy to come to Kansas and see your Granny and Paw Paw, huh?"

17

"You're sure you can manage while I'm gone?"

Matthew gave her a puzzled look. "We always do."

Jenny glanced around her spotless kitchen. "Yes, but that was when Hannah was here to help. She has her own family now."

Phoebe walked into the kitchen. "What am I, chopped liver?"

A strangled sound escaped Jenny's lips. She stared at her grandmother. *"What?"*

Grinning, Phoebe poured herself a cup of coffee and sat down at the kitchen table. "It's an expression. I'm sure you've heard of it."

Openly laughing now, Jenny nodded. "Yes, but I've never heard my Amish grandmother use it."

Phoebe shrugged and helped herself to a cookie from a plate on the table. "You pick up things."

"Apparently." Jenny frowned when she saw the time. She sighed. "Well, I'd better get going." She bent to hug her grandmother and then walked outside with Matthew.

"You're sure you have time to drive me?" she asked as he helped her into the buggy and set her overnight bag in the back.

"You know it's slow right now. And it gives us a few minutes to be alone together."

And without that time being in a bedroom, she thought, though he wouldn't say it and neither would she. There was still distance between them, distance they hadn't managed to bridge.

They didn't often get to take a buggy ride alone together. She found herself remembering a drive before they were married. It was one of her favorite memories. Matthew had picked her up after physical therapy and they'd picnicked on her favorite McDonald's burgers near a patch of daffodils pushing through a late snow. He'd taken her there because she'd been so tired of the dreary winter and the pain and the therapy. His thoughtfulness had been just what she needed.

The leaves had all fallen from the trees now, creating a carpet of gold and russet and brown on the road as Jenny and Matthew wended their way into town.

"I left dinner in the refrigerator, all you have to do is —"

Matthew glanced at her and grinned. "We'll be fine."

"But —"

"We'll be fine."

"Well, you don't have to sound like I'm dispensable," she told him, feeling a little miffed.

Then he did something that surprised her. He picked up her hand and kissed it. "You're indispensable, I assure you."

"So you say." She lifted her chin and turned to look out the buggy, pretending to be miffed, but when she turned, he was grinning at her.

"We don't like it when you're away but we know it's important for you to do it sometimes for your work," he said quietly. "And it's been good for the *kinner* to help more."

"They do so much — especially compared to *Englisch* children."

Matthew shrugged. "Hard work is good for everyone. *Kinner* here know how to do their share. And they love it."

The Amish didn't believe in public displays of affection so after he parked the buggy, Matthew always gave her a big hug and a kiss before they got out. She wondered if he would do it today since they were still walking around each other a bit.

But he gathered her in his arms and kissed her without reservation. Her heart turned over at the gesture and afterward, she rested her forehead against his.

He acted as if nothing had happened between them. When she drew back, she looked into his deep blue eyes, searching for something to say.

"Life's too short," he said quietly as he stroked her cheek. "When you come back, let's talk some more and see if we can get past this for good."

Nodding, she started to get out of the buggy but he touched her arm. She turned and looked at him.

"I know it's hard to forgive. But even though I told you that I felt I had to honor your father's wishes to stay away from you, that didn't mean I didn't regret that I didn't go back and talk to him again."

It was the first time he'd said that. Jenny stared at him.

"I told you, it wasn't easy for me. I wish you could believe that. And understand it."

"I'm trying," she whispered. Then she remembered what one of her college professors had once said: "When people say they'll try, eighty percent of the time it doesn't get done. Just say, 'I will' and it *will* get done."

Jenny took a deep breath. "I will," she promised.

She watched him get out of the buggy and reach into the back for her overnight bag. Pulling a note from her purse, she laid it on his seat and got out. He walked her into the terminal and waited with her until it was time for her to leave.

She told herself not to look back. The first time she'd left him and the children after the wedding, she'd nearly gotten up and left the train. But she'd forced herself to stay on it, to go see her editor. Matthew had insisted she go in the first place, saying her work was important. And did she want the *kinner* to see that she was afraid to leave, that she was a quitter? he'd asked. Or that she thought she had to hang close, never let them learn to take care of themselves without her? That wasn't good, he'd maintained.

Smiling at the memory, Jenny leaned back in her seat and got comfortable, then began writing on a yellow legal pad.

"Hi there!" an older woman said as she took the seat near Jenny. "Sorry, didn't mean to bump you."

"It's okay," Jenny told her, trying not to

rub the elbow the woman had hit with her oversized purse.

"I'm going into the city to see some plays. Where are you going?"

"The city. But it's for work."

"Work?" The woman eyed her curiously, taking in Jenny's Plain clothing and the pad on which she'd been writing. "What kinds of work do you do?"

"I'm a writer."

The woman considered that. "Well, how about that. What kinds of things do you write?"

It should be easy by now to talk about her writing, thought Jenny. But it had always been so personal to her. The television news reporting had been different, somehow. Yes, some writing had been involved, but that had been just straight reporting and delivering to the camera.

So she told the woman — her name was Adele — about the book she was working on in as few words as possible. Adele clapped a hand to her chest. "Why, I know who you are! I used to watch those broadcasts. My, look at how well you're doing."

Jenny knew that she looked like she was doing well now. She no longer limped, her scars had faded, and although she didn't always love that she'd gained weight, she knew she looked better than when she'd been rail thin after the car bombing. The emotional, well, that was pretty much okay, too. She hadn't had a nightmare in more than six or eight months now. But the fact that she hadn't conceived made her wonder if the abdominal injuries hadn't permanently rendered her infertile.

Her stomach was queasy again, no doubt because of the motion of the train.

"I read where you became Amish," said Adele. She reached into her purse and withdrew a bag of cookies, held them out to Jenny who refused them with a polite smile, then took one for herself. "I just admire them — the Amish, I mean — for practicing forgiveness and all."

She sighed as she ate another cookie. "I should let you get back to your work." With that, the woman turned to her magazine and, absorbed, munched on her cookies as she read.

Forgiveness. Jenny reflected on how she hadn't been practicing that lately. Before her grandmother had fallen ill, she'd sat at her own kitchen table and reflected on how she wasn't a saint. She'd envied her sister-in-law being pregnant and not been happy that she hadn't been able to conceive.

Then she'd found out that her grandmother had written her father to inform him that Jenny fell in love with Matthew, the boy next door. The boy who was Amish. She'd known how Jenny's father had broken away from the Amish and wouldn't want her to marry Matthew. And then — then to find out that Matthew had promised her father that he wouldn't pursue her against his wishes.

She'd been so upset for so long and struggled so hard to understand, to accept. To forgive. Gradually she'd begun to understand her grandmother's actions and to accept them. She'd finally begun to forgive. Remembering how her grandmother had sent her the quilt in the hospital with the note that said "Come. Heal." had helped. Whether Phoebe had done it as a way of undoing what she'd done years ago didn't even matter. Things had worked out.

That quilt, that note, had begun her road back here, to heal, to be reunited with Matthew. To find love and her faith and a way of life she had never imagined. She'd healed.

And she'd begun to feel a peace here she'd never imagined.

Some said everything happened for a reason. Maybe there was a reason for why she'd been separated from Matthew, why she'd gone to college when she really hadn't wanted to. Why she'd been injured so badly overseas and suffered and then, after all those years, returned to Matthew.

And maybe there was some reason why she hadn't conceived.

Did she have to know to trust God? Could she just . . . be? When she thought about it, did she really have a choice? Did she want to let what had happened years ago separate her from the family she loved? From her grandmother, her husband, her children?

Yes, her children.

She remembered how it had felt to realize how quickly she could lose one of them to an injury when Joshua had been hurt, how quickly life could change.

Remembering how he had apologized for getting hurt and causing his family pain and expense, Jenny doodled aimlessly on her pad. He'd said he hadn't obeyed his parents' rules about safety. That made her think about how Matthew had said if she understood how the Amish insisted on obedience, on obeying the rules no matter what, on putting the good of others, of the community, above his own, she would understand and be able to forgive and go on. He'd even admitted when pressed that he had sometimes regretted that he'd gone against his beliefs, his upbringing, and pressed her father to talk to him again.

But this man she'd had a second chance to love . . . if she thought about it, one of the things she loved about him was that he did the right thing. She'd thought he hadn't loved her enough and that's why he hadn't refused to listen to her father. But those rules he lived by, the *Ordnung* and the Amish culture, had shaped this man she loved.

She remembered how when she'd first returned to Paradise, Matthew had often taken her to the place they'd picnicked as teenagers. He'd carved a heart and their initials into a tree and said he'd intended on showing it to her. But her father had come that day, talked to him, and taken Jenny back home with him.

He wasn't a talkative man but she needed to remember that he'd shown her so many times since they reunited that he loved her.

When Matthew went to get into the buggy and saw the folded note on the seat, his heart felt like it would burst from his chest.

He stood there staring at it for the longest time, as wary as if he'd encountered a poisonous snake. Finally, he made himself reach for it and climb inside the buggy to read it. Was she leaving him? Maybe she'd decided she couldn't ever forgive him.

No, he couldn't believe that. She was a loving woman, a compassionate one. Eventually, when she had a chance to think more, when she realized how much he loved her and she loved him — because he was convinced she loved him — she'd forgive him. They'd made such inroads to this tough patch in their marriage lately.

He had to believe that.

They'd been given a second chance. Not many people got those. She'd recognized that once and been grateful. Now he had to trust that God would help keep them together.

Because if God wanted them together, nothing, no one, could tear them apart. Not even them.

The ride into New York City gave Jenny time to think about all that had happened the past couple of months. She was glad she'd come to some sort of resolution with her grandmother. What Phoebe had done was done and there was no going back and fixing it. Jenny had come to forgive her grandmother for contacting her father and letting him know about Jenny falling in love with Matthew.

And when she'd touched the quilt that

one afternoon, the one her grandmother had sent to the hospital after Jenny was injured . . . well, that was an attempt to make things right after all those years, wasn't it? If her grandmother hadn't invited her to her home to heal, Jenny wouldn't have had a second chance with Matthew.

And Matthew . . . what he'd said about her not really understanding the Amish way if she didn't realize that he'd had to obey her father's stricture to stay away from her. It pained her to realize he was right. Obeying authority, respecting it even when it went against what you wanted — especially if against what you wanted — well, that was part of the ultimate obedience to God.

She stared out the window at the fields they were passing, squares of brown, gold, ochre, and fading green that so looked like patches on a quilt. She was bound to this family and this land and these people like the stitches that bound the quilt squares, woven into a tapestry of love and faith.

Peace settled over her like her beloved quilt and she sighed and slept.

18

"Miss? Miss?"

Jenny woke and found the woman who sat next to her staring at her in concern.

"This is your stop, isn't it?"

Blinking, trying to focus, Jenny saw that it was, indeed. Thank goodness the woman had remembered from their brief conversation at the beginning of the journey.

"Yes, thank you!" she told her fervently. She gathered up her things and prepared to disembark. "I can't believe I slept so long. I've been so tired lately."

The woman's glance went to Jenny's abdomen. "Are you?"

Even though Jenny wasn't very alert yet, she caught the implication. Maybe it was because Hannah and her grandmother had asked her such a question recently.

She shook her head and tried to smile. "No. We've just had a lot going on at home."

"Do you have children?" The woman who

appeared to be in her late sixties smiled at her.

"Three," Jenny told her. "Joshua, Mary, and Annie."

"That's a small family for the Amish, isn't it? But then again, you're young. Maybe God will bless you with more."

He'd have to do that with adoption but that wasn't really a subject Jenny wanted to share with a stranger and besides, there wasn't enough time. The train was already slowing for her stop.

"Well, just think, I met a celebrity," the woman mused. "Can't wait to tell my friend, Cynthia."

"I'm hardly a celebrity."

"Sure you are. Or you were. And such a nice one."

Surprised, Jenny thanked her.

"It was nice to hear how you ended up getting married and all. Going in to New York to do some television work?"

Jenny shook her head. "I'm seeing my editor. I'm working on a book."

"Well, it was so nice to have met you," the woman said.

"I enjoyed meeting you, too." She tucked her writing pad into her carry-on.

"Think about writing about your story," the woman suggested. "Not just the ones about the children overseas. I mean your love story, about meeting the man you loved when you were a teenager and met again."

"I'll think about that," Jenny said although she doubted she'd share something so personal. And things still felt a bit tenuous right now in her marriage.

But hope. Yes, she had hope.

"Well, you take care of that business you have in New York City and get back to your family. And have a wonderful Christmas. It's not far off now."

Christmas. The woman was right, thought Jenny as she disembarked and saw the decorated store windows. Maybe after she finished seeing her editor she'd have a little time for a little Christmas shopping. It wouldn't be for glitzy gifts — those weren't exchanged by the Amish. But something small might be nice.

There was a display in a nearby window, little snow globes of the city. Annie had seen a snow globe in a store in town one day and been fascinated in it. She might like it. Joshua was easy. All she had to do was find something like a book about horses and he'd happily settle in his room with it for hours. And Mary, sweet, quiet Mary. She loved that journal Jenny had given her once. A new one would be welcome, Jenny was sure. Maybe some fabric to make a dress — Mary was becoming quite the seamstress — that would be good.

And Matthew . . . she was sure just holding out the hand of forgiveness was all he wanted.

Suddenly woozy, she nearly missed her step. A man caught her arm and steadied her. She turned and thanked him.

"You okay?" he asked.

"Yes," she said, giving him a grateful smile.

But she walked over and sat down on a bench when the woozy feeling continued. It must be that her body, not fully awake, was reacting to the rocking motion of the train, she told herself. Once she felt recovered, she hailed a cab and went on to the hotel.

She'd just settled in when she got a call on the hotel phone. It was Matthew.

"Sorry I didn't call before," she said, pulling off her jacket and sinking down on the bed. "I just got to the hotel."

He talked to her for a few minutes and then she could hear Annie, impatient as always, asking to talk to her.

"*Mamm,* my teacher loved my short story!" she cried when she got on the phone. "She wants me to read it after the school Christmas play!"

Jenny congratulated her, wondering if she

was going to become the second writer in the family. Joshua got his turn and wanted her to know that the doctor said his wrist was healing nicely. Mary came on and reported that her baby cousin had smiled at her that afternoon.

Warmed by the sound of their eagerness to talk to her, to share their day, Jenny sat there on the bed for a long time after Matthew had come on again and they hung up.

She unpacked her things and found a plastic bag she hadn't put in the carry-on. Glitter fell out of the bag when she opened it. The children had made her cards and Annie's had a clump of glittered letters on the front.

"Have fun," the card said on the front. Inside, she'd written, "Love, your daughter, Annie." The cards the other children had created were just as sweet — although they hadn't used the abundance of glitter Annie loved.

Just what she needed, she thought. Smiling, she pulled the coverlet from the bed over her and lay staring at the cards for a long time before she fell asleep again, still dressed in her clothes, and slept through the night.

The meeting with her editor, a blond dynamo in her thirties, lasted several hours. Sally wanted to show her the marketing campaign for the book that would be released in the spring.

Once that was over, they ate lunch in a small restaurant near the publisher's and caught up on all the news about their families. Sally shared photos of her twins who it seemed had grown a foot since Jenny had last seen them. Jenny told Sally that the Amish didn't like having photos taken so she didn't have any to share but Sally said that she'd painted such wonderful word pictures of them in the years that they'd known each other that she felt she could see them.

"Maybe one day you'll be able to bring your husband and children to the farm to meet mine," Jenny said as they parted.

"Or you can bring yours to the city," Sally suggested. "Jenny, are you feeling all right? You look pale."

"Just a little rundown, I expect. I told you about all that has been happening."

Sally bit her lip as she continued to regard at Jenny. "When's the last time you went to a doctor?"

"A while," Jenny admitted. "But I'm fine. I think I might even do a little shopping before I go home."

But she found herself staring at her reflection in a shop window after Sally hurried back to her office and wondered if she should call her doctor while she was here. She'd been dragging for too long now.

When the receptionist heard her name, she told Jenny to come over right away. "The doctor was just saying the other day she wondered how you were doing. I know she'd want me to get you right in while you're in town."

So Jenny climbed into a cab for another wild New York City ride that had her wondering if she'd keep her lunch down on the way.

Jenny's doctor was happy to see her, just as the receptionist had said she'd be and ushered her right into her office. She sat in a chair next to Jenny instead of sitting behind her desk.

"So, any luck getting pregnant?" she asked, looking hopefully at Jenny's waist.

Jenny shook her head. "I thought about asking you for a referral to a fertility specialist like we discussed last time. But it's so expensive. We have so many things the money might be better spent on. Besides, I'm not sure it's the right thing. I mean, if it's God's will for us to have a baby, we will."

She sighed. "Well, I have to tell you, I'm

still working on that last part."

Dr. Ross patted her shoulder. "It's not an easy thing for any couple of any religion to face problems getting pregnant. And I'm sure it's not easy having those problems and living in a community with such large families."

"I already have a large family in the eyes of some people," Jenny said. "Three is a lot if you think about it. And Matthew and I are talking about adoption."

She bit her lip, then plunged forward. "I don't want to be unhappy every month, wanting another child. Matthew's agreed to adopt."

"Good for you!" Dr. Ross exclaimed, looking genuinely happy. "I've seen too many couples grow apart because they can't conceive."

The doctor rose. "Now, why don't we see why you're feeling so tired lately. Not that being a mom and a homemaker and a writer won't do it, right?"

Jenny changed into a paper gown, produced a urine sample, and winced as a few vials of blood were drawn. Then she climbed onto the exam table and Dr. Ross came in.

A few minutes later, the doctor pushed back her wheeled stool, stood, and stripped off her exam gloves.

"Well," she said. "There's nothing that an infertility specialist can help you with."

Jenny immediately went back to the hotel, checked out, and got on the next train home.

She couldn't stand being alone in the city for one more minute after the doctor visit. This time she had no trouble staying awake on the trip home, her thoughts and emotions just one big jumble.

All she wanted now was to be home with her family. The longer she was on the train, the more desperate she felt to be with them.

Then she realized that she was going to arrive home at an awkward time. Rather than wake Matthew, she found a cab and told herself the expense was worth it. So she'd have to find a way to stretch the budget. Matthew wouldn't be upset with her. He'd understand when he heard the news, she told herself.

Letting herself into the house, she glanced at the kitchen clock and saw that her family would be getting up in about an hour. The burst of adrenalin that had driven her home, the stress of it all, fizzled. Her feet felt like lead and the stairs ahead looked like they stretched for a mile. Dumping her carry-on and purse, she curled up on the sofa, drew the quilt on the back of it over her, and fell asleep immediately.

Dreams chased after each other, images of children playing hide and seek, running in and out of dark places and into sunlight, back into darkness and then back into the light.

A butterfly landed on her cheek and fluttered its delicate wings. She brushed at it and it giggled. Jenny smiled at the familiar sound and with her eyes closed, reached out and grasped Annie.

"You're back!" Annie cried. "Hey, *Daedi,* Joshua, Mary! *Mamm's* back!" she yelled.

Jenny released her and pressed her hands to her ears. "And has lost her hearing!" She grabbed Annie again and hugged her tightly.

"You're squeezing me."

"Too bad," Jenny told her. "Oh, it's so good to be back."

"You're home early!" Matthew exclaimed as he walked into the room, dressed but his hair still tousled from bed. "Why didn't you call me? I'd have come to pick you up."

"Couldn't wait," she said, releasing Annie.

He eyed her uncertainly. "You alright? Everything go okay with your editor?"

She nodded. "The meeting went fine." She accepted a hug from Mary and Joshua.

"I have something to tell all of you," she

said, taking a deep breath.

"Wait," said Matthew, walking over to retrieve a fat envelope from a nearby table. He handed it to Jenny. "Me first. Just this once."

She stared at the address on it. "You called them?"

He nodded. "They said they'd put an application in the mail the same day and they must have. It came yesterday."

How to tell him? she wondered. "I don't think I can do it."

His face fell. "You changed your mind?"

"Yes." She patted the place next to her on the sofa. "Here, sit down."

"Okay," he said slowly. He looked at the children and they looked at him.

"But we like 'doption," Annie said and her bottom lip quivered. "*Daedi* got the papers."

Joshua and Mary nodded.

"I just don't think I can take care of two little babies by myself, even with the help of all of you," she told them.

"Two," Matthew repeated, clearly confused.

Jenny pressed her hand to her abdomen. "Yes. It would be too much for me. I'm sorry."

And then Mary squealed and clapped her

hands. "You're going to have a baby?"

Jenny nodded.

"You," Matthew said. "But you —"

"Didn't think I could. But I went to see the doctor while I was in New York City," she told him, enjoying his bafflement. "I thought I was sick from something going around. That the exhaustion was from caring for my grandmother when she was sick. Then I blamed it all on stress." She knew he knew what stress she was talking about — the upset between her and her grandmother, and their own marital problem it had caused. "I decided to see her while I was there. I'm not sick. I'm pregnant."

"A *boppli,*" he said and he shook his head. His expression was changing from bafflement to joy. "Can it be true?"

She nodded and he stood and lifted her in his arms to swing around and then clasp her to him.

Laughing, she cried, "Stop!"

"Oh, sorry!" he said immediately and he bent to place her gently on the sofa. "I didn't hurt the baby, did I?"

"Of course not, silly!" She held on to the sofa armrest, waiting for the world to stop spinning. "I'm still having trouble with the nausea, that's all. Let's not move me around too much too quickly."

And then as the children crowded around her, hugging her, telling her how happy they were, she started crying.

The children backed away, looking concerned. "It's okay," Matthew told them.

"Happy tears?" Joshua asked.

"Ya," Matthew agreed and he was grinning.

But he looked concerned when Jenny couldn't stop crying. He gathered her into his arms and shushed her, saying that she needed to stop or she'd make herself sick.

Safe in his arms, feeling a tremendous relief, Jenny sagged against him.

"What's all the commotion?" Phoebe wanted to know as she walked into the living room. "Why Jenny, you're back early."

Jenny pulled back from Matthew and wiped her eyes on the handkerchief Matthew handed her. Then she held out her hand to her grandmother who came to sit beside her on the sofa and stare at her, concerned.

"Tell me: What do you think about being an *urgrossmudder* again? A great-grandmother?"

GLOSSARY

aenti — aunt
allrecht — all right
bauch — stomach
boppli — baby or babies
bruder — brother
Daedi — Daddy
danki — thanks
dawdi haus — addition to the house for grandparents
eldre — parents
en alt maedel — old maid
Englisch or Englischer — a non-Amish person
fraa — wife
grosssohn — grandson
gwilde — quilt
grossdochder — granddaughter
guder mariye — good morning
gut — good
gut nacht — good night
gut-n-owed — good evening

haus — house
hochmut — pride
hungerich — hungry
kaffi — coffee
kapp — prayer covering or cap worn by girls and women
kich — kitchen
kind, kinner — child, children
lieb — love
liebschen — dearest or dear one
Mamm — Mom
mann — husband
nee — no
onkel — uncle
Ordnung — The rules of the Amish, both written and unwritten. Certain behavior has been expected within the Amish community for many, many years. These rules vary from community to community, but the most common are to not have electricity in the home, to not own or drive an automobile, and to dress a certain way.
Pennsylvania Deitsch — Pennsylvania German
redd-up — clean up
rotrieb — red beet
rumschpringe — time period when teenagers are allowed to experience the *Englisch* world while deciding whether to join the church.

schul — school
schur — sure
schwei — sister-in-law
schweschder — sister
sohn — son
urgrossmudder — great-grandmother
verdraue — trust
wilkumm — welcome
wunderbaar — wonderful
ya — yes

DISCUSSION QUESTIONS

Please don't read before completing the book as the questions contain spoilers!

1. Jenny studied to join the Amish church before she married Matthew. She knows that she — and her Amish friends and family — aren't saints. But she experiences unaccustomed envy when her sister-in-law conceives. Have you ever envied someone? What was the situation? What did you do about it?
2. Jenny inherited a ready-made family when she married Matthew: little Annie, Mary, and Joshua. Many people have stepchildren these days. Do you? How are they the same — or different — from your own children?
3. Chris — Jenny's brother-in-law — also converted to the Amish faith. Did you convert to a different religion when you married? How did you adjust?

4. Hannah — Jenny's sister-in-law — practiced forgiveness when she was injured by a man who carried a grudge against Chris. What do you think about the Amish practice of forgiveness? Do you think they are right to refuse to prosecute those who try to harm them or in some way break a law?
5. Jenny's family loves to tease her about her cooking. Many people don't know how to cook these days. Do you like to cook or do you prefer to buy ready-made food or eat out? If you like to cook, what's your favorite thing to cook?
6. Jenny is devastated when she finds her grandmother ill. Since Phoebe is her only living relative, she experiences real anxiety at losing her. Have you lost a beloved mother, father, or grandparent? How did you cope?
7. When she goes to get clothes for her grandmother, Jenny unexpectedly finds a letter that changes everything for her. Have you ever discovered a family "secret" and had it change how you felt about someone you loved?
8. Friends of Jenny's decide to make a major change in their lives, downsizing and living simpler. Have you ever done this or thought about it?

9. Joy, Jenny's friend, asks her if she's ever considered adoption. Have you adopted? What do you think of adopting?
10. When her stepson is hurt, Jenny discovers she has much to learn about God's will and obedience to rules and to God. Sometimes it's hard to be obedient to God or to have faith that He has a plan. Sometimes it takes faith you feel you don't have at the time. How do you deal with that?
11. Jenny's relationship with her husband changes when she discovers he kept part of the secret. It affects their marriage. People say "don't go to bed angry" but their distance isn't because of anger but because of a difference in culture. How have you resolved differences in your marriage or significant relationship?
12. Jenny wrestles with what she calls "unanswered prayer." Do you feel if you don't get the answer or thing that you've prayed for that God hasn't listened or given you what you prayed for? How do you feel? What do you do?

AMISH RECIPES

Potato Soup

6–7 large potatoes, peeled
1 medium onion
2 quarts milk
Salt
Pepper

Chop potatoes and onion and boil in salted water until fork-tender. Drain and return to saucepan. Mash potatoes somewhat (leave a few chunks for texture) and pour in milk. Warm without boiling, simmer for an hour. Add salt and pepper (white pepper is best) to taste. If soup is too thin, add a teaspoon or two of cornstarch to thicken it.

Serve with some crumbled cooked bacon, grated Cheddar cheese, and some chopped chives (optional) for a soup that tastes like a big, stuffed baked potato. So good on a cold day or serve chilled on a summer day for vichyssoise (blend the soup so it's very smooth).

AMISH MACARONI SALAD

2 cups uncooked elbow macaroni (or any shape macaroni you prefer)
2 stalks celery, chopped
1 small pepper (red, green, yellow, or a mixture)
2 teaspoons pickle relish (sweet or dill, whichever you prefer)
2 tablespoons mustard
1/2 cup sugar
2 teaspoons white vinegar
3/4 teaspoon celery seed
1 tablespoon chopped onion

Boil macaroni according to package directions, drain, and cool. In separate bowl, combine remaining ingredients and pour over drained macaroni. Stir until blended. Chill in refrigerator for at least two hours (best if chilled overnight).

Add cup or two of drained tuna, chopped cooked chicken, or ham, and you have a wonderful cool summer salad.

AMISH BREAD SOUP

A simple fruit dessert for any season

Homemade bread or sweet Hawaiian rolls

from the grocery store
Fresh fruit in season
Heavy cream or ice cream

For each serving, tear up bread — home-made bread or Hawaiian sweet rolls — and place in a soup bowl. A slice or slice and a half of the bread or two or three rolls should be right for an individual serving. Top with your favorite summer fruit. Ripe peaches, plums, strawberries, or any kind of mixed berries will do nicely. Thawed frozen fruit will also work — even canned pie filling. However, fresh fruit in season is best. Top with heavy cream or ice cream. This dessert is a busy Amish *fraa*'s favorite.

WHOOPIE PIES

For the cookies:

1 cup shortening
2 cups sugar
1 cup hot water with 2 teaspoons baking soda
4 1/2 cups flour
3/4 cup cocoa
Dash of salt
3 eggs
1 cup milk (buttermilk is best)
2 teaspoons vanilla

FILLING:

4 tablespoons flour
1 cup milk
1 cup sugar
1 cup shortening
1 teaspoon vanilla

(OR, you can use that marshmallow fluff in glass jars found in the grocery store in the baking section)

Preheat oven to 375 degrees.

For cookies: Mix the dry, then the wet ingredients. Drop mixture by the teaspoonful onto a greased baking sheet, taking care to space far enough apart so cookies don't blend together. Bake for 8–10 minutes, cool.

For filling:

Mix flour and milk and cook in a saucepan, beating until smooth. Add sugar, shortening, and vanilla. Cool. Spread onto one cookie and top with another.

Then stand back and watch out for the hordes of children and men who will descend and devour these!

ABOUT THE AUTHOR

Barbara Cameron is the author of more than two dozen books and three television movies, as well as the winner of the first Romance Writers of America Golden Heart Award. She lives in Edgewater, Florida.

The employees of Thorndike Press hope you have enjoyed this Large Print book. All our Thorndike, Wheeler, and Kennebec Large Print titles are designed for easy reading, and all our books are made to last. Other Thorndike Press Large Print books are available at your library, through selected bookstores, or directly from us.

For information about titles, please call:

(800) 223-1244

or visit our Web site at:

http://gale.cengage.com/thorndike

To share your comments, please write:

Publisher
Thorndike Press
10 Water St., Suite 310
Waterville, ME 04901